KRISTIN: BLUE BLOOD RETURNS

THE BLUE BLOOD RETURNS SERIES, BOOK 1

STACY EATON

NITEWOLF NOVELS

FOREWORD

Forty years ago, Kristin Greene joined a new world in the series, *My Blood Runs Blue*. That series consists of 4 full length novels and one short story. While it is not necessary to read that series before reading Kristin, it will give you major insight into some of the things they discuss in this book and series.

My Blood Runs Blue Series
My Blood Runs Blue, Book 1
The Pulse of Blue Blood, Book 2 (Short Story)
Blue Blood for Life, Book 3
Mixing the Blue Blood, Book 4
Blue Bloods Final Destiny, Book 5

KRISTIN

40 YEARS LATER

I stared at the picture on the wall of my office as I slowly swiveled my chair back and forth. So much had changed since that single moment in time. Forty years had passed, and wars had been fought—both human and vampire. Things were vastly different than they had been, and I found myself missing those simpler times.

I was now in charge of the United States VMF territory and had been since Alex's death eighteen years earlier. Twenty-five years ago, there was a revolt within our world, and while previously there had been only three masters around the world, now there were twenty-one. Each of us had territories, some smaller than others, but we oversaw the race that resided and visited under us. We also stayed in close contact with one another and, for the most part, got along.

A few years after the revolt, our entire race broke into two main factions. Even the smallest territories had rebels that attempted to overthrow the current masters. There were many here in the United States that were opposed to me being the master of our region, and they had divided off. There were many more that stood behind me—or at least pretended to.

Sadly, about three years ago, our breed and lifestyle had become

1

known to humans, and even after three years, fear and violence sparked when it came to humans and vampires. Many of our breed spent more time in the shadows of the night to avoid the humans, rather than going about their regular business.

It was a constant fight with humans to prove that we weren't hell-bent on destroying their race. It didn't matter that we had been around for centuries or that it had taken them this long to learn we existed. They didn't want to accept that we preferred to live in coexistence with them—well, at least our side did.

I continued to stare at the picture as I dwelled on the past. It hung right beside the door and served as a constant reminder of how quickly life could change. Friends could become foes; lovers could leave. Mates could die, and everything could turn upside down in an instant. Well, a flash in my lifetime, not to humans.

There was a knock at my office door, and Joshua pushed it open. "It's time to go, Mistress."

I contemplated him for a moment. Over the last few years, Joshua had become an essential person to me—a constant in my life—with his broad shoulders, deep-set dark-green eyes, and quiet nature along with his unwavering support. I stood, then walked around my desk to pause in front of the picture. I took in every smiling face one at a time, and my heart ached for all that was lost, the people I loved, the friendships that I had once cultivated.

"Mistress?" Joshua said softly, and I turned to him.

"I'm ready." He gave an abrupt nod and allowed me to pass before stepping to my side and putting his hand to my lower back. After we entered the elevator, I stared down the hall, wondering what I would find when the doors opened two floors down.

"How many people are here?" I asked Joshua.

"Sixteen. Eight of ours, eight of theirs," Josh stated with a brief look my way.

"Eight, huh?" I laughed slightly, hoping it would ease the tension in my shoulders.

Joshua snickered as he turned my way again, and our eyes locked. Many years ago, I had met Joshua when he had worked for Alexander.

KRISTIN: BLUE BLOOD RETURNS

Joshua could hide his presence from most of our kind, and his assistance had been instrumental in helping to rescue Trent, Mick, and his wife from Leo and his gang of thugs when human-turned vampires were new to us.

In the back of my mind, I truly believed that incident had been a turning point in our history. Somehow Leo and my father Burke had discovered that human-turned vampires had special abilities; at least the females did. Back then, my sister, Angelina, had been working with Leo. In fact, Leo and Angelina had been bonded, and both of them had worked with my father.

I was glad that Angelina had since changed her ways. Of course, if I hadn't killed our father, she might never have, but she did, and that's what counted. She was an essential part of my life. After getting to know her, I didn't ever want to be on the opposite side of the battle-field again.

And a battlefield was what we were dealing with now. "Did they say what exactly they wanted?"

"No, Mistress."

I sighed. I wasn't a fan of my title, but sadly, I was stuck with it. Since Alex had been known as Master when he was in charge, I'd received the title when I'd taken over after his death.

The door to the elevator opened, and I stepped out. Once again, Joshua put his hand to my lower back. It was for more than just being gentlemanly; he was protecting me. Almost anywhere that I went, Joshua was at my side, always touching me. His ability to hide his presence from others now leeched into me if we were in contact since I had taken his blood—I continued to feed from him quite regularly to keep that bond between us strong. He didn't do that with everyone, only with me and occasionally, my sister. He had shared his gift with Alex too when times had gotten bad; unfortunately, it hadn't saved Alex.

Joshua escorted me down the hallway. Two human men in suits stood at the door to the conference room, both eyeing me critically.

"Josh, did we remove their weapons?" I asked in his mind, not that I was worried about human weapons.

"Yeah, Kris, we removed them. They balked at it, but they gave them up when they realized it was futile to argue."

I cast a sensual smile over the two men at the door. Both of them fought not to return it, but one cracked, and I felt his lust pulse toward me as he let loose a handsome smile. I gave him a wink as I passed.

In the conference room, there were six more men that I didn't know, but I quickly figured out that only two of them were there to speak with us. The other four were for protection. Did they honestly think we would hurt them? Or that those men could protect them if we decided to go into a feeding frenzy and devour their life essence? Humans were so fucking simple-minded.

"Evening, everyone," I said as I rounded the table and took my seat at the head of the long conference table. Clayton Lakin sat to my left, and beside him were two other male elders, Beckett and Henry. To their left were Scarlett and Hazel, two of the female elders on our board. In the corners of the room were more of my people: Jett, Ryker, and Lorna. All of them worked for the VMF as sentinels in the field but spent more time these days protecting us here—my very own secret service—oh, yeah—not!

Sometimes it irked me that I was not the one doing the protecting, but instead hidden behind thick walls, dark glass, and glamours that tricked people's minds. I missed the old days sometimes. Okay—most days, I found myself missing some part of my former life. Right now, I'd take a dull foot patrol in a heartbeat.

Joshua stood behind my chair, and I let my gaze drift over the four men giving protection to the two seated at the table. Seriously, did we really need all this muscle in one room?

The level of gravity in the room reminded me of when I used to attend court after I'd arrested someone. All the stone faces shifting carefully, searching for any telltale sign of guilt or weakness. I wanted to throw a joke into the room just to kill some of the tension, but I didn't.

"Gentlemen." I eyed the men at the opposite end of the table, damn bureaucrats. "I'm Kristin Armstrong. I appreciate you coming to us at this hour, and I'm sorry for being late. I was on a call."

The older gentleman nodded. "Thomas Singer, and this is Hugh McMurphy."

I smiled pleasantly. "Pleasure to meet you, gentlemen. Do you mind telling me what government agency you are with?"

Singer shifted slightly in his chair. "I'm with U.S. Immigration and Customs; Hugh is with the Department of Homeland Security. We currently work together on a task force."

I tried not to frown as I leaned further back into my comfy high-backed leather chair and crossed my legs as if I didn't have a care in the world. "And what can we possibly do for this task force between ICE and DHS?"

The two men glanced at one another as if surprised that I would be able to speak their acronyms so effortlessly. They had no clue of my past, but then again, I had very little on them as they'd requested this meeting at the last minute, and I was interested just enough to entertain them on a whim.

I studied them both. Thomas Singer was an older man with a full head of white hair, probably in his late fifties or early sixties. His nervous energy flitted about the room, and I didn't need to peek into his head to see what was stressing him. He didn't want to be here, and he was scared to death of us.

Now, the other man, Hugh McMurphy, was quite the opposite. He regarded me openly as I shifted my gaze to him. His dark-blond hair was peppered with short strands of silver around his temples, and I would peg him for being around forty, maybe forty-two at the most. He had an attractive round face and light-blue eyes that studied me almost as hard as I did him. He wasn't nervous, and as I reached out to him. I saw inside his mind that he thought I was rather sexy for a dangerous woman, but he also thought that being dangerous might be why he thought I was sexy. Was Agent McMurphy a bad boy looking for some fun? I couldn't help but chuckle softly; I wouldn't have said no to that. My days of being a good girl were long gone.

"Well, it's more what we can do for you," Singer finally responded gruffly and collected my attention again as I raised a questioning brow his way. "With the knowledge of your kind becoming more pronounced, people are still concerned, and we need to take a proactive stance in trying to calm their fears."

"Proactive stance? We've been around for a long time, Mr. Singer. I would think that by now, most people realize that we are not here to hurt them. The existence of our breed is not fresh news. Why is this suddenly a concern?"

"As I said, Mrs. Armstrong, your"—he hesitated as if unsure what word to use—"people are out there more often, and our people are still scared. Besides, we only recently figured out who to speak with about these matters. You don't make it very well known that you run these hooligans."

"Hooligans?" I laughed. "Now that's a word that I haven't heard since before you were born, Mr. Singer."

"How long have you been around?" Mr. McMurphy asked as soon as I finished speaking. His tone was low and husky, and it made me take another long look at him. I hadn't expected his voice to be quite so deep—or seductive. Hmm.

Clayton spoke up. "Our breed has been around for thousands of years." Singer and McMurphy glanced at one another again. I wasn't sure if Agent McMurphy had been referring to our breed or me in particular, and I was thankful for Clayton keeping this on business. "And we have been peaceful, law-abiding citizens all that time. I don't know what angle you all are working here, but just spill it already."

"Well, I don't know about law-abiding or peaceful," McMurphy said slowly. "Your people wouldn't have come to our attention if you had been living that way."

"Just like any other civilization, there are bad people, or hooligans, as you so eloquently referred to them earlier. We can't watch everyone all the time," Hazel replied dryly.

"Funny that you call yourself a civilization," Singer said as he laced his fingers over his ample belly and leaned back as if he were in control of this meeting.

Beckett asked, "Why is that?"

Singer shrugged. "Because you all act as if you were your own little country. You have your own government, your own laws, your very own leader." He lifted his hand toward me as he spoke as if to prove a point.

"It has been necessary since the start of time to have a governing body, Mr. Singer," I stated. "Our hierarchy has been in place for a long time to oversee our breed and keep them in line."

"You haven't done so well recently, Mrs. Armstrong," he replied tersely.

"Do you want to start quoting statistics, Mr. Singer? Because I'm pretty sure that the human population is responsible for a much higher percentage of criminal activity," I said, trying to keep the annoyance out of my voice. "I could have one of my analysts come in here with the numbers. We track that sort of thing."

Mr. McMurphy put his hand up. "It's not about statistics or criminal activity. We want to help you, Mrs. Armstrong."

"That was mentioned previously, but I have yet to hear what it is that you wish to be of service for," I stated dryly.

He glanced at Singer. "We'd like to work with you and have you assist us by providing a census of your people and any of their special skills."

My brows jumped ever so slightly, and all four of the elders turned my way, protesting into my head. "Enough!" I snapped back at them mentally.

"A census?" I laughed lightly. "You want a list of my people? Why? So that you can herd us all into a confinement camp, while you tell us that you are trying to protect us?"

Both men shook their heads, and Singer looked a little nervous, but McMurphy answered. "No. We do not want to put you all into a camp."

"Then what the hell do ICE and DHS think they are going to do with a list like that? We aren't breaking any laws, and those that do are dealt with."

"Yes, through your justice, but not ours," Singer stated hotly. "You have previously said that your people are no different than ours. If that is the case, they should be required to follow the same rules of justice."

Clayton laughed loudly. "You want to run them through a court of law? There isn't a jail out there that could contain one of our kind."

Singer shifted in his seat uncomfortably, but it was McMurphy who spoke. "No, that's not what we are saying. We want to make sure that your justice is fit for the crime. The fact that you kill members of your society makes you your own court of law—judge, jury, and executioner. Your people, citizens, whatever you call them, should be protected. They do have constitutional rights."

I fought not to roll my eyes. You have got to be kidding me. "I'm sorry, gentlemen, but you don't seem to understand the world *we* live in—*have* lived in for centuries. While our people follow our rules, it is to protect them *and* your human race. The only time a member of our breed is removed, is when they have violated those laws. It's kind of like your death penalty."

"You don't have the right to put someone to death." Mr. Singer sneered my way.

I was very tempted to flash to the other side of the room, put my hand around the asshole's throat, and hiss into his ear that I had every right. Instead, I focused on the anger simmering inside of me. "I have every right as the mistress. Those of our breed that harm humans are removed. We do *not* tolerate that—we never have—and we sure as hell won't allow you and your government or task force or whatever the hell it is to control how we have done things since the start of our time."

McMurphy was staring at me, and I knew he noticed that my eyes had changed color. I let my steel-gray gaze linger on him for a moment before he shifted slightly in his seat. Nerves? I didn't think so. I think my intensity just turned up the volume on his lust for me. Too bad that I had other things to do tonight.

"Gentlemen, if that's all you came here to discuss, I believe our business is concluded." I went to stand, but McMurphy held up his hand.

"Wait, Mrs. Armstrong, we seemed to have gotten off topic here.

We really did want to speak to you about ways to protect your people."

I stared down at him. "Your concern is noted, Mr. McMurphy, along with Mr. Singer's disdain. While we appreciate your offer, we aren't interested in your assistance. Thank you for your time. Gentlemen."

I heard the other elders get up from their seats as Joshua escorted me from the room.

"She can't just walk out on this," Mr. Singer growled.

"Don't worry; I'll find a way to talk to her, Tom. Calm down," Mr. McMurphy said as I walked down the hallway. Yeah, good luck with that, I thought to myself as I reached the elevator.

Lorna was behind the other elders, and I knew that Jett and Ryker were still in the conference room and would show our guests out. We loaded into the elevator, and it wasn't until the doors closed that Scarlett began to speak.

"They want more than what they are asking for," she said.

"Yeah," Beckett replied, "I am pretty sure they want to use our people, the ones that might be able to assist them, anyway."

"Well, that's not happening," I stated. "I have no plans to get into bed with the U.S. government."

Scarlett chuckled, "Although someone from the government sure wanted to get in bed with you."

Several of us laughed as the elevator doors opened. I stepped out, Lorna and Clayton behind me. I was pretty sure the rest were going to head down and out of the building now.

"Lorna, can you ask Lainey to come to my office, please?"

"Sure, Kris," she replied before she split off down another hallway near my office.

Lorna had come to work with me when she was in her early twenties. After Julian and Lyssa died during a raid on the VMF office out west, Clayton and Lorna had moved here to help me. It had been thirty-five years since Julian's death, and my heart ached every single time I thought of him.

Now Lorna was a full-blooded vampire mated to Paul, one of our traveling sentinels. Their daughter Lainey, who was twenty, was my current assistant.

Joshua left me at my office door, and Clayton came in with me and took a seat on the side couch. "I have a bad feeling about this, Kris."

"I do too, Clay. I'm not sure if it's because they want to know what we are capable of or because they think they can gain control of us, but I don't like it."

I took a seat in my chair and looked at Clay, his gaze locked on the large photograph near my door, and his voice was soft, sad, as he spoke. "I sure wish we could go back in time."

I lifted my eyes to the picture. "Yeah, sometimes I wish that too, Clay."

HUGH

"She can't just walk out on this," Tom snapped as Mrs. Armstrong left the room.

"Don't worry; I'll find a way to talk to her, Tom. Calm down." One of the men that had shown us into the conference room waited at the door for us to follow. Tom and I left without saying anything further, our entourage of unarmed guards in front and behind us.

I hadn't wanted to bring them, but Tom had insisted. He said that we needed protection walking into the viper pit, but I doubted that the six men with us could have taken the two vampires that were leading us out—especially as they were unarmed. I'd seen vampires fight before, and I knew our men were no match for them.

Perhaps if we hadn't shown up with so many people, Mrs. Armstrong might have been more comfortable talking to us. Or maybe she'd never be open to speaking with us. I sighed as we reached the elevator and piled in—all ten of us crammed into the metal box. You couldn't turn, or your dick would smack the next guy.

When we arrived on the first floor, I burst from the elevator as if I'd been forceably projected from it, and we returned to the lobby and reunited with our weapons. Tom and I went out front and stood on the sidewalk leading to the parking lot; our men fanned out around us, scanning all directions.

"I'm going to stay here," I told him.

"Why?" His face screwed up with disgust.

I shrugged. "Maybe if it is just me, Mrs. Armstrong might be more open to talk, or listen at least."

"I doubt that," he scoffed. "But it might be worth a try. Keep these men with you."

"No, Tom. You take them back to the office. They aren't going to do anything to hurt me. Besides, as I said, if it's just me, she might talk."

"You're insane to go back in there alone."

I laughed. "I'll be alright. I'll give you a call later and let you know that I'm still alive. If I don't call you by eleven, you can send a search party for my bloodless body."

He shook his head. "That's not funny, Murph."

I slapped his shoulder. "I'll be fine, Tom."

"Make sure to call me later, Hugh."

"I will." I watched him walk away with all six of the men flanking him protectively.

There was something inside of me that was telling me to stay. I wasn't sure if Mrs. Armstrong would speak with me or not, but I had a strong desire to find out. Was it because I had been insanely attracted to her and felt this undeniable urge to be near her? The moment she had walked into the room, practically no one else existed. A few times, our gazes had collided, and I'd felt my entire body come to life. Things tingled in me that I didn't even know could fucking tingle. I had to wonder if she sensed it too. I knew that nothing would happen between us, but the desire was still there, throbbing through my veins.

I returned to the lobby of the building, bypassing the room where I'd previously stored my weapon, and found the bar. The building was once a busy hotel; now, I guess it still was, but I wasn't sure how many rooms they had available for guests. I was aware that quite a few vampires now resided here; at least that's what I had heard.

As I went to step into the lounge, one of the men from upstairs stepped in front of me, halting my progress. "Do I need to remove your weapon again?"

"I mean no harm to anyone," I responded. "I'm not stupid enough to think that I could do that and live to see the sunrise. It's been a long fucking day, and I just want a drink."

He stared at me hard for a moment as if trying to read me, nodded, and then walked away with a smirk on his face.

I really could use a stiff drink right about now, and with any luck, Mrs. Armstrong would find out I was still here and come down to speak with me.

At the bar, I ordered a scotch on the rocks and planted my ass on a stool. I glanced around at the other patrons in the place and tried to determine if they were human or vampire. It wasn't as hard as I suspected it would be. The humans were all going about their business—blasé to the world, but the vampires watched my every move. Even if they weren't looking in my direction, I was pretty damn sure they were still keeping tabs on me.

I was almost finished with my drink when I heard a soft voice behind me. "Why are you still here, Mr. McMurphy?"

Damn if her voice wasn't as fucking sexy as she was. I swallowed the mouthful of liquor and turned slowly toward her, my eyes locking onto her bright-blue irises. "It's Hugh, and I was hoping if you weren't too busy, I could buy you a drink and apologize for my companion's behavior earlier."

She lifted an elegantly manicured eyebrow. "Do you think that buying me a drink will get me to come around and give you the information that you requested?"

I shook my head. "No, but I was hoping it would allow us to talk for a few minutes without all the hotheads around."

She chuckled and glanced over my shoulder to the bartender. "Jeff, refill his and pour one for me."

"You're usual, Mistress?"

"Yes, please."

"Mistress?" I asked as I turned back to her, and she laughed briefly as she shook her head. The sound went right to my cock and made it twitch.

"Let's take our drinks to a table." She reached around me, brushing her shoulder against my arm and thanking the bartender. My arm tingled where she had casually touched it, and I had the sudden urge to touch her again with a different part of my body to see if it happened again.

Instead, I followed her to a small table near the back of the bar, enjoying the sight of her long red hair hanging down her back and how her hips swished back and forth like a gliding pendulum. Surprisingly, she sat with her back to the room. I had pegged her for someone who would want to see everything. I shifted around her and took a seat on the opposite side of the small cocktail table.

"So, why do they call you Mistress?"

She spun her glass for a moment, and I noted that she had short unpainted nails. Not something I would have expected from a classy lady of power. "Alexander was the Master; as his mate, I was known as the Mistress, although I didn't use it until Alex died, and I took over. Personally, I fucking hate it. I thought Widow would be better."

"You were married to Alexander?"

She shook her head, and her glorious hair swung around her shoulders. Damn, I wanted to bury my hands in those waves. Fuck my hands; I wanted to drape those locks over my naked body while I got off.

She looked like she was about to laugh, but sobered before she responded. "No, not married like humans. We were mated. It's a different bond, a much deeper connection."

"But you took his last name?"

"I did, but only because of my position. I didn't take my first mate's name."

"You've been mated twice?"

She frowned for a moment. "Mated four times and married once."

I cocked my head. "Married?"

"Back before I transitioned into this world, I was married to a human man. He was a cop; he died in the line of duty."

"Wait, what do you mean you transitioned into this world?"

She lifted her glass and stared at me; her eyes turned a darker shade of blue. "That is a story for another time."

Was I imagining that her eyes were changing color? I'd noticed in the conference room earlier that they looked like they went from blue to gray in the beat of a drum. Okay, a story for another time. I had a feeling that the woman in front of me wasn't just a story or a novel, but a fucking library full of vibrant tales and knowledge. I was ready to apply for a library card so I could start checking them out and reading every line.

I moved our conversation back to the previous topic. "Are all the men you were mated or married to dead?"

Her smile was almost sad. "Yes."

"I guess that would make you more like a black widow than a mistress."

She sipped her drink, staring at me over the top of her glass. "But I didn't kill them. Rogue vampires killed most of them, not me."

"Is that why you don't want to work with us? You have it out for the vampires that killed your mates? You want to take justice into your own hands for losing the love of your life?"

If I hadn't been staring so intently into her eyes, I might have missed the shift of her eye color. It was fascinating—she was fascinating. "I can't say that Alex was the love of my life, or his son, Trent, who was also my mate."

I laughed. "Wait, you were mated to Alex's son? Was that before or after Alex?"

She grinned, her eyes sparkling slightly. "I was mated to Alex first, then to his son, and then a few years after Trent died, I mated to Alex again."

"Okay, so that's three matings; who was the fourth?"

She opened her mouth to respond, but before she could answer, a man approached our table, and I met his watchful gaze. His eyes were dark blue; his features almost chiseled to perfection. As he stepped around the mistress, he dismissed me.

"Mom, Lainey said your call would be ready in fifteen minutes."

"Thanks, Rex. I'll be up shortly." The two of them stared at one another, and then she nodded almost imperceptibly. The man shot me another look before he stalked off.

"That grown man is your son? He looks like he is almost my age."

"In your world, Rex would be forty now."

I began to cough after I sipped from my glass. "Forty? He *is* my age! How do you have a child that old? You don't look any older than him."

"Once we transition, our aging slows down tremendously. Trust me; I'm old enough to have a son your age."

She had used that transition word again, but I knew it would get me nowhere to ask about it. Instead, I looked her boldly up and down. Damn, I had always had a thing for older women, but she probably had years on my mother. She was striking, without a mar to her complexion, her deep-red hair long and wavy, and what I could see of her body was incredible. I could only imagine what she would look like spread out naked before me. I suppressed a shiver filled with the desire to find out.

"Well, don't mind me saying this, but you look damn good, Mistress."

She tilted her head to the side, a seductive smile slipping over her lips as she tugged her bottom lip under her teeth just long enough to make my dick twitch again. "Thank you, and you may call me Kristin."

"Kristin," I replied as we stared at one another. Was I the only one feeling the desire spiraling around us?

A loud laugh on the other side of the room broke our connection, and she took a long drink from her glass. The slim column of her neck was visible to me for a moment, and I pictured my face to her neck as I devoured every inch of it. I tore my gaze away as I found it locked to the vein pulsing under her ear. What the fuck was wrong with me? I'd never fantasized this bad about a woman before.

I cleared my throat and glanced around as I shifted in my seat. Kristin set her glass down on the table. "Well, Hugh, it was a pleasure talking to you, and thank you for the drink, but I have a video conference I need to attend."

Without conscious thought, I reached over the table and touched her hand with the tips of my fingers. "I can wait for you."

She glanced at my hand briefly. "Why would you want to?"

"Because I want to talk to you, Kristin."

She leaned forward, sliding her hand over the top of mine and lowering her voice as she said, "You want to talk, or—" A split second later, her soft voice slipped through my head. *"Or you want to see me spread out naked for you?"*

I blinked and then stared at my drink. Had I had more than two drinks, or was this spiked with something? She laughed as I lifted my confused gaze back to hers; her eyes were now light blue as she removed her hand from mine.

"I'll have Ryker take you to my apartment. I'll meet you there when I'm done with my call." Before I could even reply, she was out of her seat, and one of the men from earlier this evening was heading my way. Yeah, I doubted that he was going to take me to her apartment. He was probably going to show my ass to the door.

Surprisingly, he led me to a different elevator and put his thumb against a biometric pad to bypass the settings. The doors closed, and the elevator began to ascend quickly. Why did she want me in her apartment? Was it so we could talk? Or had she somehow known what I was thinking? Did she actually repeat the same thought that I'd had about her into my mind? A friend of mine had told me that some could read minds, but she had never admitted to being able to speak to anyone mentally unless she had taken blood from them. Was this confirmation that it went way beyond that?

If it did, we were screwed. If they could get into our minds without any trouble, we would never have the advantage. They would know what we wanted before we even opened our mouth. Was that what happened today? Had Kristin seen something in our heads that had put her off? Is that how they had stayed quiet for so long?

The elevator stopped on the ninth floor, and Ryker chuckled loudly as he stepped out, going toward one of the five doors that I could see off the lobby area. Could he hear what I was thinking? Is that why he laughed?

He unlocked the door with his thumb on another pad and held it open for me. Was he taking me to a prison? Was I going to be held captive? I stepped through the door and stared at the room in front of me. Well, hell—if I was being held captive, it was going to be in the most delightful place I'd ever been.

The elegantly decorated living room was filled with cream and beige furniture. On the opposite side of the room, a spiral staircase led to an open loft. I could see a desk, couch, and a few bookshelves up there, but not much else. The dark-haired man went around me and reached for the remote to the television. "You into football?" he asked.

"Yeah," I replied as I approached the seating area and observed him further. I was tall, six two, but he was taller than me, by probably two inches. While my body was lean, his shoulders looked a bit more jacked than mine, which made his waist look a little slimmer.

He nodded and dropped the remote to the couch. "You want a beer?"

"Sure," I said as I sat on the edge of a suede chair and watched him head across the room. He wore black cargo pants and boots. If I didn't know he was a vampire, I would have thought he was military.

Ryker pulled open a small fridge at the bar and removed two bottles. He came back and handed one to me before he plopped down on the sofa as if he lived there. Shit, maybe he did. Or perhaps he was another one of her kids.

Ryker snorted, and I glanced at the television to see a commercial. Hopefully, he was laughing at that and not me.

I glanced around, wondering what the hell I was doing here. I'd wanted to talk to her, see if I could get her to understand what we had been proposing earlier. I hadn't considered having a private audience with her in her living quarters. What the hell should I say to her?

"You're a lucky man," Ryker said with a sly grin, and I noted that his eyes were an odd red-brown color, almost burgundy.

"Why is that?"

"It's not often that humans get invited into the inner sanctum." He paused and thought for a moment. "No, I don't think she ever has. At least not while I've been working with her. She must like you."

"The inner sanctum?"

He laughed. "Yeah, usually when the mistress is with a human, she takes them to one of her hotel rooms, screws them six ways to Sunday, practically sucks them dry, and then leaves them alone to sleep it off for a few days."

I think my jaw fell open a little bit. "Um, I'm not here to sleep with her. I only want to talk."

"Yeah, right, man." He took a long drink from his bottle. "I can feel your jacked hormones over here. They are so strong; you're giving me a fucking hard-on, and I'm not usually into men. I would totally do the mistress if I had the chance—fuck, yeah! She is one hell of a hot woman. I've seen her in action before, almost lost my cool right on the spot."

I frowned at the side of his head, and he laughed, grinning back at me. "I was kidding about being sucked practically dry. She doesn't do that—not normally, but she will make you think you have died and gone to heaven. That I can promise."

He had to be wrong. That wasn't her intent, was it? I thought about the words that had echoed through my head downstairs. Had she not somehow known what I was thinking? Was she going to feed on me, suck me dry? Something akin to a shiver jolted down my spine, but I wasn't sure if that was from fear or excitement.

"Just go with it, man; you won't be sorry." Ryker remained quiet for the rest of the time, his focus on the television. I tried to let it capture my attention, but my eyes kept wandering around the room. There were pictures scattered about, but I wasn't close enough to see any of them, and I wasn't sure my curiosity would be appreciated.

It was maybe forty minutes and another two beers later when the door opened, and she stepped in. Her gaze slipping over mine to Ryker, she scolded him. "Get your shoes off my couch, Ryker."

"Sorry, Mistress," he said with a laugh as he stood. "You need anything else?"

"No, that will be all. Thank you," she replied, not even looking my way.

Ryker glanced at me, winked, and strutted toward the door. A deep voice whispered in my mind that sounded a whole lot like Ryker's. *"I envy the shit out of you, man."* In the hallway stood another man who glared daggers at me. He was far from envious.

The door closed, and I shifted my attention back to her. She was watching me carefully and then turned and walked toward a hallway. As she went, she removed the suit jacket that she had on and disappeared through a door.

Okay, maybe she had to use the restroom or was changing clothes. I sipped the last of my third beer and waited. About five minutes later, her voice slipped into my head again. *"Are you going to come in here, or do I need to come out there?"*

Was I really hearing this shit? Or was it wishful thinking? There was only one way to find out. I set my empty beer bottle on the coffee table and slowly began to approach the door where she had disappeared. I came up short at the threshold. She was lying in the middle of a king-sized bed, naked and propped up on her elbow.

"Is this how you imagined?"

Holy—fucking—shit. Instant erection. My gaze slipped over her full perky breasts, her toned stomach, and neatly manicured groin area. She had the perfect body. "Kind of like I imagined."

She peaked a brow. "Were you thinking something more like this?" She rolled to her back, spreading her legs, and I almost lost it right there as my eyes locked on the extraordinarily sexy woman in front of me.

Suddenly, the tie around my neck was restricting the airflow. I swallowed the overwhelming wave of lust that threatened to take me down and somehow ground out a response. "Yeah, that's more like I imagined."

She smiled, lifting her hand and crooking her finger at me. "Get undressed and join me, Hugh."

I took two steps, then paused. "What if I'm married?"

She laughed. "Do you think that I care about that?"

"No, but maybe I do."

She sighed and rolled back to her side. "Are you married, Hugh? Is there someone that is at home waiting for you? A little woman who is wondering where you are so late at night?"

I'd never been so damn happy to be single in my life. "No."

Her eyes brightened slightly, and then she lay slowly back, spreading her legs again. "Then I suggest you get undressed and get over here, Hugh."

Yeah, like I was going to say no to that.

ANGELINA

$\mathcal{I}$ was glad to be home. I'd been traveling for three weeks, trying to figure out where the Portage family was living now, but I still wasn't sure. I'd reached out to every contact that I trusted, and even a few that I didn't.

I was pretty sure that the prick was holed up in Kentucky or Tennessee or one of those other boring mid-country states, but I didn't have a clue as to which one, and everyone had been tight-lipped. Kris wasn't going to be happy, but that wasn't anything new these days.

I did have to hand it to her, though. She dealt with the constant shit much better than I did. By now, I would have killed half of our breed for the stupid shit they did.

I was pretty sure the only ones that she wanted dead were the Portages and their followers. They started the faction that had branched off years ago when she had taken over as Master or Mistress or whatever the fuck you wanted to call it. They had started the revolt and had taken a lot of people with them.

Joseph Portage needed to grow a backbone and get with the times. Women could be rulers now; hell, the U.S. had already had two female presidents. We didn't see him revolting against them, or maybe he had. I was irritated as I got off the elevator onto my floor and found Joshua standing outside my sister's door.

"Why are you out here?" I asked him.

"Your sister has company," he stated a wee bit sternly.

"In her apartment? That's not like her," I said as I went to pass him. "How long have they been in there?"

"About an hour."

"They done?" I asked as I slipped my hearing out but didn't sense any wild breathing or bodies slapping together.

"Yeah, they're done."

"Good. I have business to discuss with her." I pushed open the door, and after a quick glance around the living room, I went straight to her room. She was lying upside down on the bed, her foot in a man's lap as he rubbed it. Well, look at that: sex, food, and a foot massage—lucky girl.

"I'm next," I declared as I stepped into the room. The man practically jumped out of his skin and yanked a pillow over his groin. "Honey, you don't have anything I haven't seen a thousand times."

My sister rolled to her stomach. "I didn't think you were going to get home until tomorrow."

"I couldn't find anyone else to push around," I stated and then grinned at my sister. "Looks like you've been busy."

I checked out the attractive man sitting against the headboard; for a human, he was rather tasty-looking. My gaze went to his neck, and I licked my lips. "You ready for another round, hot stuff?" His eyes widened as I perched on the edge of the bed.

"Leave Hugh alone. Hugh, this is my sister, Angelina. Don't pay any attention to her; she was just leaving."

"Nice to meet you," he said, his voice much deeper than I had expected, and I stared into his light-blue eyes. And—bingo. That's why she took this guy to her bed. Damn blue eyes.

"Nice to see you, Hugh." I let my gaze roam audaciously over him.

"Lena, go in the other room. I'll be there in a minute."

"Fine, ruin my fun." I sighed dramatically. "Here I am running all over the country trying to find these pricks, and you're back here going to town with every guy who has his eyes."

"Lena—" I heard the anger in her voice, felt it blast through the room.

I sprang off the bed. "Sorry! I'm going." I didn't bother to look back. I knew I would see the frustration and pain in her eyes. I always saw that whenever she was reminded of the men from her past.

I poured myself a drink as I waited. Truth be told, I was somewhat jealous. Hugh was a handsome man, and my sister did look rather satisfied, well, at least in one way. I knew she hadn't fed from him, and she needed to feed soon. Over the years, our metabolism and our blood had changed. Both Kristin and I needed to feed more regularly than the rest of our breed. While most of our breed could enjoy bagged blood, we did better with fresh in our veins. Yeah, we took from our breed, but human blood was vital for us—essential for our survival. We keep that quiet, along with the details about how dangerous the blood running through our veins was. Only those very close to us knew.

I was halfway through my drink when Kristin came out in a t-shirt and jeans. "Was it good?"

She gave me a droll look. "Pour me one of those."

I refilled my glass and one for her. "Why didn't you feed?"

"Because I didn't want to."

"Kris, you have to feed." She glared at me. "And, I'm sorry for that earlier comment."

"Whatever." She took the glass.

"Where is your friend?" I asked as I glanced back at the bedroom door.

"He's taking a shower."

"Wow, you not only brought him to your apartment to screw him, but you let him use your shower, too. Next, you'll be telling me that you aren't going to compel him to forget."

"I'm not."

I almost choked on my drink. "What's so special about this guy? Besides his eyes and sexy-as-hell voice?"

"Nothing. Now, what did you find out?"

Something was on her mind, and I decided not to push it—at least right now. "Not anything good, that's for sure. I reached out to all of my contacts, and then some. Either people don't know where he is hiding, or they aren't saying. It's the same shit, different fucking month."

Kris frowned. "Someone has to know something."

"Yeah, I agree, but the man's location is a tightly kept secret. I have no idea how he can do that unless he's a complete hermit. I did find something out, though. Portage has a new mate. He's not with Tracey anymore, but with a woman named Diane, and they have a kid named Zander."

"How long has he been with this other woman?"

I shrugged. "No clue. The person that mentioned it said quite a while."

"Alright, do we know anything more about Diane? Maybe we can trace her family and find them that way?"

"Nope, nada, and before you ask, I don't know anything else on the kid either."

"Do you know if he's transitioned?"

"Not for sure, but I'd have to say that he probably has. One guy mentioned that his son does all the business for his father."

"And his name is Zander?"

"Yep, Zander Portage."

"Well, let's do some digging and see what we can find on him."

"Already on it. I asked Paxton to look into it when I got back tonight. I don't think we will find anything. We didn't even know he had a son, and I'm pretty sure that we thought we had his family tree down pat."

"Yeah, well, if Joe Portage has another family, there is a lot we don't know."

"I will tell you that if I ever see Joe Portage, I'm going to put a stake between his eyes before I put it into his heart. What a bastard he is."

A sound had both of us looking toward the bedroom door where Hugh was coming out, his tie hanging loosely around his neck, his charcoal-gray suit jacket thrown over his arm. "Are you talking about Joe Portage? I wasn't eavesdropping; I just thought I heard you mention that name as I stepped out."

"What do you know about Joe Portage?" I inquired immediately.

He shrugged. "He's been on our radar for a while."

"Why?" my sister queried before I could. What radar did the guy have going?

"Like you, he oversees certain people. We wanted to discuss the same things with him that we did with you."

"Do you know where he is?" I probed, bolting to my feet.

He shook his head. "No, I was hoping that Kristin might know that."

"Yeah, well, we are both in the dark there," Kris said solemnly.

"What did you discuss with him?" I asked her.

"I'll tell you about it later," she answered and went to Hugh. "You should get going. Your day might be over, but mine is not even halfway through."

He paused at the door, and I sat back down, watching them from under my bangs. "Can I see you again? I'd like to finish that discussion."

"You left your card, right?" she said to him.

"Yeah, I did. My cellphone number is on the back. Call me when you have time to talk."

"I will, and thank you, Hugh."

He stared down at her like he wasn't sure if he should kiss her goodbye, or maybe he was trying to figure something else out. I didn't know and didn't fucking care.

Kris solved his dilemma by opening the door, stepping up on tiptoe, and kissing him briefly on the lips. As she stepped back, they continued to stare at one another. No way! Did my sister actually like the guy? He was hot, but he was human. She smiled at him and turned away.

Josh glared at Hugh, and I chuckled. Josh was a little territorial when it came to Kristin. Not because he was in love with her— although we all knew he was—but because Josh felt like it was his sole purpose on Earth to protect her—especially since he hadn't been able to protect Alex.

Kristin asked Josh to show Hugh out and told him she'd see him in the office in a little while.

After she closed the door, I spoke. "So who was that hottie, and why were you screwing a strange human in your apartment?"

"Hugh McMurphy, Department of Homeland Security."

My eyes almost bugged out of my head. "You thinking of making a career change and going back into law enforcement?"

"No. Hugh showed up here today with another guy from Immigration. They said they wanted a list of all of our people and what special abilities they might have."

I gawked at her and then stuck a finger in my ear as if I wasn't sure I'd heard her right. "Say what?"

"Don't worry; we aren't giving them the list. I only met with them today because we have heard rumblings that they have formed a special task force to find out more about us several months ago. I've kind of been waiting for them to knock on my door. We don't know the true purpose of their task force, so it doesn't hurt to get close to one of them to find out."

"No, it doesn't, but what the hell would they even want a list of our breed for?"

"To be honest, I'm not sure. I was actually about to find out more when you decided to barge in on Hugh and me."

I grinned. "Hey, you were done. I didn't know that you were into pillow talk now."

"I'm not into pillow talk, Lena, but Hugh was relaxed, and I was hoping he'd tell me a bit more about the real reason they want the names. I know that's why he came back tonight. He hoped to speak with me alone, and there was a powerful mutual desire there between us. I figured it was a good thing to use to get him to talk."

"What excuse did they give you when they first asked for the list?"

"Said they wanted to protect us, but I'm not so sure that they don't want to round us up." She looked at me pointedly. "I'm sure you've heard the rumors of some of our people going missing."

I nodded. "Yeah, what does that have to do with them?"

"Hugh and his counterpart said the list was for our protection, and also to make sure that our people know they have rights, but I have to wonder."

"Rights?" I said indignantly. "What rights? We allow them to live."

"Yes, but they seem to think that our serving up our own justice is not appropriate."

"Fuck them! Who do they think they are?"

"The government," she replied with a sigh. "It was only a matter of time before they decided that they needed to exert control over us."

"That's not happening."

"Yes, I agree, but we also don't want to piss off Uncle Sam. We are going to have to figure out what they are really up to, and then go from there."

"How many of our people are missing?"

"I think the last I heard there were twenty-six that have disappeared."

"What if they have just gone underground?"

"Maybe."

"Or they could have jumped sides and are hiding with Portage."

"They could be, but the timing of this just makes me wonder." She tapped her fingers on the arm of the chair. "I think that Hugh's task force has something to do with it."

"Why didn't you take his blood then? You could have figured it all out much easier."

"I don't know. There is something about Hugh." She stared at the carpet for a moment, frown lines marring her forehead. After a moment, she blinked and smiled my way. "I want him to trust me, to show him that I want to trust him, and then see if there is any way we can use that friendship to gain something. Maybe he will tell me the truth. Maybe he won't. I don't want to use tricks to get into his head—not right now. If I can get him to trust me, maybe he can help us locate Joe Portage."

"That would be a plus, along with you getting a little rumba in the sheets while you do it."

"Hey, look who is talking."

I grinned at her. "I know, I know." I threw back the rest of my drink. "And on that note, I'm going down to the bar to find myself a little midnight snack. You might not have been hungry tonight, but I'm famished, and I fed just the other day."

"Oh, I'm hungry; I'm just holding back right now. I'll walk out with you. I need to go back to the office."

"Oh, I saw Garrett on my way up. He told me to remind you that the family dinner is Saturday."

She sighed. "Yes, the family dinner. You're going to be there, right?"

"I wouldn't miss it for the world. Not often that we get all our kids and ex-mates into one room."

"Your ex-mate," Kristin said with a laugh. "All of mine are dead."

I turned to her. "Does that ever bother you?"

"No," she said with a straight face. It was only a slight shift in her eye color that told me otherwise.

KRISTIN

"*L*ainey, can you get Jacques Berger, Harry Davies, and Ben Tremblay together and set up a time for a conference call?"

"Sure, I'll do that right now. What time do you want me to set it up for?"

"As soon as possible," I told her, and she disappeared to make it happen as Ryker came into my office.

"Mistress, one of the men from your earlier meeting is still here."

I leaned back in my chair. "Which one?"

"McMurphy. He's in the bar now. Do you want me to get rid of him?"

Now, why was he still here? Was this his way of trying to talk to me alone, or did he want something else? "No, I'm interested in finding out why he is still here. I'll go down and speak with him myself."

"He said he was just here for a drink, but you were on his mind." He smirked.

I laughed, "Can you tell Lainey to send someone down for me about fifteen minutes before the call?"

"Sure." He smiled and was gone.

I was only four feet out of my office when Joshua showed up out of nowhere and startled me as he asked, "Where are you heading?"

"Down to the bar to have a conversation with Hugh McMurphy." He nodded, and I saw his lips purse as he joined me in the elevator. "You do know that I will be safe going into my own bar, right?"

He grinned. "Not taking any chances."

"Well, make yourself scarce when you are down there, please. I'm hoping if I can get the guy to lighten up some, he might tell me the real reason for him coming here today."

"Yes, Mistress."

Hugh was sitting at the bar, and I joined him. He didn't seem that surprised that I had, and I knew he had been hoping that I would get word he was here. After taking drinks back to a table, I tried to get a better read on him. While his mind was wide open, I wanted to use my old police instincts to figure him out. It was more fun and reminded me of where I had come from and how far I had gone in the last forty-one years.

I wasn't surprised to both see and feel his sexual interest in me and realized that it might be the perfect way to break the ice. He was a very handsome man, and his mature sexuality oozed from his pores. I could do with a proper release.

Rex came to tell me the call was coming up, and he paused beside me. *"What are you doing with him?"*

"Trying to figure out what he wants," I replied.

"He wants to screw you six ways to Sunday," Rex snapped.

"Yes, I am aware of that, but there is something more."

"Whatever. Are you alright with him?"

"Yes," I nodded, and then he turned and walked away without any further comment. He was just like his father, Trent. He always wanted to know what I was up to, although he knew that I could take care of myself.

I told Hugh I had to make a call and was getting up when I sent Ryker a message. *"Ryker, take Mr. McMurphy up to my apartment."*

"Um, your apartment, Mistress? You don't want him in another room?"

"No, my apartment. Stay with him until I get there."

"Yes, Mistress."

I was in the conference chamber two minutes before the call and took a seat in my chair, wondering what I could get out of Hugh besides a good time. After I pushed the button for the hologram camera, I clicked on the receive button, and Canadian Master Ben Tremblay's image wavered slightly as it came into focus a few feet away.

"Evening, Kristin. How are you?" he said as he smiled kindly and crossed one leg over the other. Ben and I spoke quite often as a lot of our breed crossed the borders between our two countries. For a few minutes, we exchanged pleasantries about family and business before Jacques Berber, the French Master, and Harry Davies, the British Master, appeared in a semi-circle around me.

After a few quick hellos, we got right down to business. "Have any of you been contacted by your local governments about giving them a list of our people and special abilities?" All three of them looked immediately concerned as they glanced at one another and said no. "Well, expect it."

"What is happening there, Kristin?" Harry asked.

"I was approached tonight by ICE and DHS about providing such a list to them. We heard that they started a new task force to deal with our breed several months ago, although we don't know much about it. The security is tight, so we haven't heard much, but neither have they. It has taken them a while to figure out who I am and how to reach me. Today they stated that they wanted to protect us and make sure that our breed was being treated fairly. They were questioning the government we have in place for the breed."

Jacques growled. "They have no rights when it comes to our breed."

"I agree, Jacques, but I have a feeling that all of our governments are going to put more pressure on us to give them information about our people." I sighed. "They also made mention of our way of handing out punishment. Said that our race needed to know their rights."

"Their rights?" Ben snapped. "Our people know their rights and their place."

"Most of them do," Jacques replied dryly. "Kristin, did you, by chance, locate that man you were looking for?"

"Joseph Portage, no, not yet. I expect a report on that tomorrow when Angelina returns. I'm sure that if she had some solid intelligence information on him, she would have called me. Since she hasn't, I have to assume that she hasn't learned much."

"The guy can't hide forever," Ben hissed.

"We'll find him, Ben. I promise you; we'll find the son of a bitch. Once we do, we can figure out where to go from there. I might have another way to get some information, though."

"What is that?" Harry asked.

"Well, right now, I have the DHS guy in my apartment. I'm going to build a friendship with him, see if he will come to trust me, and then maybe I can figure out what the government really wants. I'm concerned that they either want to confine us someplace, or they want to exploit some of our abilities."

"Build a friendship?" Jacques grinned. "Oh, Kristin, I do enjoy how you build friendships."

I chuckled. Yeah, I'd not only slept with him but fed from Jacques many years ago when we had first met. Being not only a Master but an elder too, his blood had given me a strength that I had missed since Alex had died.

"Just be careful that you don't share too much with him," Harry added, always the careful one out of our group.

I shook my head. "I don't plan on telling him much, Harry. He will get just enough from me that he will see that I want to help him, but that I'm leery. If he thinks that I want to trust him and work with him, I might be able to get more from him. Besides, having an in at the DHS office, or whatever task force they have started, might be good for us."

For the next twenty minutes, we discussed some other issues in the breed, including the subject of missing people before we bid each other goodbye. Each of us said we'd reach out to other masters to see if anyone had contacted them for the same reason.

After signing off with them, I sat there for a moment, thinking over our missing people. Ben said he had five people missing that he was just made aware of, but Jacques and Henry both said they weren't aware of any. Both of them said they would look into it, though. There were three options here. One, they had been killed. Two, they had changed sides and were now working against us, or three, they were being held someplace.

After a few minutes of dwelling over that, I told Lainey I'd be upstairs for a little while and that I didn't want to be bothered. She said she would hold down the fort until I returned.

Like usual, Joshua followed me to the elevator. "You can go; you don't need to come up," I said to him as I pushed the button to call the elevator.

"I'm staying." His voice was tense, and I put my hand on his arm.

"Look, I know you don't approve, but I have a purpose for this." The elevator opened, and we stepped in.

He looked at me hard. "You need to feed; please tell me you are going to at least use him for that."

I shook my head. "No, I don't plan on feeding on him, at least not tonight."

He glared at me. "Why not? You need to. I don't like that guy; something about him is off, but you need to feed."

"I will, soon," I told him.

Joshua turned toward me, taking my face in his hands, his touch and gaze both tender. "You know I'm always here for you, Kris."

I leaned forward and kissed him tenderly. "I know you are, Josh."

He wrapped his arms around me and kissed me harder. I got swept up in the feel of his mouth on mine for a few seconds and then pulled back. "Not now."

"You know how I feel about you," he stated huskily.

"I do, and you know I care about you, too."

"But you don't love me."

"Josh, I do love you, just not the way you love me." The story of my life.

He sighed and stepped back as the elevator door opened. "I'm not giving up."

I smiled at him as I stepped off, not sure how I should respond to it. Inside my apartment, I dismissed Ryker and Josh's words and stared at Hugh for a moment. He did intrigue me, and I headed to my room without a word. I got undressed and lay down on the bed, calling out to him mentally.

The look on his face when he saw me was almost comical, but the instant desire in his gaze and the vibration of his lust that filled the room kept me from laughing.

Hugh leisurely undressed, pulling his tie from around his neck as he slowly moved toward me and stared at every inch of my body. My hands drifted over my stomach and lower, and he swallowed hard. I remained where I was, teasingly stroking parts of my body as he removed his clothing. His gaze followed my hands, and when he removed his boxers, I smiled to myself, knowing that this was going to be good.

He stood at the edge of the bed, his fingers drifting over my legs, his eyes locked at the apex of my thighs, and he licked his lips. That one motion was enough to make me want to throw him to the bed and devour him, but I didn't. I let him have control over the situation. He grabbed my ankles and yanked my ass to the edge of the bed. I chuckled as he dropped to his knees. This man liked to be in control—and I was all for that.

His hands spread me wide, and he groaned as he leaned forward and put his mouth to me. I stroked the top of his head, enjoying the feel of the soft strands as I let myself go and enjoyed the moment. He was good, and his tongue helped release the tension of the night. His fingers thrusting into me began to build a new tension, and I arched off the bed, holding him closer to me as I climbed.

I hit the top as he continued, and he dug in deeper, lapping at my oversensitive flesh until I couldn't take it any longer. I pushed his face away as I rolled to my side and got on my knees. "Stand."

He did, and I took his rock-hard erection in my hands, licking my lips to prepare them for the first taste. As I pulled him deeply into my mouth, I stared up at him. His hands came to the sides of my face, and he stared down in wonder. My teeth trailed over his sensitive flesh, and he hissed as his head rolled back on his shoulders. I brought him almost to the point of no return, and then I laced my fingers with his and began to lean back, pulling his body down to mine. His face hovered over me, and he let go of my hands to brush the hair back from my face. He stared at my lips and then into my eyes.

I cupped the back of his head and brought our mouths together to share our first kiss. His tongue was just as masterful in my mouth as it had been between my legs. His hips shifted as I widened my legs for him, and he plunged deeply into me. My mouth pulled from his on a gasp as he filled me. His gaze was mesmerizing as I stared up at him, and my mind began to descend into the past. Before it could pull me under, I yanked it back. I didn't want to think about Julian now, not here, not with Hugh.

We didn't speak; we let our touches do the talking. Hugh went to his knees, lifting my hips to an angle where he could thrust deeper, his thumb brushing the sensitive bundle of nerves that cried for his attention again. He squeezed my breast almost painfully before he leaned forward and bit at my nipple. My orgasm exploded through me, carrying him over at the same time.

His weight was welcomed as he collapsed on me, and we calmed ourselves. My hands drifted over his back lightly; goosebumps peppered his skin.

He chuckled and rolled to his side. "That was—wow."

I snickered. "Wow, huh? A rather impressive term."

He lifted on an elbow. "I'm not sure my mind could come up with a more impressive term right now."

"I guess you enjoyed that, then?"

His eyes searched for something as he stared down at me. "Enjoyed? I think I'd have to say that was the best sex of my life."

I laughed loudly. "Oh, really?"

"Yes," he said thoughtfully. "You are a beautiful woman, Kristin, but I sense much more in you than just your beauty and passion."

Well, what was I supposed to say to that? I didn't have to reply, though, because he began to speak immediately after that. "I think we should talk."

"Talk? We just had sex, and now you want to talk?"

He nodded and shifted on the bed to put some distance between us, leaning against the headboard. "Yes, I think we should talk."

"Well, alright then. What do you want to talk about, Hugh?"

"How about you tell me more about you? Like how old you are?"

I rolled over to my stomach, and he leaned forward and grabbed one of my ankles, pulling my foot into his lap. I rolled to my back as he began to massage my foot. Damn, I might need to keep him around for a little while if he liked to do massages.

"Do you really want to know?"

He nodded.

"I'm almost seventy-six."

His hand paused. "Seventy-six? Are you kidding me?"

"No, why, did you think I was older?"

"No, I just can't imagine a woman of that age being that damn good in bed."

I laughed. "Yeah, well, you aren't so bad yourself for an almost forty-year-old man."

He smirked and resumed his ministrations on my feet. "Glad you think so." He paused and stared at me for a long time. "I hope this wasn't just a one-time thing, Kristin."

"Why?"

"Because there is something about you that intrigues me." Interesting choice of words for him to use since I had thought the same thing about him.

"Well." I sighed as I heard the door open in the living room. I immediately felt her presence and wanted to shout out to her to go away, but she was in my bedroom a moment later.

"I'm next!" Angelina announced, and a little voice in my head whispered, no way, honey, he's mine.

HUGH

Few things surprised me in life, especially in my line of work, but having sex with Kristin had shocked the hell out of me. When I first stepped in her room and removed my clothing, I'd anticipated a quick, but pleasurable fuck. I did not expect to feel like I had just connected with her in some odd way. When had it happened? How had it happened?

I sat against the headboard, my head spinning on the whys of it all. Was it because of what she was? That couldn't be it. I'd been with a vampire before, and I hadn't felt like this. Had she put me under some strange spell that I didn't know about? I had to admit that even though I'd researched and paid close attention to the vampire race since it became public knowledge, I still didn't understand a lot of it or what they were capable of—although I wanted to know it all.

I had a feeling that even though the vast majority of people knew they existed, they didn't have a clue as to what they could do either. That was my goal. I wanted to know, needed to understand them. Yes, maybe I had an underlying reason for being here that pertained to work, but my personal interest was just that—personal.

When her sister arrived, I was surprised and uncomfortable to be face-to-face with Angelina Michaels, especially since I was buck naked in her sister's bed. Angelina had a reputation, and it wasn't just in the bedroom. There were stories that went back over forty-five years of her violence, both to vampires and humans. In our office, I had much more information on Angelina than I did on her sister, and I wondered how much of that information was correct.

I studied her for a moment; she was just as beautiful as her sister, although she seemed a bit more reserved, except for her innuendos.

As Angelina got off the bed to leave, she mentioned something about Kristin sleeping with guys who had similar eyes. Similar eyes to whom? Someone she was mated to perhaps?

I knew I wasn't going to get any answers to that question right now. I'd have to wait and see what happened. Kristin sighed as her sister left.

"Well, I guess my playtime is over. I need to get back to work."

She climbed from the bed and disappeared into her bathroom for a few moments. I was collecting my clothes when she came out and feeling a bit frustrated that I hadn't gotten a chance to talk to her. With one look at her gorgeous body, my frustration switched to a primal one, and I was instantly ready to go again. To hell with talking, I wanted her riding my cock again. She smirked as she looked at my hard dick.

"Another time," she said with a wink. "You're welcome to use the shower before you leave." She began to dig around in a drawer.

"You wouldn't mind?"

"Not at all. Help yourself."

"I'm going to take you up on the shower." I came to stand behind her, staring at her reflection in the mirror above the dresser. My hand brushed her side, cupping her breast and rolling her nipple between my fingers. "And the other invitation, too. The one for another time."

Her chest arched into my palm for a moment. "I'll hold you to that."

I rubbed myself along her back while I ran my nose up the column of her neck. She smelled sweet, good enough to eat again; was that her perfume? "You sure your work can't wait a few minutes more?"

She laughed. "Not unless you want my sister to come in and join us."

My brows popped; now as exciting as that might be, I wasn't sure I was ready for the two of them together. I planted a kiss on Kristin's neck and then grinned at her reflection. "Yeah, I'll just go take that shower."

She chuckled as I walked away. "Make sure to leave your number. I'll call you when I have time."

"I'll do that." At the bathroom door, I glanced back and saw her frowning. Was it something I said? Or was her mind on other things already?

I glanced around her large bathroom, the fixtures all gold, the counters marble. It was as opulent as the rest of her place, but not flashy, and I found myself liking it. I would have been blind not to see the male body soap in her shower—that I didn't like quite as much. How many men did she bring in here? Who had put it there? Was she in a committed relationship with someone? Maybe the guy that she was always with? Perhaps I should have asked her that when she asked if I had someone waiting for me.

When I finished showering, I dressed and was heading out to the living room when I heard them mention Joseph Portage. We had been searching for that man for a while, but he was a ghost.

I knew why we were searching for Portage, but why were they trying to find him? Was it because he was waging war against just about everyone? Probably, and if Kristin was searching for him, I had a feeling it was to kill him.

She showed me out, asking me if I'd left my number before brushing a kiss over my cheek. The man outside the door glared at me as I left. Did he not like Kristin with other men? It was apparent that he was close to her, but just how close? Shower close?

We stood in the elevator as it went down, and I studied him. He was intense-looking, a bit taller than me, green eyes, short cut brown hair. He turned to me as if he knew what I was doing, lifting a brow my way. "I'm not your type."

"You're not mine either," I replied. I knew that the best way to get respect from these guys was to show them that you weren't afraid. "What I was wondering was if you were her type."

He turned away, but not before I saw the slight frown on his brow. "What the mistress does is none of your business."

"Maybe not right now."

He turned so quickly that I didn't see it. Suddenly, he was right in front of my face, our noses almost touching. "Don't think for a second that you are more than a quick fuck for her. She's too damn important to our people to get involved with a human male. You are merely food and a plaything to her." He lifted my chin roughly, looking at my neck on both sides. "Although I guess you weren't up to her standards since she didn't take your vein."

I didn't reply. I didn't know what I could have said because I was pretty damn sure he was right. I was nothing to her, and never would be, but I didn't back down. After he let go of my chin, I kept my eyes locked on his.

He slowly stepped away, a little smirk on his face. Was that because he knew he had practically scared the crap out of me? Or because he knew his words hit home?

"At least you aren't stupid enough to think that there will ever be anything between you," he said gruffly.

I frowned. "How do you know what I was thinking?"

"You project some of your thoughts loudly," he said as the door opened on the bottom floor.

"You really can hear my thoughts?" I asked.

He turned to me, smirking again. "Oh, yeah. I can hear them, and I can hear your heart thudding hard in your chest with fear. I hear every beat and the sound of your blood rushing through your veins."

"Can she?"

He laughed. "Man, we all can. Now get out. I have work to do."

I stepped around him and left, heading straight to the front door. I pulled my cellphone out of my pocket, noting it was almost ten-thirty. I dialed Tom's number as I hit the sidewalk.

"Did you get anywhere with her?"

The best damn orgasm of my life, I thought but replied, "Not yet, but I think I might be able to. I didn't get much of a chance to talk to her tonight, but I have a feeling she will call me again. When she does, I'll speak to her then."

"Fine, I'll talk to you tomorrow."

I told him goodbye and hung up. There was no way that I was going to say to him that instead of talking, I'd been having earth-shattering sex. Damn, her body hummed like a fine-tuned instrument. By the time I got in my car, my dick was throbbing again.

I sat behind the wheel of the car for a moment, staring at the hotel. Why hadn't Kristin fed on me? Everyone I had spoken with tonight seemed to think that was my purpose. Was there something wrong with my blood?

~

*I*t was three days later before I received a phone call from a number I didn't know. My watch vibrated, and I glanced down to see a request for a voice-only call. Odd, since most people did projection calls now. I frowned as I tapped the earpiece tucked into my ear. "Hugh McMurphy."

"Hello, Hugh, it's Kristin."

I leaned back in my desk chair as her sexy voice zipped straight down my spine and lodged in my groin. I had been working late, and the office was quiet now. "Hey, wasn't sure I was going to hear from you."

"It's been a hectic couple of days."

I bet it was. It was crazy for me. In fact, there had been a small break in what I was working on, and I might have a lead as to where Joseph Portage was. I wasn't going to tell her that, though. I did not doubt that if she knew, she'd get to him before we could, and he'd be dead before we could speak to him.

"Yeah, for me too. How are you?"

"I'm fine, thank you. Are you available later?"

Just the thought of seeing her again was causing something to stir below the belt. "I could be. What did you have in mind?" Please say another romp in the sack.

"How would you like to come over for a drink? I'd like to talk to you."

"Just a drink and some conversation?"

She chuckled huskily. "Let's start with that. We'll see where it goes from there."

"Okay, what time?"

"Would ten be too late?" I glanced at my watch. It was almost eight so ten wouldn't be a problem.

"That's fine."

"Alright, I'll meet you in the bar at ten."

"I'll see you later, Kristin."

"Looking forward to it, Hugh." She hung up before I could say anything else.

I logged out of my computer, gathered my things, and then headed home. I had enough time to grab a bite to eat, shower, and then get over to her hotel. I felt like a kid that was just offered a trip to the candy shop.

I ate leftover stew when I got home, and then showered, dressing in jeans and a long-sleeved dark-blue Henley-style shirt. The shirt made my eyes look brighter blue, and I was hoping she would notice. Her sister's comment had stuck with me the last few days, and I wondered if I could use that to my advantage.

It was ten minutes before ten when I walked into the hotel and saw Ryker standing near the far elevator. He grinned at me, and I lifted a hand his way. At least not all of them hated me being around.

In the bar, I paused to glance around but didn't see her. Instead, I went to the bar and ordered a scotch on the rocks. "Also, pour one of whatever the mistress likes. I'm meeting with her."

His brow lifted slightly, but he kept his mouth shut. The bar was crowded tonight, and voices competed with the music that was playing on the overhead speakers. There was a noticeable softening of the voices a few minutes later, and I immediately glanced at the door to see Kristin had stepped in.

I scanned the room; many people watched her as she approached me, and I was rather impressed by the amount of respect and curiosity that she garnered from these people. "Hello, Hugh. Right on time."

"I have a habit of always being ten minutes early," I said.

She smiled as she collected her drink from the bar. "Ten minutes early, or you consider yourself late, right?" I nodded, and she laughed and began to walk away. I followed her to the same table we had sat at before. "I'm the same way. I think it has something to do with when I was a beat cop. I always made sure I was there with plenty of time before my shift started. I didn't want the guy who had just worked twelve to get stuck on a last-minute call."

"You were a cop?" I wasn't sure why that surprised me, but it did.

She studied me. "What? Your research on me didn't tell you that?"

I shook my head. "To be honest, there is very little information about you."

She sipped her drink. "Is that why you are here? Are you trying to fill the gaps and get more information about me for your task force?"

"No, my reason for being here tonight is strictly personal."

"Is it? Are you seriously trying to tell me that if you learned something personal about me, you wouldn't be typing it up in a report tomorrow to add to your database?"

I thought about that for a moment. "Honestly? I think that might depend on what it was. If you're going to tell me about the men you've been in love with, the things you like to do for fun, the kinds of foods you enjoy eating, what else you like to do in bed, then no. It won't. If you are going to tell me about your people, what they can do, then maybe."

"I won't talk about my people," she replied after a few seconds.

"Then I guess we're going to talk about what else you like to do in bed."

"Why talk? Why don't we just go try out a few things?"

A slow grin spread over my lips. "I thought you would never ask, although not to turn down what could be a rather exhilarating night, I thought you wanted to talk."

She leaned back in her seat and spun her glass slowly as she watched me with light-blue eyes. "Alright, so we'll talk."

"What would you like to talk about?"

"How long of a conversation do we have to have before I can get you back up to my apartment?"

"Is that what you want, Kristin?" A sly smile slipped over her lips, and I lifted my drink and downed the rest of the scotch. "Then, consider the conversation over."

ZANDER

"**I** heard someone else was trying to locate you earlier this week," I said into the phone.

"People are always looking for me; who was it this time?"

"Angelina Michaels."

My father chuckled huskily through the phone. "Oh, really? The Angelina Michaels? Well, I'm greatly honored. Where was she asking?"

"One of my contacts in Lexington called me the other day, told me she was sniffing around trying to find you."

"You know she's not the only one trying to locate me, Zander."

"Yeah, I know." I sighed. "Zeus did mention my name to her, though."

"Why would he do a stupid thing like that?"

"I think he was trying to stay on her good side. Said she has a serious reputation for being scary."

"If she's anything like her father, she is."

"Well, when he mentioned my name, she seemed surprised that you had a son. I guess that information never filtered back to them."

"I've worked hard to keep your name quiet all these years, Zander. It was for your protection. I did not doubt that any enemy of mine would have come after you had they known you existed. It's why I wanted you to carry your mother's surname."

"Yeah, well, I'm a Portage, so I'm keeping my name."

"If they know about you, Zander, they will be looking for you too."

I smiled to myself. "Let them come. I'm not afraid of them, Dad."

He was quiet for a moment. "Well, it might help us out in the long run."

"Yeah, how?"

"I'll tell you when the time is right."

"Whatever." It was always the same old bullshit with this man. Still so damn secretive and guarded after all these years. First, it was wait until you transition; then, it was just a couple more months. Months turned into years, and it drove me up the fucking wall.

"So, tell me how things are going? Have we been able to pull more people over to our side?"

"Yeah, we've had a few more join us. Not as many as I would have hoped for. Some are getting antsy with the way things are going under the mistress. She really pissed off a lot of people when she announced that human-turned were illegal."

"Good. I have a feeling that things are going to get even tenser in the next couple of weeks. Keep working on them," he paused, "and since word has gotten out, you are going to want to be even more careful. I have no doubt they would come after you."

"I'm not worried about that, Dad. You know I can take care of myself."

"Zander, stop being so naive. You know that I have a lot of enemies, but you are still very young in this world. You've only been transitioned a few years. You have no real clue about our world. I sheltered you from much of it."

"But you have been instructing me about our world since I was old enough to understand. Hell, even before I was old enough. You always told me that I was going to be instrumental in helping you gain the position that you deserve."

"Yes, you will be, but I don't trust the mistress or her sister. If they felt you were a threat, I have no doubt that they would try to take you out immediately, Zander."

"I'm not sure they would. I have a feeling that if they could get to me, they'd bring me in and try to get all the information out of me that they could about you and your plans."

"And then they would kill you."

"Maybe, or I would kill them. It doesn't matter. Eventually, I'm going to have to deal with the mistress and her sister. Whether it's to talk to them or kill them, most likely the second."

"Don't get cocky, Zander. You still have a long way to go before you can come up against the mistress. Especially if she is with her sister; they are are more powerful than most vampires."

"Yeah, have you seen what they can do?"

"No," he said softly. "But I have heard enough of the stories. Most people who do see what they are capable of never live long enough to speak about it."

I laughed. "You make it sound like they are untouchable."

"I didn't say that, Zander. I said they were dangerous, and you should remember that."

"I will, Dad." I sighed. I was damn tired of him telling me that people were dangerous. I had heard the stories since I was a child. My father being able to influence me with his mind to never speak of our world to humans. Even if I had wanted to, I physically hadn't been able to.

That's how he kept his location a secret from so many. His ability to implant in their minds that speaking the truth would instantly kill them. To be honest, I wasn't sure if that would actually happen or not. I'd never seen anyone defy the order.

Anyone who came in contact with him or worked directly for him was given the same command: Never reveal his location to anyone, not even me.

You would think that I would at least know where he was, but nope. Even I was kept in the dark, which was another thing that pissed me off. I had seen him only a few times since I had transitioned two and a half years ago. I did, however, see my mother, but even she was unable to tell me where he was.

"Be patient, Zander; the plan is underway. I've been working on this for a very long time, but it is finally in motion."

"If you say so," I replied drolly.

I hung up from my father and turned to stare out the window of my condo. The surf below was angry tonight as a storm was brewing. There was a storm coming; that was for sure. We all knew it, and it wasn't just the weather.

The war that my father had been waging against the society was on the verge of finally happening. Yes, many, many years ago, he had made a play for the Master position of the race, and he had almost succeeded. Alexander Armstrong had been killed, and that's when his mate had taken over. I was only a teenager then, but I remembered it well.

In fact, my father had allowed me to be there to watch. I'd stood back in the shadows, surrounded by men who worked for my father to protect me. As I stared at Alexander, something deep inside of me had screamed to come out of the shadows. Had it been my father's hatred for the man that had been ingrained in me for so long? Was it only my wish to see my father succeed? I hadn't known the answer then, and I still didn't know it now.

I wanted my father to take over as the Master, and yet part of me didn't. Was that only because I knew that once he commanded our breed, I would eventually have to take it over? I wasn't sure that was what I wanted—at least not now. I was too young even to consider such things, but wasn't the Mistress young by our standards?

That was part of the issue with her overseeing the breed. Many thought that she was too young, only seventy-something, compared to many of our elders who were hundreds of years old. My father was over three hundred, and I had a hard time imagining living that long. How much had changed in the world in his years? How much would change in my lifetime?

I closed my eyes, bringing back up the image of Alexander being held down by my father's henchmen. I'd had this almost undeniable urge to rush forward, to do something. Maybe part of me wanted to drive the stake through his chest to please my father. Or maybe there was a part of me that had sought to release him.

In the years since Alexander had been removed from the Earth, I'd dreamed of him. Odd dreams that didn't always make sense. It was like a part of me knew him; part of me understood him. I chalked it up to having spent many years learning about the man. Perhaps I had been taught so much about him that I felt a part of me really did know him. Maybe I was just making all this shit up.

"Zander, sweetie," Laura called from behind me as she approached and put her arms around my waist, cooing in my ear. "We have to go; they are waiting for you, my love."

I sighed as I put my hand over one of hers on my chest. "Yeah, I'm coming."

I turned to Laura, staring down into her pretty face. This was a match that my father wanted, but for some reason, I held back. My eyes tracked over her dark-brown hair, her pouty lips, her caramel-colored eyes, and I inhaled her aromatic scent of ginger. She was a good woman, several years older than me, but I just didn't feel it.

I wasn't ready to settle down and mate to anyone. There was so much more that I wanted to do, to see, to find before I decided to take a mate.

The image of a woman came to mind. Her features were cloudy as if I were trying to pull her from a dream. The only thing that ever brightened with the image was the way her eyes shimmered in silver.

I didn't know who she was, had never seen her before, but like Alexander, I felt that part of me knew her. Or perhaps should know her. Had someone schooled me on her when I was younger? Was she a famous elder? Was she my destiny—the one that I held out for?

A moment later, the image was gone, and as hard as I tried, I could not recall it.

"Hello?" Laura said as she cupped my cheek. "Where did you go, Zander?"

I laughed slightly. "Nowhere. Just thinking about something that my father said." I kissed her lightly and stepped away. "Are you coming with me?"

"Of course, darling. I'm not going to let you run around town by yourself."

Yeah, of course, she wasn't. I had a feeling that everything that I did was reported back to my father by her. That's how he knew every step I made, every person I spoke with.

I had confronted him once about it, but he had brushed it aside, saying that he needed to keep me safe and had people watching out for me for that reason. I wanted to call bullshit on that, but I kept my mouth shut. My time to speak would come.

Until then, I would deal with Laura and my father. I tucked her hand into my arm and led her out to the waiting transport.

KRISTIN

J sat on the roof of the building, staring at the dark sky above me, trying to count the stars. No matter how long my lifetime was, I'd never count them all, but that didn't stop me from trying.

The door opened to the private patio that I'd had constructed here. It was as close to freedom as I got these days. No matter where I went, I had an entourage of people around me. Some to help me, some to protect me, but there were times when I just wanted to scream at them all to go away. The roof patio was my only slice of personal paradise—off-limits to everyone unless directly invited—except my sister, who had her own entrance.

My sister approached, and I sipped from my crystal glass. "I told Joshua that I didn't want to be disturbed."

"Yeah, and I told him I didn't fucking care," Lena answered as she took a seat in the lounge chair beside me. "You just can't help yourself, can you?"

I turned slowly toward her—confused about what she was referring to. "What are you talking about now?" She pointed at the sky, and I pursed my lips. "You realize that this is the only place where I can be alone, right?"

"Yeah, it's also where you can stare up at the stars and feel sorry for yourself."

I guffawed. "I'm not feeling sorry for myself."

"Okay, then what are you thinking about?"

"I was contemplating what Hugh said to me the other night."

"Was he as good in bed the second time?" She grinned, and I let one of my own spread over my lips.

"Oh, and the third and fourth times, too."

"Hmph—" She frowned. "No wonder you don't want to share him."

I chortled. "I'm sure I'll get bored once I have what I need from him."

"Yeah, what is it exactly that you are trying to get from him again —besides a record number of orgasms?"

I snickered. "You are just jealous."

"Hell, yes, I'm jealous!" She slapped a hand on her thigh. "I can't remember the last time I was with a man that I wanted more than once, especially a human male."

I shrugged. I didn't want to talk about Hugh and the relationship that I had with him. Not that it was a relationship—was it a relationship? "Did you need something?"

"I wanted to remind you of dinner," she replied.

"Ah, yes, the family dinner." I pursed my lips. I wasn't sure why Rex and Garrett were pushing for us to have one, but they were. I glanced at my watch; forty-five minutes until I needed to be down there. Why did it feel like I had a noose around my neck, and it was tightening the closer it got to the time?

"Sounds like everyone is going to be here," she commented.

"That's nice," I said drolly.

She laughed. "No, it's not. They are up to something, and you know it."

"Yes, I do. I just haven't figured out what it is yet. Have you?"

She shook her head and changed the subject. "Did you ever find out what your boy toy wants from us?"

"Not completely. Hugh said again that he wanted to help protect us, which I have doubts about. I'm not sure how they could protect us, not from the wars we fight."

"Do you think maybe he means by the war that the humans want to run against us?"

"Maybe, but he mentioned again that they were interested in what abilities our people have. He said that they could be useful."

"Useful?" She chuckled darkly. "As in, they want to *use* us."

"Yeah, I have a feeling that might be the real reason that they want to know more about us. I picked up on a few things from Hugh, and they were conversations he'd overheard about if they had certain abilities, they might be able to achieve things."

"What are they trying to achieve, Kris? It sure doesn't sound good."

"I agree, it doesn't, but I don't know. What I do know is that my gut is saying all of this is tied to our missing people."

She turned to me. "Why the hell haven't you sucked everything out of his mind already?"

I shrugged. "I'm trying to see if I can trust him. I want him to tell me. Besides, Hugh is very good at hiding his thoughts from me."

"You're kidding?"

"No, it's rather impressive. It's like Hugh clears his mind when he's around me, or he's been taught, really well, how to hide his thoughts."

"Maybe you blow his mind, and the only thing he can think about is your body." She laughed, and I joined her.

"Oh, those particular thoughts are loud and clear." I peered at my sister. "And he thinks you are rather beautiful, too, although you scare the shit out of him for some reason."

She snorted as she threw her head back. "Sorry, no threesomes with my sister and her boy toy."

"That is *not* what I was suggesting. Although I joked with Hugh about that, I think it scared the crap out of him." I laughed. "Besides, what I was stating was that maybe when I've gotten what I need from him, you can have him for a while."

"Since when do we share men?" she asked and then put her hand up. "Forget I said that. We have shared quite a few, haven't we?"

I sighed and scooted off the chaise lounge. "Yes, we have, and a few of those men are expecting us to be downstairs soon. I should go change."

"Yeah, I'll see you down there in a little while."

"You're staying here?"

She leaned back and stared up at the stars. "I'm going to take up where you left off in your counting. Maybe between the two of us, we can get the job finished."

I laughed softly as I headed back inside. Joshua stood inside the door, and I forced myself not to sigh. "You did not have to wait for me, Josh. You know I am safe up here."

"You are never safe," he stated huskily.

"Why do you think that? Is there something that I don't know?" His hesitation was just long enough that I knew something was up. "What's going on?"

He hesitated for all of two seconds. "Someone tried to get in by way of the service elevator. Security caught him on camera just before he took it out."

Anger radiated through my chest. "Who?"

"His name was Vince."

"Was?"

"Yes," he said, just above a whisper.

I stepped around Joshua. "Why wasn't I informed about this when it happened?"

"Because you were busy at the time," he stated.

I spun back around and was in his face, and he jerked back in surprise. "I am never too busy that I could not be notified that someone had gotten into the private section of this building. What did he want?"

"He didn't say."

"He didn't say, or you all didn't give him time to say anything?"

"Rex didn't ask," Josh finally replied.

I lifted a brow. "Rex? Rex took him out?" He nodded. "Then I will speak with my son. In the meantime, if something like this happens again, I want to be notified immediately, is that clear?"

"Even if you are indisposed?"

"Yes, even if I am screwing someone, Josh. You do not keep things from me. Do you get that? You could have easily slipped into my mind to let me know that someone was in the building. That is why I continue to take your blood so that you can easily communicate with me whenever it is needed."

"I didn't want to bother you."

"Yeah, well, I suggest you bother me next time, Joshua, or your services will be put to use doing something else. Is that understood?"

He looked apprehensive as he nodded. "Yes, Mistress."

I was tempted to lean forward and ease his tension, but he needed to know that I was serious. I nodded abruptly toward him and then spun to take the stairs down to my apartment.

I was on the livid side as I changed clothes and brushed out my long hair, pulling it back and quickly pinning it up. No one should be keeping anything from me, especially not a breach of security.

When I finally got myself calmed down, I found Josh standing outside my door. I nodded to him, and he followed me to the elevator, standing quietly at my side. I hit the stop button just before we got to the ground floor and spun on Joshua, pushing him against the far wall, his head bouncing off the panel with a firm clunk.

"Do not ever keep stuff like that from me again. Do you understand me, Josh?" I leaned forward, my lips almost touching his. I felt his lust building under my hands, but he didn't touch me back. He nodded slowly. "After dinner, you will come back to my apartment. I need to feed."

"Yes, Mistress." He breathed toward me, and I shifted so that our lips weren't touching, but our breath mingled. I leaned forward and nipped at his bottom lip, and he sucked in a sharp breath. Before he could respond further, I was back on the other side of the elevator, and the stop button had been released.

He adjusted his suit jacket and returned to his position beside me.

"Let's get this damn dinner over with," I growled as the elevator door opened.

"Yes, Mistress." He smiled slightly from beside me, putting his hand to my lower back and escorting me off the elevator. We walked down the hallway toward one of the smaller ballrooms. How many people were coming tonight? Typically, when we had a family dinner, it was in one of the private dining rooms, not a ballroom.

Ryker stood at the door and opened it for us as we reached it. "Mistress," he said with a nod, and I stepped into the room and paused.

There were over thirty people in the room, and I let my gaze slide over them all. Trent's and my son, Rex, was standing with his half-brother, Garrett, who was fathered by Alexander. Beside them was my sister and her daughter Abina. On the other side of Abina was her father, Cameron. I smiled at him. It had been a while since I had seen Cam. I was immensely glad that he had come.

In another cluster stood Clay with his granddaughter Lorna and her mate Paul with their daughter, Lainey. Beatrix, Alex and Courtney's daughter, was with them too, along with her four-year-old son, Galen. She had yet to be mated, but I had heard rumors that she was interested in Jett.

Lindsey and Donovan stood off to the side with Skylar, Mick, Novah, and her daughter, Violet. Both Donovan and Mick were human-turned, and I hadn't seen either of them in a long time. The sight of Mick made me instantly think of Olivia and Gabriel, and I tried not to let the pain of their decision descend on me.

Novah was new to our inner circle, and while I appreciated her style, I wasn't sure I trusted her, especially since she had her eyes set on Rex.

Off to the far side were several of our sentinels, Matt, Conner, Steven, Bill, Jett, Cora, Lydia, and Paxton, and already seated at the back table were the elders from my board, Beckett, Henry, Scarlett, and Hazel. With them were two more men that I knew but wasn't well acquainted with: Richard and David.

"Wow!" I said as I forced a smile. "This really is a big family dinner." Rex and Garrett approached me. "What is the occasion?"

Rex and Garrett glanced at one another, and I observed them cautiously. They were up to something, and I wasn't sure I liked that.

Usually, the boys were slightly at odds. When they came together, it always meant trouble.

"We know that things have been hectic and stressful recently," Garrett said before he kissed my cheek. His dark hair was longer like his father used to wear it, and tonight it was pulled back at the nape of his neck. "We just wanted to give you a nice evening."

"Well, that's very kind of you." I lowered my voice. "But I don't believe you for one second. So please explain what you two are doing."

Rex laughed, the sound so much like his father, as he put his arm around my waist and pulled me forward. "We aren't up to anything, Mom. Come on. Have a seat so we can eat."

He led me to a table in the center of the room and held my chair out. "Is there a special occasion that I have forgotten?" I asked as I took my seat.

Again, my boys glanced at each other, and then Rex looked back at the elders' table, while Garrett laughed. "No, just enjoy yourself, Mom."

Angelina came to sit at my table, a brow raised. *"They are making me nervous."*

"Yeah, me too."

She laughed into my head, and then everyone else got seated. Rex stood and lifted his glass. "I'm glad that all of you were able to attend tonight. It's been too long since we were able to do something like this, and we need to return to doing it. Family is important, even in our way of life, and those of you here are family, or may one day be family."

I frowned as I glanced back to the elders' table; both Richard and David were staring at me. I forced a smile their way and returned my focus to Rex.

"I'd like to take a moment to remember those who were part of our family at one time and have moved on. I'll start with my father, Trent Myers." He lifted his glass high and then gulped his drink.

Garrett lifted his glass. "To my father, Alexander Armstrong." Many people raised their glasses and murmured his name.

"To my mother, Lyssa Lakin," Lorna said, and her daughter put her hand over hers.

"To Rosa," Cameron stated with his glass raised high.

"Cheating bastard," Angelina hissed under her breath, and I tried not to laugh.

Angelina shoved her chair back and stood, glancing around at everyone with a massive smile on her lips. "To Burke and Susan, our *crazy-ass* parents, may they forever rot in hell," Angelina said with dramatic glee, and I rolled my eyes amidst laughter in the room.

My sons glanced at me, and I stood, holding my glass up. "To all of those who we have loved and lost—and there are many. You will never be forgotten or replaced."

As I lifted the glass to my lips, I whispered his name into my mind. *To you, my Jules.*

Dinner got underway, and there were tons of laughs and talking amongst everyone. By the time we got to dessert, even I had relaxed and was enjoying the atmosphere—it had been too long.

It was as we finished that things changed quickly as Clay and Beckett came to my table with Richard and David. Beckett spoke as I stood. "Mistress, I know you have met these two elders before, but we wanted to introduce them to you again. This is Richard Mears and David Montauk."

I nodded to each one in turn. "It's a pleasure to see you both again. Thank you for coming tonight. I hope you are enjoying yourselves."

"The pleasure is all ours," David replied in a voice that carried a touch of southern in it.

"It was an honor to receive an invitation," Richard stated.

And just who invited them? Were they here on other business and since they were here, we were sharing hospitality? I had noticed that Beckett said that *we* wanted to introduce them to me again.

Beckett looked slightly nervous as he studied me. "Mistress, if we might have a few moments of your time."

"Is there a problem that I need to be made aware of?" I asked immediately.

"Well, no, but a few of us have discussed the fact that it has been eighteen years since Master Alexander has passed. We think it might be time for you to mate again."

Something shifted in me; just the tiniest flicker of anger ignited in my belly. "Excuse me?"

He shifted on his feet nervously. "The board has discussed this at length, and we feel that you might be taken more seriously by the breed if you had a man ruling at your side."

I closed my eyes for a second as that earlier flicker suddenly engulfed me, and I knew that when they opened, my eyes had turned silver for all four men shifted back.

"Out!" I snapped.

Several of the chairs at the other tables began to slide back, and I glanced around the room. "If you are not an elder, then leave this room—now!" The room began to clear out, although I felt the presence of Rex, Garrett, Lena, Joshua, and Cameron still in the room, along with the four elders.

"Would you like to repeat what you said?"

"I believe you are well aware of what I said, Mistress." He swallowed—hard.

I laughed rudely. "Oh, yes, I am well aware of the words that left your mouth, Beckett, but I was hoping that you might have misspoken. I was merely giving you a chance to take back those words."

"No, we have given this a lot of thought and consideration. Both Richard and David would be good matches for you. With your...blood consideration, there are not that many in which you can choose from."

"My blood consideration?" I peaked a brow. "You mean the fact that my blood will kill any vampire that is not old or strong enough to withstand it?"

"Yes," Beckett said as he lifted his chin. "Kristin, we are going to war soon, and we feel that our people will listen to you better if you have a man at your side."

I glanced between Richard and David. "No offense to either of you, but I'm not interested in having a mate."

I stepped forward and seethed into Beckett's face. "And if you ever broach this subject again, I will put a stake in your chest. You do not tell me what I am going to do, or whom I shall mate. Do you understand that, Beckett?"

"Kris." A hand landed on my arm, and I spun toward it, coming face to face with Clay. "We are only trying to find the best way to get through this. You could use the support, and you need someone you can regularly feed from."

"I feed just fine, thank you," I hissed.

"You do not feed nearly enough, Kristin. Taking small amounts from a variety of people a few times a week is not feeding properly. You know that," Clay said.

"*Kris, you need to take a step back and calm down while we think this over,*" my sister's voice whispered into my head.

I turned to her and knew she was right—well, about calming down. There was no way I was going to think any of this over. I was ready to tear all their heads from their bodies. Without another word, I stepped around Beckett and headed toward the door.

"Mistress, you can't leave now!" Beckett called out.

I lifted my hands, palms toward the door, and sent out a mental message to anyone who was outside to open the door. Both doors whipped back as I reached them, and I called over my shoulder, "Yeah, well, fucking watch me."

LENA

"Oh, man! Did you all just screw the pooch," I said the minute my sister was gone.

Clay glared at me. "Lena, you know as well as we do that she needs help."

"Actually—I don't. I think my sister has done a fine job. If she needs help, then I will help her. She sure as hell doesn't need a man around." I took a moment to eye up David and Richard and found them severely lacking—even for my tastes. There was no way Kristin would go for either of the stuffy shirts.

"Aunt Lena," Garrett said softly. "Mom needs someone strong in her life. Someone that she can rely on and feed from regularly."

"She feeds from lots of people," I said hastily.

"Yes," Clay replied. "But she needs a strong bond that can help her heal if she is injured. It's not like we want to take her power away; we know that she has done a great job, but she needs help. She needs to be stronger. If she were mated to an elder, her strength would be that much greater, and her ability to heal if she were hurt would immensely improve."

I glanced at Garrett and Rex; boy, was Kris going to give them hell later. "Kristin is not going to mate with someone to secure her health or to make her look stronger by having a man at her side. Kris mates for love."

"She has had her love—twice in fact," Scarlett said as she approached our group. "It's time that she focuses on our breed."

Only twice? I thought it was three times. I huffed out a breath and glanced around.

"You think that she's not focused on the breed every single minute of the day? Do you realize the only thing that is truly important to her is having control over her life, and now she has none! She has given it all up!" I growled at the group. "You guys don't know her like I do. Forty years ago, it was all about her controlling her own life, and she has given up all of that control to live here in a fucking fortress. She can't even leave the damn building without half a dozen people with her, but she lives this way because she believes in the breed. She believes in what she is doing—and she's damn good at it too!"

"The dangers are all around us," Rex said. "She needs to be protected as much as she can be. We aren't trying to take her control away, Lena."

I laughed. "You aren't? You sure as hell sound like you are. You just handed her two men on a silver platter and said which one looks good enough to eat? Pick one because you're going to bleed for him, screw him, and then he's going to be the new Master. You weren't even giving her a choice in the matter, Rex."

Everyone glanced around, looking at one another, and Garrett sighed. "I'll try to talk to her."

I pointed at him. "Oh, no, you won't. You'll be lucky if your mother will speak to you in the next century. I will talk to her and try to calm her down, and then maybe you all can have a rational conversation when she doesn't want to tear you to pieces."

Suddenly, Joshua appeared at my side. "She's gone."

"Gone?" I asked.

"Yeah, she left the building."

"No, I'm sure she's probably up on her patio."

"I looked; we've looked everywhere. She's gone, Lena." The usually reserved Josh was close to panic.

"Relax, she's a big girl, Josh. She can take care of herself."

"See," Beckett held his hand out. "She's irrational. She needs someone around her to keep her calm. I knew she wasn't old enough to deal with this."

"Give me a break, Beckett. You just blindsided the woman. It's not against any rules for her to go off on her own. She'll be back after she calms down. She might not be centuries old, but she is the scariest damn vampire I have ever seen. She can handle herself and anything you throw her way."

"We'll see about that," he muttered and began to stalk off.

"Do you have any idea where she would go?" Cameron asked. "I can try to speak to her. You know I can calm her down."

"No, I don't." I turned to Josh after responding to Cameron. "Do *you* have any idea where she might have gone?"

He shook his head.

I sighed as I put fingers to my temples and rubbed them—what a night. "Okay, let me think for a few minutes. In the meantime, I'm going up to the balcony; maybe I can feel her someplace out there."

"I'll come with you," Cameron said. I was going to tell him to get lost, but whatever.

I turned to Josh as we left. "Check the security cameras and see if you can tell where she left the building."

"I already have Jett doing that," he responded.

I turned and put my hands on his shoulders. "Kristin is going to be alright, Josh."

He nodded, and I left him staring after me as Cameron and I got on the elevator.

"Did you have any idea that was coming?" Cameron asked.

"No, and please don't tell me that you did."

"I knew nothing about that. I think she's doing a great job. I don't understand why they suddenly want to push for her to be mated."

"Because they are controlling bastards," I hissed. "God, she's given up everything to watch over the breed, and they do this to her."

"Angelina, I can understand where they are coming from, kind of. I mean, they want her to be safe and strong. She does need someone to bond with so she can get what she needs."

"Oh, trust me, Cam. She can get plenty of blood. She has no shortage of volunteers. She just chooses not to feed as often as she should."

He chuckled as the elevator door opened, and we walked to my apartment door. "I'm sure she does, but we need to change that. Maybe if she were feeding more regularly, they would see how strong she is."

I opened the door and went toward the staircase that went up to the patio. Our apartments were identical, and the only two that had an entrance to the roof. Not that I needed to use it as she did. I was able to come and go as often as I wanted. No one was gunning for me, at least not in the way they were for her.

At times I wished she wasn't the leader of our breed. If she weren't, she could leave this godforsaken building once in a while. Sadly, that wasn't the case. Man, I missed those earlier days when things were settled, and we'd hit the bar together, catch a movie, or stay up at all hours talking over the bullshit we did when we were growing up.

Not that we grew up together. Kristin and I were separated at birth, and it wasn't until Alex was kidnapped many years ago that we learned we had a sibling. Not just a sibling, but a twin—although, we were as different as night and day at times.

Our father, Burke, had raised me, and I had known since I was young what I was and what I would one day become. Kristin had not. Our mother had staged her own death, using her sister's body in place of her own, and Kristin was raised as a human and knew nothing of our world.

Kristin had killed our father when she came to rescue Alexander the first time that she was mated to him. Although she wasn't mated to him when she saved him. She had mated to his son, Trent—by accident. When Alex had gone missing, Trent meant to bond with her to protect her from Alex's pain but took it just a little too far.

It worked out in the end, and their relationship had been a good one, for the most part. Sometimes Trent tried to be overbearing, or he'd get a stick up his ass, but he was good to her, and she had loved him. She had also loved Alex—and Julian. We can't forget good old dad!

I stared out into the night, my mind lost in thoughts of the past as I dwelled back to the earliest memories I had. Back when Kristin was Calista, and Calista was mated to Julian. At that time, my soul had been in that of a child, their child, Anastasia. Julian's son, Damon, had been the one to kill Calista and me back then by bleeding us out quickly, but he didn't have enough time to stake us. Because he didn't do that, our souls were not lost forever, and we had been reborn— reborn as twin sisters.

I reached out into the night, trying to feel something, but the only thing I could feel was Cameron beside me. "Can you please go sit down; you are too close."

He laughed. "You used to like it when I was close."

I rolled my eyes. Yes, once upon a time, I was mated to Cameron, but that was before he decided that I wasn't enough, and he found sweet little Rosa. Or maybe I had been too much for him. That was probably more correct.

I closed my eyes and tried to focus on Kristin, endeavored to feel her somewhere out there in the night, but I couldn't. She was completely blocked off.

As I stood there trying to locate her, I slipped back in time again to when I had first come face-to-face with Kristin. We had seen each other previously in passing, but this was the first time we had spoken to one another. We had been in the center of a wind vortex that my human-turned, Olivia, had created. I had needed her help, the help of all of them, and that's why I had turned Kristin's best friend, Livy, into a vampire. I needed a bridge to get Kristin's attention, and luckily it had worked.

The man that I had been involved with—bonded to—was breeding human-turned females to find ones with special abilities that he could use to take over the breed. It was always about taking over the breed. I frowned. Back then and now, it was the same. Who could control us the most? Who could make sure we stayed in line, did their bidding? I was so fucking sick of it.

Leo had been disposed of, and then I had almost been killed. Along with me, Olivia and Gabriel, her mate, had almost died because they were only bound to me when Leo's brother, Fitz, shot me. I wondered what Olivia and Gabe were doing now. Who were they double-bonded to now that Trent was dead? The complexities of our world made me exhale loudly.

I attempted again, sifting through the vampires out there, searching for the strongest one. It was faint when I first felt it, and I turned to the east and smiled. There you are, sister, dear.

I let my shoulders relax. Now that I had an approximate on where Kris was, I knew who she was with and what she was doing—I could feel it through our bond. She was fine for now. I'd let them know in a few minutes that I had located her, and I would be the dutiful sister and go with them to bring her back to her prison.

"What are you smiling about?" Cameron asked from the seat he had taken.

"I know where she is."

"Okay." He went to get up, and I put my hand up to stop him.

"She's fine, and she will remain that way for a little while."

"Where is she? What is she doing?"

I grinned at Cameron. "She is with her human friend."

His brows popped up. "She has a human friend?"

I laughed. "Yes, a man she met. For some reason, she has taken a shine to him, although I'm not sure if it has more to do with the fact that he's on the new vampire task force thingy or that he has bright-blue eyes."

"Oh, does he know who she is?"

"He does. He came here on business and met with her and the elders. They hit it off, and now I think they are both using one another, not only for sex but for business. I think they are feeding off each other—not literally—trying to figure the other one out and see what they can help each other with."

"Who is the guy?"

"Hugh McMurphy. He works for the Department of Homeland Security."

"Huh." He nodded and looked thoughtful for a moment. "Well, good for her."

"Do you want to see Kristin mated to one of the elders?"

"No, I want to see Kristin happy and safe."

I nodded. "Yeah, me too."

He laughed. "I remember a time when you wanted her dead."

"A lot has happened since those times, Cameron." I eyed him carefully. "A lot has happened."

HUGH

*I*t had been a few days since I had last seen Kristin, and I couldn't get her out of my head. It was like something inside of me was continually searching for a way to get back to her. Maybe it had been too long since I'd been in a relationship with anyone—not that this was a relationship—or perhaps she had cast a spell over me. Could she cast spells?

Three years ago, I didn't think that vampires existed, so who was to say that a vampire couldn't be magical or that there weren't magical beings out there someplace. Or was I just losing my fucking mind?

In all seriousness, I wondered several times what the woman could do besides lead people and be utterly tantalizing in bed.

I was keenly aware that there would never be anything between us besides the intense sex and possibility of a fragile friendship in the future. However, that didn't stop me from oddly—almost obsessively—wanting more. It wasn't just the sex that I wanted; something deep within me wanted to know what it would feel like to have her slide her fangs into my neck and pull the blood from my vein.

It was twisted and fucked up, but it was on my mind. Every time I thought about that, I gave myself a fucking hard-on too. I knew it was wrong, especially in my position, but a part of me didn't fucking care.

I had spoken to her earlier today for a brief moment and had been hoping she might have time to see me tonight. Frustratingly, she'd had a previously scheduled family engagement that she needed to attend. Who exactly was her family? I'd met her sister, seen her son, but how many other members of her family lived in that hotel?

I kicked back on the sofa, watching a football game and drinking a beer while my mind spun in circles from my life to my job to Kristin. They all seemed to lead right back to the next one in a vicious circle— although thoughts of my life acquired the forefront of my mind most often.

Yesterday, I had my annual physical, and everything appeared to be perfect. The problem was that I felt like a bomb was ticking in my chest. It was as if my minutes were limited, and I didn't quite know what to do with that. Perhaps it was fear because both my father and grandfather had passed away early in life, and my subconscious was keenly aware that I was approaching the big four-zero, the same age that they were. Okay, so it was much more than perhaps. I was extremely fearful about hitting my next birthday.

I reminded myself that medicine was so much better now than it had been forty years ago. If the doctor said I was alright, then I had to believe him.

My job was intense and stressful, and I wondered if it would be my downfall. Last year, DHS, in cooperation with ICE, had created a new task force to deal with the vampire population. They had asked for volunteers to work on it, and I'd been one of the first ones to raise my hand. I was utterly fascinated with their lifestyle and what they could do, and it consumed me those first few months because the information was so hard to acquire. I sucked up every tiny morsel that I could learn, and our task force slowly began to track and record them.

Some were easier to track than others as they were blatant about what they were and what they could do. We had figured out early on that while some of them were a pain in the ass, they weren't the ones in charge. They were what we assumed was the bottom rung of the society. We had loosely associated the breed of vampires with something that had been around for years: gangs.

The bottom level did the dirty work and didn't care what people thought of them. Then came the middle class; they rode the coattails of society—neither good nor bad. We did not doubt that there was also a higher class, and then those that led. Perhaps the upper class and the leaders were the same, but we weren't sure yet.

There had been little known about the leaders until a recent interview in our office. Now we knew for sure that there were two significant factions located not only here in the U.S., but worldwide. One of them appeared to be on the up-and-up, while the other was anything but.

Tom Singer and I had hoped that reaching out to the faction that Kristin controlled would allow us to learn more about them and see if there was a way that we could help. Our bosses did want us to obtain a list of their abilities, hoping that if another war came our way, human or vampire, that we might be able to use those with abilities to put a stop to it. I had little doubt that they also wanted to use them for their own reasons. Who wouldn't want a superspy on their side?

Then there was Kristin herself. What I had seen of her—oh, man, what I had seen—was incredible. I knew that she was much more than just a means to earth-shattering sex; she was a strong woman who knew what she wanted. It was also apparent that she took her responsibilities seriously. What would it be like to rule over a society of immortals? What did her day consist of? What kinds of things did she have to oversee? What would it feel like to have her suck from my neck?

A knock landed on my door, and I glanced at my watch to see it was almost eleven. I frowned as I set my beer down. Who the hell could be at my door at this time of night?

"Display door camera," I called out, and a window popped up on my eighty-inch television screen. What the hell?

I jumped to my feet and moved quickly to the door. "Kristin? What are you doing here?" I glanced into the hallway, seeing no one else around.

"Hi, Hugh. Sorry for the surprise visit. Can I come in?"

I stepped back. "Of course. How did you know where I lived?"

She laughed as she stepped in. "How do you think?"

Right, of course, she had checked up on me. I closed the door and watched her as she drifted slowly around the living room. Her hair was pulled up tightly to her head, and she wore a gauzy blouse in black that was elegant, and holy crap, practically see-through I noted as she turned sideways.

"Not that I'm not happy to see you, I am, but what are you doing here?"

She turned to me, crossing her arms over her chest and looking frustrated and somewhat unsure. "Do you have another beer?"

"Sure," I told her and went into the kitchen to retrieve one. She took a tentative sip after I gave it to her and then sat down on the couch.

"I needed to get out," she said softly.

"Is everything alright?" I asked as I took a seat beside her.

She turned her blue eyes to me, and in them, I saw a mixture of sadness and frustration. "It will be."

I took her hand. "Talk to me, Kris; tell me what has you so upset."

"I can't, Hugh."

"You can, Kristin. You just choose not to."

She watched me for a long time, and I felt as if she were trying to make a decision. She stood abruptly. "I'm sorry. I shouldn't have come here."

I was on my feet as soon as the words left her mouth, and I took hold of her forearms. "Kris, sweetheart, you can come to me anytime." I didn't know what was going on, but I didn't like the fact that she was upset, and I didn't want her to push me away. It was as if I needed her to trust me, to let me further into her life.

Her chin dropped to her chest, and she stepped forward into my arms. I held her tightly, knowing that this was what I needed to do. I had to be there for her.

"Talk to me," I whispered against her ear as I brushed my lips over her head.

She pulled back, looking up at me with so much pain in her eyes. "I just needed to get away. This was the only place I could think to come." She laughed a little manically. "Would you believe that you are the only person I really know who doesn't live in my building? Jesus, I'm the fucking leader of our breed here in the U.S., and yet I don't know a damn person who lives around here."

"Maybe it's time to change that," I suggested, and she sighed in response. "I'm here for you, Kris. Does anyone know where you are?"

She shook her head. "At least not yet. I know they are looking for me, but I don't care."

"How did you get out? I thought you never left the building without a dozen people with you."

She gave me the smallest hint of a smile. "I got pissed off at something and walked out."

"They just let you walk out?"

"No, they didn't know I was going. I'm sure they figured it out pretty quickly, especially Joshua, who watches me like a hawk."

"He is rather protective." I cupped her cheek. "I'm glad you came to me, Kris. I was just thinking about you."

Her smile began to grow. "You were, huh?"

"Yeah, I always seem to be thinking about you."

The smile vanished. "Is that because of your job?"

I shook my head. "No, it's because of who you are. An incredibly beautiful, intelligent, strong, sexy woman that I can't seem to get enough of."

Her hands slipped up my chest and to the back of my head. "Then let's see if we can rectify that, shall we?"

Like I was going to tell this goddess no. I leaned forward and kissed her tenderly. My hold brought her closer to my body as the kiss deepened. I pulled back. "How long do you have before they find you?"

She shrugged. "Does it matter?"

"It does if I want to take my time and love every inch of you."

Her eyes brightened. "Then we will have the time."

I shifted my hands to her hair and began to remove the clips that secured her long tresses. They slowly began to fall, and when I had all the clips out, I ran my fingers through the luxurious waves to comb it out. Her eyes closed, her lips parted, and her head tipped back as if she were in heaven. My lips went to her neck, and I ran hot kisses along the column, pausing once to bite at the tender skin.

She whimpered as she held my head in place as if she were asking me to bite harder. I shifted her head to the side so I could reach her neck better, biting down on the column of her neck just under her ear. She practically crawled up my body as I released the skin and caressed the spot with my tongue.

A moment later, she was tearing at my t-shirt. Not just trying to get it off me, but literally tearing it from my body. My knees went almost weak at the animalistic way she did it. She lifted her face to me, her eyes crystal blue, the tips of her fangs just visible behind her full lips; my dick throbbed, and her mouth ran hot kisses over my neck. The rasp of her fangs ran along my skin, and I thought I would orgasm right then.

I had imagined what it would be like. The need to know what it was like pushed me on, and I cupped the back of her head, holding her mouth to my neck, practically begging for her to take my blood—but she didn't.

She pulled herself away from me, smiling seductively as she stepped back and pulled me by the hand toward the hallway. My gaze drifted to her shirt, where her erect nipples peaked through the fabric, and my dick throbbed harder.

We barely got into my room before I was cupping her breasts and then bent down to mouth them through the rough material. I dropped to my knees, working quickly at the waistband of her leather pants to get them off. I needed to taste this woman. I needed her like she was what would keep me alive.

She went to remove her top, but I stopped her. "Oh, no, keep that sexy thing on."

She chuckled huskily as she sank to the edge of my bed, and I practically dove between her legs. She held my head in place, straining against me as I hit all the right spots and pushed her over the edge. She rolled over, getting on her knees and backing up. Oh, fuck yeah. My pants were gone in a second, and I slammed into her from behind.

One hand held her hip in place, and the other ran up her spine, under her shirt, and back down before grabbing her other hip and crashing into her again. I was so close to finishing when she jerked away, rolling over and moving back on the bed. I crawled onto it with her, and she pushed me down to my back, climbing over my hips and seating herself on me.

Her long hair spilled over her shoulders, and I brushed it aside so I could watch her breasts move through the material as she rolled her hips. I gripped them, squeezing tightly as I knew she liked that and felt her body squeeze me intimately as her head fell back on a moan. I could still see the tips of her fangs, and I wanted so badly for them to be buried deep in my throat like my dick was in her body.

I curled a hand around her neck and pulled her face down to mine. "I want you to drink from me." The words were husky as they left my mouth, and her eyes widened ever so slightly at the invitation, but she shook her head. "Why?" I stopped moving my hips and held her face in my hands.

"Because I don't want to ruin this, Hugh."

"Ruin it? Wouldn't that make it better for you, for us?"

She closed her eyes for a moment, and when she spoke again, her fangs were retracted. "You make it better for me. I just want us to be a man and a woman. For just a little while, I want to forget what I am, what you are, and just feel us."

I caressed her cheek, leading her lips to mine, where we kissed unhurriedly for a few moments. "Then let's be just us, baby."

She didn't have to say anything, but I saw the thankfulness in her eyes as she began to move over me again, and the two of us eventually tumbled over the top together.

Kristin lay with her head on my chest, her fingers drifting over my stomach a few minutes later when she sighed. I squeezed her hip. "What's wrong?"

She leaned up on her elbow. "Time for me to go; my watchdogs are here."

I laughed. "Your watchdogs, huh?"

She kissed my nose. "Yes."

"How did they find you? Are you wearing a tracking device?"

She shook her head. "No, my sister can feel me."

"Are they going to be upset that you left?"

She threw back the sheet that was covering us and sat up. "Oh, a couple are upset, but I can deal with them."

"How many are here?"

She stood and cocked her head. "Three in the hallway, three more on the street."

"How do you know that?"

She shrugged. "I can feel them."

"Huh," I grunted. "Just like that, you can feel them?"

"Yes, it's like they all have individual signatures, and when they are around, I feel them."

"Can you only feel the people who work for you?"

She shook her head as she slipped her feet back into her heels. "No, I can feel them all, which also means that right now, they can feel me too."

"That's dangerous for you, isn't it?"

"Yes, it's why Joshua is always with me. He has the ability to hide my presence."

"Well, then you better get back to him," I told her as I got out of the bed and pulled my pants on. "I don't want you to get hurt because of me."

Her smile was crooked. "I can take care of myself, Hugh."

"I have no doubt that you can." I put my hands on her hips. "But I'd rather you not have to defend yourself because you came to me. Next time you need me, you call, and I'll come to you where you are safe."

She touched the side of my face, looking contemplative. "I like you, Hugh. It's been a long time since I found myself liking someone for who they are, not what they are."

I laughed. "We really don't know each other that well. You realize that, right? I know we always say we are going to talk, but we usually end up in bed almost immediately."

"Yes, true." She leaned forward and kissed me. "I know you better than you think, though." Her gaze drifted to my neck. "And thank you for the offer. I will take you up on it sometime, but not right now."

"Whenever you want, whatever you need, Kris." She winked and then was gone. The sound of the door clicking softly in the other room was the only thing that told me that I hadn't imagined her being here in the first place. I glanced back at the rumpled sheets on the bed, frowning.

KRISTIN

Fury rushed through me as I disappeared into the night and a few blocks away. I hailed a transport for hire, and as I sat in the back, I realized that I had nowhere to go. We had moved here to Philadelphia years ago, and I had barely been allowed to leave the hotel.

Suddenly, an address popped into my head, and I compelled the driver to take me to it. I wouldn't have forced him if I weren't alone, but I didn't have my phone with me, which meant that I didn't have my payment app.

I sat back as the transport operator navigated the streets, dwelling over how much of my life had changed. When had I become a prisoner within my own home? When was the last time that I had paid for anything on my own, done anything on my own? I couldn't remember, but it had to be over ten years.

How had my life gotten so out of control? I suddenly wished that I was behind the wheel of my old Dodge Challenger. I could practically hear the roar of the throaty engine, feel the vibration around me as it moved down the roadway. Cars, or transports as they were now called, had no vibration, no particular sound but the slight whirring of the electric motor. There were few cars left that used gasoline, and most of those were in museums. I had one, but it was tucked neatly in storage.

It was time for a change. Maybe I hadn't been as strong as my breed needed me to be. Perhaps by staying sheltered, I had not been there for my kind as I should have been. It was time for me to get back out there, time to show people that I meant business.

The driver pulled up in front of Hugh's building, and I quickly compelled him to forget he had ever seen me and go on about his night. I found my way to Hugh's door, pausing before I knocked to wonder if I should be here at all. Around me, I felt the presence of others of my kind, but I closed myself off from them. They might feel me, might know that someone powerful was around, but they wouldn't know who, or exactly where.

Hugh looked shocked that I was here, probably almost as surprised as I was myself to have come to him. The thing about it was, I did like Hugh. There was something different about him, something deep within his DNA that called out for me.

As he pulled me to his neck, asking me to take his vein, I wanted to. Damn did I want to, but I didn't want him to be just that for me. I had taken a thousand human veins in my life, but to take Hugh's gave me pause. It was as if I knew that having his blood run down my throat might change me, change my purpose, change my life, and I couldn't take that chance.

His scent was almost smoky, rich as it filled my lungs, his emotions high as he waited for me to strike, but that chance that things would transform held me back. I was seriously in need of blood, but I would not take his—not tonight.

I left him in his room half-dressed and flashed out to the hallway where I paused in front of Joshua, Ryker, and Conner. "Not a word," I said to them as I brushed past and flashed down to the street using the stairs from the fourth floor.

Angelina stood on the sidewalk, hip cocked to the side, a smirk on her face as I came out the door. "Did we have fun?"

"Get in the car," I snapped toward her but smiled afterward to ease the harshness of my words.

Cameron held the door for me, and I slipped inside with Angelina right behind me, Joshua and Ryker following. Josh immediately put his hand on my knee, effectively hiding my presence from everyone, as Clay glared at me.

"That was stupid," Clayton snarled.

"What? The fact that you all went behind my back and are trying to force me into mating with someone for political reasons, or because I walked away?"

He cocked his head, giving me an annoyed look. "No, running the way you did, Kristin. You realize that didn't help your case any."

"Bullshit, Clay," I growled toward him. "They are going to think what they want to think. I don't need to be mated to be strong. I'm fucking stronger than any of them."

"This is not about physical strength!" he lashed out and then inhaled loudly to calm himself. "I know that you are strong; you know that; the people in this transport know that, but the other elders feel it would be better for you to be mated."

"What is this? The nineteen sixties? Women do not need to be mated. We can have their own voices. We can be leaders. We don't need men to do things for us."

"I know you do not, but Kristin, you are aware that for all of our existence, there have only been men in power."

"And I have been in power for eighteen years; why is it now important that I have a mate?" I glared at him. "Do the elders feel as if I have failed as a leader? Do they really wish for me to hand the reins over to a male?"

"No," he said quickly. "This is not about you handing the reins over, Kristin. This whole thing is about you being safe. You need a mate to help you heal. Perilous times are coming, and you will need to be strong. You know how much stronger you are when you have a mate."

I turned and looked out the window. I could see everything clear as day, but anyone looking at our passing vehicle would see only darkness with the tinted glass. Not that there were a lot of people on the streets. In fact, at night, humans rarely left their houses. Their fear of us kept them indoors.

I sighed. "Clayton, I can understand that reasoning, and I do agree. I am stronger when I am mated, but I will not take another mate until I find the right one. I will not allow the elders to put men in front of me like a fucking buffet to choose from. It's not going to happen. When I find someone that I feel is appropriate, then I will take the steps necessary."

Angelina was staring at me from the side. "Are you serious? You're going to let them dictate that you get mated?"

"They aren't wrong, Lena. I do need a mate for my strength and to help me heal. Not just because things might get ugly here soon, but because it's time to make some changes."

Joshua stiffened beside me as Cameron asked, "Changes? What changes?"

"I'm tired of being locked up in that damn building, for one. I need to live again. I need to be out there to show our breed that I'm strong, that I'm there for them."

"No," Clayton growled as Joshua's concern slipped into our bond. "You can't take those kinds of chances, Kristin."

"The hell I can't. Who is going to stop me? You? Ryker? Joshua? No. I'm tired of being locked up in a fucking prison, Clay. I need to get back out there; I need to see what's going on, be part of life again before I lose my damn mind."

"Kris, I realize that you've been hidden away for a long time," Cameron stated, "but it's for your own protection."

"You realize that I could kill every single one of you in this vehicle before you could bat an eye, right?"

Clayton and Conner shifted in their seats as Angelina laughed. "She's right, guys. She's more dangerous than you all give her credit for."

"You've been out of the game for a long time," Cameron stated. "Things have changed."

Before they knew what was happening, I had reached forward toward Ryker and Conner and removed their weapons, putting a stake over Clayton's heart and a gun to Cameron's head. Everyone looked shocked, especially Josh.

Angelina clapped her hands and laughed. "Oh, goodie! Now there is the sister that I love!"

"Do I need to prove anything else to you men?" I said as I stared between the two of them. Clayton swallowed and pushed the stake away from his chest while Cameron shook his head.

"No," Clayton said gruffly. "We get it; you need a few field trips. We'll make sure they happen, but you still aren't going out alone. That little jaunt over to your human's house is the last one you get."

"I refuse to be locked up anymore, Clayton," I said as I handed Conner and Ryker back their weapons. Both of whom were grinning at me for getting the upper hand. "I will also decide where I go, when I go, and who I take with me."

He shook his head, knowing that it wasn't worth the fight. At least he could go back to the elders and tell them that I would consider mating with someone when I found the proper male to mate with.

Everyone was quiet as we returned to the hotel, and I was hustled inside, with Joshua's hand on my back. Beckett paced the lobby, and I glared at him as I walked past and to my elevator with Josh, Cam, and Angelina at my side.

We were in the elevator when Angelina spoke privately to me. *"You didn't feed from him; why not?"*

"I'll explain later."

"Well, at least go shower and then take Josh's vein. You look weak."

"Why do I need to shower? I don't plan on having sex with Josh."

She wrinkled her nose. *"Because you smell like you've been around a barbeque pit. Your human's scent is potent."*

"You can smell him on me?" She gave me an are-you-kidding-me look, and I saw the flash of a question in her eyes. *"We will discuss that later."*

When we got off the elevator, I told Josh to wait for me in the living room and went to shower. As I took my clothing off, I realized that I really did smell smoky. Hugh's scent was oddly strong for a human man, and it made me wonder—not for the first time.

STACY EATON

I dressed in comfortable slacks and a button-down blouse and returned to the living room to find Joshua standing at the window, staring down, a drink in his hand. "I poured you one; it's on the bar."

"Thank you," I told him while I went to retrieve it. My hand was almost around the glass when Joshua pushed me against the bar, his hands tight on my arms.

"How could you do that?" The words seethed out of him. "How could you run out like that and take that kind of chance with your life? All you had to do was ask, and I would have taken you anywhere."

"That would have defeated the purpose of being alone, Josh."

"What if something had happened to you?" The tension in his hands lessened, and he removed one and brushed it down the side of my face. "I'm not sure I could take it if something happened to you."

"Josh," I said softly, "I know you think that I am your responsibility, but I'm not. I appreciate everything that you do for me, I do, but if something happens to me, it's not your fault."

"How can you say that? I swore to protect you, Kristin."

"And like I said, I appreciate that, but—"

He pushed my chin to the side, running his nose down my neck, and I felt his fangs graze the surface. A shiver jetted down my spine. God, it had been so long since someone had taken my vein, so fucking long.

"Do you know how badly I want to taste your blood? To have it course through my veins?"

"It would kill you, Josh."

He pulled back. "Would it? Would it really? With all the blood that I feed you, do you honestly think that your blood wouldn't recognize the source?"

"We don't know that, and I'm not willing to take the chance," I said to him, but part of me wanted to. That dark part of me that wanted to feel someone deep in my throat, pulling at my life force. That part wanted it something fierce. So fiercely, that my entire body began to hum.

He stared at me one second longer, no doubt feeling my reaction, and then he struck. The feel of his fangs sliding into my throat put me

86

on an instant high, and I held his head to me as he drew from my vein —knowing at the same time how wrong it was. My body shook with the second pull, and then he was pulling out, backing away from me.

Fear took over the high as I saw his face. He shouldn't have done that. "Josh!" I cried out as he winced and stumbled back. "Josh!"

I caught him before he hit the floor, and he curled in on his side, holding his stomach as he groaned.

"Lena! I need help!" I shouted to my sister mentally, and two seconds later, she and Cameron were in my room.

"What the hell?" Cameron yelled.

"Oh, shit! Did he drink from you?" Lena asked.

"He did. He said that with as much blood as I take from him, my blood should know that it's his and it shouldn't hurt him. I didn't get to tell him that it was a bad idea even to try it! He was at my throat before I could do anything, and I was too surprised to react immediately."

The door opened again, and Ryker and Jett rushed in as Cam spoke. "Help me get him out of here and back to his place. Call the doc up here; let's see if there is anything we can do."

I watched as they carried him out, and Angelina came to my side. She licked at my neck to close the holes that were still open, and I winced.

"How did it feel?" she asked softly, a wistful look in her eye.

I sighed. "It felt amazing—utterly amazing."

JOSHUA

I had worked for Alexander for over sixty years, had been at his side more and more as the years went on, especially after the incident with the human-turned forty years ago.

I would have done anything for Alex, and even more for his mate, Kristin. While many of us cared about her, I felt more. I loved her—had loved her practically since the day that I had met her. My feelings had only grown stronger since Alex died, and she had become my sole focus. I was stupid not to realize that focus was guilt-ridden.

I had been with Alex the night he died, although not at his side—a mistake I shall forever live with.

Alexander had been attending a meeting, and I'd stopped to speak with someone as Alex proceeded around the corner. We were separated for two minutes—one minute and fifty-nine seconds too long. With me not at his side, rebels picked up on his exact location immediately and took advantage of the moment.

I raced to him at the first flash of pain to find that they put a bullet into his left shoulder and right leg to slow him down. It was not the type of ammunition that the humans used, but instead, a unique titanium and platinum mixture that was lethal to us. Alex was surprised and went down enough that they were able to overpower him. I felt his pain, his small flash of fear before he tried to strike back at them. The three other men with him were shot in the head and then staked.

When I arrived at his side, I did not fight, even though I wanted to tear them to shreds. I gave myself up. I knew that if I tried to fight, I would be killed, and right now, I needed to stay alive. I allowed them to take me hostage so that I could remain with Alex.

I wasn't afraid to die, but my only hope in saving Alex was staying with him. My job was now to stay alive and find a way to get Alex out of this mess. As we were shoved from the van, my thoughts went to Kristin. She would have felt her mate's pain as if it were her own—the downfall to a mating bond. What was she thinking now? Could she still feel him, or had he blocked her?

I was bonded to him too, and I felt his pain, but he could have focused his energy toward her to close the bond so she wouldn't know.

Alex and I were chained down, again with the particular metal combination that removed our strength and caused us agony. Even with two bullets in him, Alex kept his head up, his eyes always on the move to everything around him. I fought to be half as strong as him.

If the blood scent on the stained concrete at our knees was any indication, they brought a lot of people here. An older man stepped out of the shadows, and his evil laugh echoed through the warehouse. My hackles went to attention, as did Alex's.

The man clapped as he came into view, his gaze trained on Alex as he grinned maliciously. "Finally. I knew this day would come."

"Portage," Alex growled, his shoulders rolling back, and I felt the pain of doing that with the bullet lodged in his shoulder.

"It's been a long time since we have seen one another, brother."

What the fuck? Portage was Alex's brother? I had never heard that Alexander had a brother.

"You are no brother of mine," Alex replied gruffly.

"Oh, but we are brothers. Of course, I was the one that was coddled by Mummy and told that I would never amount to anything because Daddy preferred you. Wouldn't Mummy be surprised now?"

"Our mother would roll over in her grave if she were in one, but of course, she's not, because you staked her."

"Not me. You killed our mother, Alexander. You killed her when you refused to allow me to work at your side."

"Yeah, so you could destroy the breed."

"No." His dark features turned hard, but then immediately relaxed again. The two of them looked a little alike; their builds were the same—tall, lean, and dark—but their facial expressions were very different. Alex looked thunderous, but Portage appeared pleased as punch. *"It was to better the breed. We are the superior race; we should be controlling this world, not living hidden lives, scuttling around in the shadows like cockroaches. We are superior, Alex. We should be taking control of the humans."*

"There is no reason to take control of humans. We have lived for centuries this way, and it will continue for centuries more. There is no reason to overtake them. They are nothing to us."

"Ah, something we agree on, dear brother. You're right; they are nothing." He shrugged. *"Hence the reason we need to put them in their place. They should be our whores, our chew toys, and we should not be cowering to them."*

Alex laughed. *"And you think that by killing me, you will be able to gain the breed's approval? Not likely, Joey."*

Portage's features went stone-cold, and he nodded at the two men beside Alex. They pulled Alex's arms out to the sides, the heavy metal bracelets clamped on his wrists. The left side of his chest was covered in blood from the bullet wound that could not heal on its own.

"I will kill you to prove to everyone that you are not invincible, Alex, and that I can get to anyone, including your mate. I wonder if she would prefer me over you in bed. I know she left you once before, mated with your son, of all people."

Alex growled, and I tried with everything I had in me to pull from the binds that held me. I struggled so much that Portage glanced my way, then nodded to two of his men who snatched my arms and kept me from attempting to escape.

"You are going to watch," Portage said to me, *"and then take a message back to your mistress."*

Alex peered my way, and I felt his words slip through my head. *"No matter what happens, you are to protect Kristin with your life. Never leave her side; never let anyone hurt her. Bond by blood with her; she will resist it,*

91

but tell her it is my last wish. She will do it for me. Do you swear this to me, Joshua?"

"I do, Master."

Portage put his focus back on Alex, and I felt sick as I watched him begin to torment him. He whipped him over and over, but Alex was brave and did not even make a sound. Then Portage took a knife and ran the blade along the insides of both of Alex's arms. Blood began to ooze and then drip from the deep wounds, but Alex kept his head up, wincing only from the extent of the pain from the metal of the blade.

I didn't want to watch Alex bleed out, didn't want to see the man that I respected and followed killed, but I couldn't look away. It was as if this was my punishment for not being at his side to protect him earlier, for not being where I needed to be in that one instant of time. I would forever live with this on my shoulders, and I would take my vow to protect the mistress with my life.

Eventually, Alex began to sag as the blood pooled around his body. The color left his face, and his head began to loll on his shoulders. Portage stood in front of Alex and grabbed his hair, pulling his face toward him, and the two men stared at one another again.

Alex's voice was raw as he spoke. "We once loved each other very much, Joey."

Portage had blinked once, then twice, and the malice in his gaze lessened. Would he change his mind, allow Alex to live? Had Alex somehow reached humanity in his brother before he would be killed?

In the blink of an eye, the evil was back as he leaned forward into Alex's face and hissed, "You never loved me. You taunted me with your greatness; your perfect son, who wasn't so perfect now was he, and your beautiful mates. You pushed me aside when I came to you and asked for your help. You always thought you were better than me. Now look who is better. Now, look at who has the perfect son, the perfect weapon. All that you have, all that you covet will be mine, Alexander."

Alex had no chance to respond as Portage ran the blade of the knife across his throat quickly.

"No!" The word exploded from my lips as I watched the last of the master's blood spill from the arteries in his neck, his eyes staring up at his brother in disbelief until they went blank. Portage let go of his head and shoved him away. Alex's body went to the ground like a rag doll, his head toward me, his unseeing eyes locked on mine. I blinked back the shock, every other muscle in my body frozen. Would they allow me to take his body? Would that be the message? Would there be a chance that Alexander might be returned to us as Kristin once had?

Portage glanced around the warehouse, and I stared at him, utterly stunned—and furious—at what he had done. His focus went toward the back of the building, and I followed it. There was a young man back there watching. Was that Portage's perfect son? The one that was a weapon?

Portage turned back to Alex and went to his side, using his foot to roll him and stared down into his face as a muscle ticked in his jaw. A moment later, he withdrew a stake from his inside suit pocket and grasped it tightly in his palm.

"No, please don't. If you ever cared about your brother, please don't." The words fell from my lips without thought.

Portage stared at me. "When you get back to the mistress, tell her I'm coming for her. Tell anyone who thinks they are going to control our breed that I will be coming for them."

No words came to my mind as he went to his knee and slammed the spike into Alex's chest. His body evaporated into a cloud of dust. I inhaled deeply, drawing Alex into my lungs, into my soul. He would forever be a part of me. My chin dropped to my chest as the heaviness of failure settled on my shoulders. I would forever bear this weight but swore then that I would protect Kristin with everything that I had in me—forever.

When his men came to me and began to beat me and kick me, I let them. My time for vengeance would come. I knew that they wouldn't kill me; they wanted me to take a message back, and I knew that my physical wounds would heal. It was the mental one of watching Alex die that would never do so.

~

I blinked and felt pain radiating through every inch of my body. I was in my room, and I felt Kristin near. I turned my head to find her lying on the bed, curled toward me. Her eyes were closed, but she wasn't sleeping; her mind was warring over things.

Her blood was still burning through my body; every beat of my heart made it flare within me. Somehow, I had lived. I had survived taking her vein. Was I alright? Was I possibly desensitizing myself to her blood over time?

Her eyes popped open, the blue so crystal clear I felt I could look straight through it to her mind. "You should not have done that," she whispered.

"I needed to," I rolled to my side, wincing at the burning inside my body. It was worse than when I'd been broken and beaten that day eighteen years ago.

"Why?"

"To prove to you that you need me." A line marred her forehead, and I touched her face with a heavy hand. "Do you remember when I returned after Alex was killed?"

"Yes."

"I told you that Alex made me swear that I would never leave your side. I would protect you with my own life, in a way that I hadn't for him. You gave me a blood oath that day."

"Yes, I did."

The memory of her scoring her wrist and holding it out to me came back to my mind. I had merely licked her wrist, taking in just a few drops of her essence, and my insides had burned like I was on fire for two days. I had survived that. Her essence drifted through my veins, and I vowed that I would never allow anything to happen to her.

"You broke that oath," I finally responded as I removed my hand away from her face. She took hold of my hand and held it tightly.

"I will never do that again, Joshua, but you must promise me that you will never take my blood again. You lived this time, but next time you might not."

"I wanted to prove to you that I would die for you."

"I know you would, but I don't want you to die for me, Joshua. I want you to *live* for me—to live beside me. I cannot be what you want, but you can be what I *need*—my friend and my protector. Do you swear this? Do you swear this on my blood?"

I squeezed her hand. "I do."

"May I try something?"

I nodded, unsure of what she wanted to do but mesmerized by her eyes as they shifted to a luminous silver, and she lifted my hand and brought my wrist to her mouth as her fangs descended. She scored my wrist, pulled deeply from my vein, and the pain inside of me began to lessen. The entire time that she fed, we stared at one another, and then the pain was almost gone, only a tingling left around my heart.

She removed her fangs, licked my wrist, and then placed a kiss to it. "I need you to live, Josh, to protect me, to feed me when I need it, and to be my friend."

"I will, Kristin." I paused. "But how did you make the pain stop?"

She smiled faintly. "I called my blood back to me, but I left just enough to make our bond stronger."

"You can do that? You can call your blood back?"

She laughed softly. "I guess I can." She shrugged as she sat up. "I didn't know that I could do that until now, but obviously I can."

I stared at her in amazement. This woman was incredible, absolutely fucking incredible.

ANGELINA

I envied my sister in a way, but then again, I didn't envy the life she had to live.

I sighed as I turned from her. "I can't remember the last time someone took my vein."

"I know." She went to sit on the couch, putting her face into her hands. "It sucks, it really does."

"Who has taken your vein since Alex died?" I asked as I took a seat near her.

"You mean the ones that lived or died?" Her laugh was brittle. "Jacques Berger did once, and Clayton has. They are the only two that have survived. Anyone younger than Alex would probably die. I think Alex only survived it because his blood was so pure, and he was so strong."

"How old was Alex?"

"Around three hundred," she stated.

"Huh, I thought he was older." I hesitated. "Josh will be alright."

"Will he? God, I can't believe I let him do that." She put her face in her hands.

"Trust me, I understand. Sometimes I just want someone to take my vein because I feel so damn full that I think I'm going to explode.

I'd rather it kill them than for me to have to keep going on with that feeling."

"But Cameron used to take your vein."

"Yes, he's older, not quite an elder, but he's older than Alex was, and I think that back when he did take it, my blood wasn't as lethal as it is now. I'm not sure if it would kill him now or not."

"I wish we knew what made our blood so lethal," she said just above a whisper.

"You know that the only thing that anyone can come up with is that we're reborn. There are so few of us that they aren't able to test the theories properly."

"I know that's the reason; I just wish we knew why. What if we eventually find out our blood is toxic even to elders? What do we do then?"

I stared at her momentarily. "I don't know, but do you think if you fed from a reborn, it would hurt or strengthen the blood? I mean, you and I can share if we have to, is that because we're twins or reborns?"

She turned to me. "I have no idea. As you said, there aren't enough of us around to be able to test that, and I've thought a lot about that myself."

"I'd like to test that sometime. Maybe we can find a couple of hot reborn guys we can experiment on."

"Count me in." She laughed. "Let me know if you find any."

"Speaking of hot guys, what about Hugh?"

"What about him?"

"You're interested in him. Why?"

She exhaled loudly. "I don't know. Maybe it's because Hugh makes me feel something that I haven't felt in a long time. I feel normal, like a woman desired. He doesn't treat me like the mistress. He has no idea what that means. I mean, yeah, he knows I'm in power, but it doesn't seem to faze him. I like that." She grew quiet. "He asked me to take his vein tonight, practically begged for me to do it."

"Why didn't you?"

"I told him that I wanted to forget the difference between us. I just wanted to be a woman that he desired, and be with a man that I wanted to be with because I felt something for him. It has been years since I have had that."

"Yeah, I guess eighteen years is a long time."

"No, it's been much longer than that. Yes, I cared about Alex, and sex was great, but I didn't feel for him what Hugh makes me feel. What Alex and I had was understanding and commitment—not passionate love."

"You know you can't keep Hugh forever."

She cackled. "I know, but for now, he makes me happy."

"Is that why you went to him tonight?"

Kristin snorted as she stood. "No, I went to him tonight because I had nowhere else to go. I was able to recall his address from the report they did on him, and that was the only place I could think of to go." She went to the bar and picked up a glass that was sitting there already filled. "I was serious about things needing to change. I need to get out, Angelina. I can't stand sitting in this building any longer, not knowing what's really going on out there."

"You know that the elders will never go for it. They might want you to mate, but they know how important you are to them. Sadly, I have to agree with them—as much as I hate that—but you are too important to be running around the city."

"See, I don't think so." I started to speak, and she put her hand up to stop me. "The way I see it, our breed needs to know that I'm there. I can't keep hiding in this damn fortress while Portage is out there pulling our society over to his side. If our people see me, see that I'm not afraid, then I think they might stand behind me more. I think they need to see me in public, mixing with humans, living life. I believe it would be good for them and us."

"Maybe, or maybe it will just bring the lepers to us."

She pointed at me. "That was another thought that I had. What if it does? Maybe it will finally get me face-to-face with Portage. I want nothing more than to tear his throat out for what he did to Alex, and for what he continues to do. You are aware that it was because of him that our existence even became known to humans, right?"

"Yes, I figured as much."

"Well, if I'm out there, maybe it will bring him out, too. Maybe they will try to come for me, and we can finally figure out where the son of a bitch is hiding."

"I still think it's too dangerous."

"Come on, Lena, you know that all I have to do is compel someone to forget they saw me, and if worse comes to worst, I can compel them to take my blood. Wham, they are dead." She grew thoughtful. "Maybe that is a good message to send to Portage."

"Too bad that our blood wouldn't kill *him*. It would be nice to pour it down his throat and watch him writhe in agony."

She chuckled. "Yes, it would, but I believe he might be too old for that. I don't know if he was older or younger than Alex. I suspect older, but I could be wrong. Shit, I didn't even know Alex had a brother until Joshua told us."

"I still can't believe they were brothers."

"Yeah, well, once upon a time, I couldn't believe we were sisters," Kristin said with a grin.

"And look how well that has turned out."

Before she could respond, the door opened to Kristin's apartment, and Cameron came in.

"How is he?" Kristin asked immediately.

"He's alright. I think he's going to pull through. If he had tried to take any more, it might have killed him, but the doc feels that his body is trying to repair itself."

"That's good," I commented.

Cameron took Kristin by the arm and pulled her back to the couch. "Sit."

"Why?"

He began to roll up his sleeve. "Because you are going to feed, right now."

"Oh, I think that is my sign to leave," I said quickly and began to turn away.

"No, stay, Angelina. If you stay, it will keep it more professional."

I laughed. "What, you don't want to sleep with my sister again?"

The look in his eyes was one of pain. "No, I don't." He glanced at Kristin. "No offense. Please stay, Angelina."

Kristin snickered quietly. "None taken."

"Fine." I rolled my eyes and went to the bar. If I was going to have to watch this, I needed a drink, or ten. I was well aware that Kristin and Cameron had been together before, at least a few times, and that she had fed from him, but it didn't sit well with me—it never had. To their credit, it hadn't been until Cameron's last mate had passed, many years after we'd separated.

I couldn't believe that even after all this time, almost thirty years, I still had residual feelings for the man. It made me wonder if he felt anything for me. The temptation was there to slip into his mind, but I refused to allow myself to do that. What Cameron felt, or didn't feel, no longer mattered to me. It stopped mattering when he went through his string of vampirettes and ended up knocking Rosa up and breaking our bond.

He had never apologized for that, not really. He had only told me once that he hadn't meant for it to happen, but it did. Unlike most vampires, and my sister seemed to be the same, I preferred my mate to be monogamous.

I went back to my seat and stared at my glass. When I finally looked up, Cameron was leaning back on the couch, his eyes closed, and his wrist to Kristin's mouth. Her eyes were open, but she stared at the floor, and I felt nothing coming from her. No desire, no undeniable urges.

Cameron opened his eyes to me, and I saw the wicked desire in them, but it wasn't for my sister. No, the way he stared at me told me that he still wanted me. For a moment, I was powerless to stop the urges within me, and I let myself soak that in. Cameron and I had always been incredible together in bed. We had excelled at that. It was everything else in our relationship that had sucked. Once upon a time, he had loved my free spirit, loved that I did what I wanted when I wanted to, but then he changed. He said I was reckless, bringing undue danger to not only my life, but to my sister's too.

He was right, and that was the start of our downfall because it didn't stop me. It made me even more reckless. It was after he left that I finally came around. Not immediately, no—for a while, I had been hell-bent on destruction, but eight years later, when Alex died, I had finally got my head on straight. I knew that my sister needed me, and my life changed.

Now, as Cameron and I stared at one another, I wondered if things could have been different for us. Could we have gotten through it? Would there ever be a future with us again? I doubted that, just for the blood reason alone—especially after witnessing what Josh just went through.

Cameron let his gaze drift down my body, pausing at my chest before sliding back up.

Kristin finally lifted her head, removed her fangs from Cameron's arm, and licked the punctures. She smiled at him, said thank you, and then stood. "I'm going to go check on Joshua."

After the door closed, I felt the charged air of the room. The sexual tension left over by the feeding was crackling around us. In the whole time that my sister had fed from Cameron, she had not released one desire into the air. She had felt nothing but thankfulness.

I tipped my glass back, swallowing the liquor in a couple of gulps and then going to the bar to put my glass on it. Nothing was spoken between us, but as I walked to the door, Cameron followed.

We stepped out of Kristin's apartment, and I turned toward my door. The moment it was open, Cameron pushed me inside and against the wall; his mouth crashed over mine in an urgency I had never felt come from him.

The sexual tension from the other room had followed us, and it was all I could do not to tear his clothing from him. His hands, so well-known to my body, were everywhere, and he was tugging my skirt up with one hand while he braced our bodies against the wall with the other.

I yanked at his waistband, undoing his belt, tearing his zipper down and freeing him. Jesus, I loved that the man never wore underwear—something we had in common. His silky cock jumped forward, and I grasped it hard enough to make him wince and moan.

My skirt was around my waist when he brought his hands to my ass and lifted me. My legs locked around his hips as he impaled himself, my head bounced off the wall behind me, his lips rough against my neck. His fangs grazed my throat, and I was prepared to beg him to take my vein. The rational side of me began to panic, and I yanked his head to the side and struck at his neck.

Yes, he had just fed my sister, but I needed him at that moment. I had to have his life essence rushing through my heart with each beat. I pulled once, twice as he slammed into me. Our bodies bounced off the wall, and I heard the drywall crack—felt the give of the material against my back.

I savored the taste of him and pulled a third time as the two of us hit that explosive moment, and I whimpered into his neck. He stopped moving after a few moments, and I removed my fangs, licking the site to close it, and rested my forehead on his shoulder as my heart calmed.

He let my legs slip to the ground and then helped me get my skirt situated again before he pushed himself back inside his pants and zipped himself up. He stared at me, his eyes jumping from one of mine to the other. So many emotions leaped around inside his gaze, but before I could comprehend them, he leaned forward and kissed my lips once, tenderly—so fucking tenderly that it almost hurt.

Then he was out the door without a word. I stood on shaky legs, staring at the closed door and blinking back tears. I didn't want to love the man still, but I did.

KRISTIN

I felt nothing for myself as I fed on Cameron. Not the building sexual lust that generally came with it and not the sense of urgency that I usually felt. It was merely nourishment for me. As if I were enjoying my favorite food in the dining room floors below.

I did, however, feel the restlessness growing in the room between Cameron and Angelina, and that is why I excused myself immediately after finishing. Angelina didn't want to admit it, but she still had feelings for him, and it was apparent that he returned those.

Ryker was with Joshua when I let myself into his smaller apartment beside mine. The television was on in the bedroom, and Ryker was kicked back on the bed, watching a hockey game.

"How is he?"

He clambered off the bed. "Mistress." He nodded toward me and then glanced back at Josh. "He seems to be healing. He's not sweating as badly as he was."

"Okay, you can go. I'll stay with him."

"Mistress." He bowed his head again before turning the television off and then leaving the room without another word.

I sank to the bed, lying on my side as I stared at Joshua. Why had he done that? Why had I allowed him to do it? I could have lost him, and I couldn't afford for that to happen—not ever. Not only because of his ability but because I genuinely cared for him.

I closed my eyes, dwelling over my earlier conversation with my sister about leaving the hotel—compound—prison—whatever the hell you wanted to call it. While she and the others might not like it, I felt in my bones that it was the right choice. I had to go out there and show myself, let others know that I would not cower to Joseph Portage. It was time to change the way we did things, and I was determined to do that—it was time to stop hiding in the shadows.

I felt Josh waking, heard the wisp on the pillow as he turned his head toward me, and I opened my eyes to study him, his dark-green eyes imploring me to understand why he did it.

The reminder of the oath he had taken to Alexander moments before he died was such a visual in his mind that it hurt my chest to watch it yet again as he played it over. My oath to him brought back to me with his words, the knowledge that I had indeed broken that, and then the pact that I would never do it again.

I pulled from his wrist to show him that I was binding myself to him again as I once had, but also to prove to him that I was serious. As I drew his blood into my mouth, I called my blood, asking for it to come back, almost begging for it to return to me—to leave him and allow him to heal properly.

I hadn't expected it to happen, but it had. How interesting that I could do that. Was I somehow compelling my blood to respond? Or was I merely compelling him to force it out? I wasn't sure, but knowing this was going to be vitally important. A weapon that I could use.

What a weapon it would be, too. Force someone to take my blood, feed them mere drops to cause the pain to start, and tell them that the only way to live was to tell me what I wanted to know. Oh, the ways in which it could be used were countless.

"I need you to live, Josh, to protect me, to feed me when I need it, and to be my friend."

"I will, Kristin, but how did you make the pain stop?"

"I called my blood back to me, but I left just enough to make our bond stronger."

He seemed awed by that thought. "You can do that? You can call your blood back?"

"I guess I can. I didn't know that I could do that until now, but obviously, I can." I paused. "How do you feel?"

He seemed perplexed for a moment. "Fucking awesome."

I chuckled. "Good. Josh, I need you to keep what I did between you and me. Can you do that? I don't want anyone else to know about this, not even the elders or other sentinels. I have a feeling it is going to come in handy in the future, but I want to keep it on the down-low for now."

"Of course," he stated emphatically.

"I'm going to let you restl stay here and be quiet so that you don't raise suspicion. I'll send someone up to feed you. I think it would be good for you to feed well."

"Thank you, Mistress."

"Is there anyone that you prefer?"

"Cora or Paxton," he said gruffly. "That is who I usually feed from."

"Very well. I'll have one or both of them brought up for you."

He laughed huskily. "I don't think I'm up to two at once, Kris."

I smiled down at him. "Just because you have two to take, doesn't mean you have to take them at the same time."

His grin was a beautiful sight to see. "It wouldn't be the first time."

I laughed. "Oh, I know it wouldn't be. I'll see who is available." I turned for the door and paused. "Get your strength back; we have things to do, and I'm going to need you to be strong. You're important to me, Joshua, and I need you to stay strong and be there for me always." I paused as a thought came to me. "Maybe it's time that you mate; that would keep you strong."

"Mistress, I'm not sure I'm ready for that."

"I didn't think I was the first time," I paused and laughed. "Or the second time either, but I did it—although I didn't know I was doing it that time. I was a little drugged up." The laugh was slightly bitter as the memory of Trent, Gabe, and Julian tricking me to drink water dosed with a sleep aid came to mind.

"Yeah, well, you might need to drug me up, too."

"We will discuss it later, Joshua. Get some rest." I winked at him and was gone.

When I stepped out of his apartment, Ryker, Jett, Lorna, and Paxton were all waiting for me. "Oh, good, you're here, Paxton."

"Mistress?"

"Can you feed Joshua for me? He could use strong blood to help him recover."

"He's going to be alright?"

"Yes, he is."

She nodded and disappeared into his apartment just as Angelina's door opened and a stern-looking Cameron exited. He glanced my way for a split second and then went straight to the stairs, pushing the lock bar and disappearing into the stairwell.

"Well, not sure what to think of that," I joked, and everyone laughed.

"Mistress," Jett spoke a moment later. "The elders would like to see you."

I exhaled loudly. "I'm surprised they weren't banging on my door. Come on, let's go let them ream me out."

The three of them escorted me down to the floor where our offices were, and to our smaller conference room. Generally, when Joshua wasn't around me, there were four of them that escorted me, but with Paxton busy, Lorna and Jett flanked me, and Ryker took the position behind me.

The elders were waiting for me when I stepped inside the conference room and closed the door, leaving my sentinels in the hallway. All of the elders were serious-faced as they observed me take a seat, and I wanted to sigh heavily, but I held it in. Nothing like getting scolded by what could be your parents and grandparents at the same time.

I leaned back, crossing my legs and lacing my fingers.

"How is Josh?" Scarlett asked.

"He's fine. He will recover in no time," I answered.

Beckett seemed surprised. "You mean he is going to live after taking your blood?"

"Yes." I sure wasn't going to tell them that I had removed almost all of it from him. That was not something that they needed to be aware of—my little secret for now.

"Well, I'm glad he will be alright," Clayton said with relief, and then his expression turned stern again.

I put my hand up. "Wait, before you all decide to chastise me for what I did, let me apologize. You took me by surprise tonight, and I lashed out. You know that I don't normally do that, but I guess there have been quite a few things on my mind as of recent, and what you were requesting—demanding—put me over the top."

I encompassed the group and found Scarlett, Hazel, and Henry nodding slightly as if accepting my apology. I focused on Beckett. "What you wish for me—to be mated—is not a bad idea. The way you went about it—was. What you should have all done was voice your opinions and concerns to me directly so that we could have discussed them. I am not a child, so please stop treating me like one."

"You're considering it?" Scarlett asked.

"I will consider it, but *I* will find the proper mate for myself. I will not allow you to dictate whom I should mate with. This is not a monarchy, and I am not searching for the correct pedigree to make you all happy. I will think about the matter, figure out who the best person will be, and then I will discuss it with them, and you also. I will not make any rash decisions."

Beckett seemed to relax in his seat. "Very well. I think we can accept that, but we don't want you to waste time. You need to do this as soon as you can."

"Beckett, I will. I do agree with you that I need to be the strongest that I can be," I paused, "which is why I have also made another decision."

"And that is?" Henry inquired.

I glanced at Clayton. "I'm surprised you didn't already tell them."

"Oh, no, I preferred not to have a hand in that." He shook his head as he spoke.

"Why do I get the feeling that we are not going to like this next suggestion?" Hazel asked with pursed lips.

"It's not a suggestion," I told her. "It is what I am going to do."

Henry laughed. "Always so strong-willed, you are."

"Yes, and that is what makes me a good mistress, is that not correct?"

"Well, what is this idea that you have?" Beckett prodded.

"I'm going to start leaving the building more often. I'm going to get out there on the streets and be around our breed."

All of them started to talk at once, except Clayton, who gave me an I-told-you-so look. I put my hand up to stop them. "Listen to what I have to say, and then you can share your disdain for the idea."

They grew quiet, and I shifted in my seat. "This is more than just me being bored and antsy. I need to get out there and mingle with our breed. I need to be seen. For too long, I have been sequestered here in this damn hotel and have expected our breed to follow me. What do they know of me? Why should they follow me? Alex protected me too much when he was around, and after he died, I became a voice, not a face. It is time for them to see me, believe in me."

Hazel laughed. "What are you going to do, go on a campaign trail?"

"No, I'm going to live my life, but I'm going to do it in a more public way. Our breed needs to know that I'm there for them, that I am *one* of them."

"But you're not."

"I am," I stressed quickly. "They need to see it and believe it. It might also help bring Portage out of the woodwork. What if we can get him to come forward? What if we can bring him to us instead of searching for him? Wouldn't that be better?"

"But we would lose the element of surprise," Henry commented.

"What element of surprise? The man is a ghost. No matter what we do to find him, we can't. It's been eighteen years. Eighteen long fucking years that we have searched for that son of a bitch. It's time that I stop hiding from him and make him come to me. When he killed Alex, he said that he would come for me. Well, I don't know about you all, but I'm tired of waiting. If we could get to him, take him out, we could bring the factions back together. We could strengthen our race so that we could fight against whatever the humans are concocting."

The room was silent for a few moments as they looked among themselves. I did not doubt that they were discussing it, but I gave them the privacy in which to do so. Finally, it was Clayton who spoke.

"I have to agree with Kristin. I think this might draw Portage out."

"I can see the idea has merit," Scarlett commented. "I agree that we should try, but you can't do what you did tonight and run off on your own. You need to remain with your sentinels."

I nodded. "I shall. I will make sure to never leave here without Joshua at my side, and at least four others."

"Six," Clayton stated, and Hazel echoed the number in agreement.

"Fine, six. That means I will be with no less than seven people when I leave this building. Josh and Angelina will remain at my sides, and five others will be brought along."

"What is it that you plan to do first?" Beckett asked with a frown.

I grinned as I stood up. "I'm going dancing."

"What?" Beckett barked. "You can't go out to a club."

"Why not? There is a club that Angelina goes to rather often. It's only for the breed and a few human consorts, but it should be safe, and they know her—and more importantly, she knows the place well. What better way to get the word out than to be someplace public where our breed is relaxed and happy while I hang out with my sister? Besides, it's been a long time since I let down my hair and had a good time."

I walked out before any of them could respond, but I didn't miss the smirk on Clayton's face, nor the wistful look on Scarlett's. If this worked out, maybe I'd take her with me sometime. She didn't seem as stuffy as the others did.

"Well?" Lorna asked, her brow lifted in question as I stepped out of the room.

I waited until we were in the elevator and then glanced around. "Make sure that you are all ready to go at midnight tomorrow."

"Where?" Ryker asked.

I grinned at the back of the elevator door. "We're going clubbing."

ZANDER

I was lying in bed, staring at the ceiling, waiting for Laura to get out of the bathroom when my phone rang. "Speaker," I spoke aloud, and the phone answered with a click.

"Zander here."

"Zander, I have some news for you." My father's voice was gruff, and I sat up, hanging my legs off the side of the bed as I reached for my earpiece and put it into my ear canal.

"Off speaker," I said. "Yeah, what news?"

He chuckled slightly. "It seems that the mistress is feeling a bit confined these days."

"What are you talking about?"

"She got upset at a few of her elders when they tried to force her to mate again. She took off on her own, and it is my understanding that she has told them now that she wishes to start leaving the property more often."

"For what? To travel?"

He laughed again. "No, to go out and show herself to her people. I'm pretty sure she is doing it to see if I will come after her. Or maybe she is just bored and needs some excitement in her life. Who knows with women."

"How did you hear this?" The shower turned off in the bathroom, and I walked out of the bedroom.

"I have my sources," he said. His fucking sources. Fuck him. I was tired of him not telling me everything that was going on. Didn't he think he could trust me? I was his son, what the hell else did I have to do to prove that he could trust me?

"Yeah, well, you know that you could let me in on the plan."

"No, it's better if no one knows what is going on. It's harder to keep secrets when too many people know."

"I'm one person. I think you can trust me, Dad."

"Can I?" he asked.

I frowned. "Of course you can. When have I ever done something that would cause you to think otherwise?"

"You haven't *done* anything." He paused. "It's what's inside your head that bothers me."

"Inside my head? What the hell are you talking about? The only thing going on inside my head is trying to figure out what you are up to so I can figure out how to help."

"Zander, when the time comes, you will be called into action. Your part will be critical; trust me. Until then, I need you to remain quiet, although I understand that you have been seen out."

"Of course, I've been out. You never said I had to stay locked in this damn house."

"No, of course not, but I suggest you limit the number of people you meet and the kind of places that you go. We want there to be rumors of you, but nothing confirmed."

Rumors? Seriously, what the fuck was he trying to do? "What is your plan? I think it's time that you told me."

"Stop acting childish, Zander. I told you that I will not explain it yet. What you need to do is keep a low profile for a little while longer. Things are finally slipping into place, and your time is coming."

I huffed as I stared out the window at the waves rushing up on the shore. "Fine, but it better hurry the fuck up. I'm sick and tired of waiting."

"Patience, my dear boy, patience. You keep this up, and soon you'll be at my side controlling the breed and taking control of our destiny. The humans will cower at our feet, beg for us to save them."

"Is that really what you want? You want to make them all cower? You not only want to control the breed, but the human world too?"

"Of course. That is my destiny, just like you are on your path to yours. I promise that you will enjoy the destiny that comes to you."

"How the hell do you know that?"

His voice was low, gruff as he spoke. "Because I know you, my son. I see what is in your head, in your heart."

He was so full of shit. No one knew what was in my head. I never spoke of my odd thoughts, of the dreams that came to me, the images that rattled around in my head.

"Yeah, whatever. Is there anything else?"

"No, but if the mistress decides to break out of the palace gates and start enjoying the pleasures of everyday modern life, you should be able to start your task sooner than later. We just have one more thing to get into place before that happens."

"Can you at least tell me what it is that you are going to want me to do?"

"Not yet, Zander, not yet. I'll speak to you again when I know more."

He disconnected, and I tore the earpiece out of my ear and tossed it to the table and pushed open the slider so I could go out on the deck. My arms rested on the railing, and I stared at the surf, the sound rushing through my head as another body of water materialized in my mind: a lake, a small lake.

I had no idea where that lake was or what it meant to me. I honestly didn't ever remember being there, but the picture in my mind was so damn real that I knew that I had. Sometime in my life, I had stood leaning against a railing and staring out at the calm, dark water.

Maybe it wasn't a memory, but a premonition of something to come. Could I possibly see the future? Was my power not only in compelling people to see what I wanted them to see, but also to see a future that had not yet happened? It was the only answer that I could come up with.

I was so stuck in my thoughts that I didn't hear Laura come up behind me. I somehow kept myself from jumping at her touch and turned to look at her as the image in my head vanished.

Laura wore a sheer dressing gown that, at most times, would have attracted my attention. Tonight, I was too frustrated with my father to care much.

"Why are you out here?"

"I just got off the phone with my father. He said things are progressing and told me to lay low for a while."

"I thought he wanted you out and about?"

"You know how fickle he is. He changes his mind like the fucking wind. He said he wanted a rumor of me to be around." I laughed roughly. "I'm so over the fucking games."

"Well, why don't you shower and come to bed. The sun is going to be up soon."

I sighed as I stared at the horizon. It was lightening, and I was tempted to stand here until the sun blazed down on me. The temptation was only fleeting, though. I wanted to live. I felt that there was a purpose that I needed to find.

"Go on to bed. I'll be there soon." I kissed her forehead.

"Come with me," she said saucily. "I want to do naughty things to you, Zander."

My eyes shifted to her body; she wasn't a bad way to waste time. "Let me shower first."

I followed her into the house and went straight to the bathroom, where I stood staring into the mirror. When I finally stepped under the water in the shower, the images of the lake washed back over me. I frowned for a moment. How had I put the thought of the lake out of my mind so wholly earlier? It was like it was there, and then someone shut the door to it, and I forgot all about it until now.

I pictured the lake again, tried to feel around me, see what else I could find, and in the back of my mind, I heard a voice. It felt a million miles away, and suddenly I could almost feel the vibration under my feet of something walking toward me. I clenched my eyes, trying to hear more—feel more, but the sounds of the wind through the trees carried the voice away.

"Come on," I whispered. "What are you saying?"

I tried to turn, tried to look toward the voice, but I couldn't. It was like I was frozen with my eyes forward, and then suddenly, I was turning, but the memory began to fade just as it landed on a cloudy image of a woman.

I squeezed my eyes shut, trying to force the image back. I needed to see what had been right there in front of me, but I couldn't, and my head began to pound. "Fuck!" I slammed my fist into the stone wall of the shower. Shards of the stone fell to the shower floor, and blood dripped from my hand. I stared at it, and for one brief weird second, I wondered why it was red and not blue.

Laura poked her head into the bathroom. "Zander? Are you alright?"

"Yeah, I'm fine." I rinsed my knuckles under the water. "Go back to bed, Laura. I'll be there in a minute."

She stared at me as if unsure if she should leave me or not and then slowly backed out and closed the door. I stared at my hand, watching the skin close as two words began to beep through my chest like a drum in the tune of my heartbeat: *blue-blood, blue-blood, blue-blood.*

ANGELINA

"*A*re we really going out?" I asked, trying to contain my excitement. "I mean, going out to have fun, not do something for business?"

"Yes, we are *really* going out, Lena. I told them that we are going to that club that you like to visit, what was the name, Darkness something?"

"Dangers in the Darkness."

"Ah, yes." She laughed. I hadn't seen Kristin so damn relaxed and happy in years.

Man, please do not let this go south, I thought as I followed her to the elevator, and Joshua joined us. He winked at Kristin and even smiled at me before he hit the button.

"You remember the rules we talked about?" he asked my sister.

"Yes, I will stick by your side while we are outside of the club, but while we are in there, you need to give me a little bit of space, Josh."

"I will, but I'm never going to be more than an arm's length away from you."

She lifted a brow. "You dance?"

He frowned. "No."

"Well, then we are going to get more than an arm's length away because I plan on dancing my little heart out."

"I told you that this place has alcohol that will give you a buzz, right?" I asked my sister before the two of them got into an argument about her dancing. "It only lasts a few minutes, but they have some chemical that they mix in it that makes you feel like you're getting drunk."

"I look forward to that. I can't remember the last time I had a buzz." Kristin grinned, and the elevator opened. Standing in the lobby were Ryker, Jett, Lorna, Paxton, and Conner.

"Looks like the gang is all here." Kristin encompassed them with a huge grin.

"Mom!" Rex called from the other side of the lobby, and the smile faltered on her lips as she shifted toward him. "What are you doing? You should not be going out; it's too dangerous."

She lifted a brow. "Who is the parent here, Rex?"

"I'm worried about you," he said.

"Well, stop, Rex. God, you are more like your father every day." I almost burst out laughing, because it was so true.

"I'm going to take that as a compliment," he growled. "Let me come with you."

"Nope. I'm going out with my sister."

"What about all of these guys?"

"Well, I couldn't very well go out without my entourage, now could I? Another time, perhaps." She spun from him and walked toward the hall to the garage.

I patted him on the chest. "Don't worry, Rex; she will be fine, and this will do her good."

"Yeah, if you say so," Rex muttered as I walked away.

We piled into our transport, and Joshua sat at her side, his hand on her knee as everyone spoke quietly amongst themselves. Josh and I were probably the only ones that picked up on Kristin's tension. I knew that she wanted to prove something, but she was also cautious enough to know that things could go wrong. Shit, with our luck, things probably would go wrong.

"Is everyone strapped?" I asked as I glanced over the group.

Heads nodded, and a few flashed weapons under their clothing.

"They aren't going to let them in with those," I told Kristin. "They don't allow weapons, and technology doesn't work in there either. It's blocked somehow. No cameras, no phones."

"Well, that's good," Kris said. "And don't worry about the weapons. You can leave that to me."

"Oh, yeah, I forgot who I was going with: the compelling queen."

The sound of her laugh filled the interior of the transport. By the time we arrived, I wasn't sure who was tenser, me or Josh. Kristin seemed to have relaxed some and looked ready to throw herself out the door so she could have a blast.

I put my hand on the handle. "Are you sure?"

"Yes, now open the damn door. Let's go."

Josh and I shared a look, and then I pushed open the transport door. Ryker and Jett appeared at my side as Lorna climbed out behind me. Behind her was Kristin, her fingers laced with Josh's as if they were a couple. The rest of the group filtered in behind us, and we approached the door.

Dominic, my favorite bouncer, was at the door. "Oh, man, she returns!" he called when he saw us.

"Hello, Dominic. It's been a while."

His gaze slipped down my body and then over my shoulder. I knew the moment he recognized my sister because his shoulders jerked back, and his eyes went wide in awe. "Mistress."

"Evening, Dominic," she said softly and stepped forward. "Do you see all the people here with me?"

"Yes, Mistress."

"Well, remember them. You will let them in whenever they want to come here, and you will never ask them questions or check them for weapons. You may not let anyone else in tonight until I am gone, and no one will leave while I am here, is that understood?"

"Yes, Mistress. You all can go right in; have a good time. I'll tell anyone else that shows up that we are full." He smiled down at my sister, and she pressed her lips to his mouth.

"Thank you, Dominic." She breathed seductively toward him.

He looked shocked and blinked a few times as she stepped away from him. "You're welcome, Mistress. Anything for you."

She threw a sultry smile over her shoulder as she entered the building, and as I passed him, he touched his lips. I rolled my eyes; men were so simple.

The inner door opened, and Dominic yelled over our heads that we were clear to enter. The guy there nodded, and we filed into the room as the techno beat began to vibrate through me. Bright strobe lights flashed in wild colors around the club, and bodies, both human and vampire, gyrated over the dance floors.

"Come on." I took my sister's hand and began to weave through the crowd toward the stairs at the back of the club. In the center, above the main dance floor, was another stage. This one looked to be floating in midair, but it wasn't. There were large cables that held it in place but were hard to see unless you were right next to them, and the sides were protected with clear glass so someone wouldn't accidentally fall off. Or maybe more like jump off—not that it would kill us.

The people below could watch the ones dancing above, which was rather hot, because many of the women on the floor above wore skirts, and not all of them wore undergarments. We reached the steps, and I leaned forward to speak with True. I think his real name was Truman, but everyone called him True. He nodded and pulled back the rope so we could pass through. His gaze locked onto my sister for a moment before shifting over the rest of our group. I couldn't figure him out; he was always quiet, always mysterious—but sexy as all get out. I'd tried to get his attention a time or two, and while he never came right out and said no, he never seemed interested either.

I was almost to the top when I heard the voice of my favorite DJ call over the speakers, "Ladies and gentlemen, the dancing queen is in the house! Angelina Michaels has graced us with her presence!"

Kristin burst out laughing behind me, and people began to look around and scream.

"The dancing queen?" she asked as we reached the top.

"Yeah, well, they know I like this place, and I always seem to get attention."

"Wait, wait!" the DJ shouted through the speakers as the music came to an abrupt stop. "What is this that I hear, not only is the dancing queen here, but the mistress herself has graced us with her presence? Where is she?"

The people below began to scream, staring up at us, and I felt Kristin's tension jump momentarily, while Josh shifted closer to her. Kristin lifted her chin higher and stepped toward the balcony railing, and the place went wild. She cast a smile around the room, and then held her hands up, and it went dead silent after a few seconds.

"I heard this was the best place to dance!" The crowd below went wild again. "I'm ready for a good time, are you?" They jumped and shouted, and whistles pierced the air. She put her hands up again, and the room silenced immediately.

"Free drinks for everyone for the next hour, on me! Now someone get me a drink!" Kristin shouted, and the people below began to chant.

"Mistress! Mistress! Mistress!" She pointed at the DJ, nodded to him, and the music began immediately. After that, things got a bit crazy, and everyone in the VIP section tried to approach her. She spoke with a few, kissed a few cheeks, let one guy dip her and lay a substantial smooch on her lips, and then she grabbed my arm and dragged me to the dance floor.

"I came here to dance. Let's fucking dance!"

People below watched her every move, and I knew that Josh was a nervous wreck as he stood on the side of the dance floor—torn as to where to be.

"She's fine, Josh. You watch her from there," I whispered into his head, and he nodded.

Lorna, Paxton, Ryker, Jett, and I were all dancing around her. Conner was off to the side a few feet away from Josh, watching everyone as they moved. She was safe, and for the moment, having a great time.

We danced until we were saturated with sweat. While we didn't normally perspire like humans, we did if heavily exerted, which was exactly what we were doing tonight.

Josh tapped his wrist as if to say it was time to go, and I touched

Kristin's arm. "Time to go."

"Okay, fine. I'm exhausted anyway."

We started to make our way down the stairs, and everyone began to scream for Kristin. Hands were everywhere as they reached out to touch her. She stopped twice to kiss two different men, and they were the kind of kisses that could turn you on, not just say hello.

Both men looked flabbergasted as she stepped away from them. I doubted that they would wash their mouths anytime soon. These vampires here were young or from the outer rim of our society. They were not top-line descendants of our elders or people that we usually associated with. That is why I liked it there. These people just wanted to have fun and enjoy their life. They didn't have personal agendas or want power.

As we spilled out the front door, Kristin laughed and threw her hands in the air. "Damn, that felt good!" A camera flashed, and she spun her head quickly. The person who had taken a picture vanished around the corner, and I saw just the tiniest movement as if she were going to go after him, but then she shrugged.

Josh wrapped his arm around her and whisked her to the transport. Back inside, everyone was bubbling with excitement, and I sat back, studying my sister. She looked almost like her old self again.

When we arrived back at the hotel, there was a crowd of reporters at the door. Word had gotten out that Kristin was out having fun. "Drop me off out front. Josh, Angelina, Ryker, and I will get out there. The rest of you go with the transport to the garage," Kristin stated.

She shook her hair back before she got out and turned to the cameras, smiling. Josh was instantly at her side, his arm around her, and she turned toward him, slowly and very passionately kissing him in front of everyone as if promising a good time to come. She grinned seductively toward the cameras before she walked into the hotel. Ryker put his hand to my back, laughed huskily under his breath at my sister's audacious display of affection, and then escorted me inside as the transport drove away, and the cameras recorded the whole thing.

Well, that was certainly going to get the news out.

KRISTIN

*a*t six in the morning, I was sitting at my desk, my feet kicked up on the wooden surface, and I was surfing the news. The virtual screen in front of me floated, and with a flick of the wrist, the images changed or the words scrolled.

I flexed my hand to stop the page. *"Mistress hits the dance floor."* It was one of many headlines that I had already seen. *"Mistress and Lover? Or Future Master?"* was another one I had seen and included a picture of Josh and me kissing. Josh was aware that when I kissed him like that, it was either a lustful urge, or I was trying to explain off why Josh was always so close to me—always touching me—making it seem like he was my romantic interest made sense.

I continued through my search and found another one. *"Who exactly is the Mistress?"* The story under that one had more questions than answers as the media scrambled to figure out exactly who I was and why I was such a big deal.

Up until now, we had kept my presence and purpose quiet, but now that the task force knew who I was, perhaps it was time to share it with the public. The article did state that I owned the hotel, and how I was protected, leading them to believe that I was someone of extreme importance.

I skimmed through a few more searches and laughed at the next one when I found a breed site talking about my outing. *"Mistress Breaks Out: Dancing and Drinking with the commoners of her breed."* In that article, there was a picture of me outside the club, my arms in the air, my head was thrown back, and I looked excited and relaxed. Behind me near the door were several patrons and bouncers all grinning as they spilled out of the club to get one more peek at me or snap a photo. I skimmed the article, chuckling at the comments that several of the patrons had made. "She was just like the rest of us; she just wanted to have fun," and "She kissed my mate; he said I couldn't kiss him again until his lips stop tingling."

The story went on describing how I had slipped into the club, ordered drinks for everyone, and then danced my little heart out for just over two hours before I left a happy and excited crowd. There was nothing negative in the article; in fact, from what I saw, my plan had worked. My people were delighted to have seen me, thrilled that they had a chance to mingle with me in a relaxed setting. Now if I could just keep it going that way.

My phone began to ring, and I called out to answer it through the speaker when I noted it was Hugh's number. "Good morning."

His voice was even huskier than usual as if he hadn't spoken much yet today. "Good morning to you, Mistress. I see that you made quite a splash in the news last night."

I chuckled. "It was fun. I needed to get out and do that. It's been a long time."

"I wish I had known; I would have joined you."

"Oh, you like to dance, do you?"

"I've been known to do it once in a while. Can't say I'm any good at those fast moves, but I sure can dazzle on a slow song."

"Oh, I bet you could. Is that why you are calling? To say you want me to let you know the next time I go out so we can dirty dance together?"

"Dirty dance? Is that a thing?"

I laughed. "It's the name of an old movie, sorry; I forgot how old you are."

"Please don't remind me that you're older than my mother." He chuckled. "So you went out; will there be a next time? I thought you didn't go out much."

"I decided that some things need to change around here, and my breed needs to know that things are well and that I am there for them, so yes, there will be a next time."

"Is that the only reason?"

"Maybe, but that's not a topic of conversation that I want to have over the phone."

His laugh was deep and sent a lustful shiver down my spine. "You know we have better conversations over the phone than we do in person."

"I wouldn't say that. I think our in-person conversations are pretty damn amazing."

He hesitated just long enough for it to be noticeable. "I saw the picture of you kissing Josh; is that something I need to worry about?"

I frowned. I didn't want Hugh to worry about anything, but then again, why not? Hugh would never be anything to me; he never *could* be anything to me. "You know Josh protects me, Hugh. Occasionally we kiss in public to give a reason why he is always around me and touching me. We make it look like we are in love. It's merely a cover."

"You told me earlier that he hides your presence while he touches you."

"Yes, he does." I gnawed on my bottom lip; maybe I shouldn't have told him that. Especially with who he is. Or perhaps that was the kind of information that would help keep him on my side. It wasn't a secret that Josh could protect me that way. You could see us, but not feel us, and our breed quickly picked up on that.

"I have to admit that it made me a wee bit jealous seeing you making out with him in front of the cameras. Are you sleeping with him, too?"

"It meant nothing, Hugh," I replied and hesitated. "Hugh, you might not know this about our breed, but we don't look at sex the same way humans do. It's not unusual for one of us to have multiple relationships."

"I am aware of that. Do you have multiple relationships going on right now, Kristin?" he asked.

"At the moment? No." I exhaled. "But that doesn't mean that tomorrow I won't decide to sleep with someone just because I'm in the mood."

"So, you're saying that what we share isn't anything special."

"I didn't say that. I told you before that I like you, Hugh; you know that. What we are doing, what you are to me, is a human consort. Someone who gives me pleasure and usually blood. You can never be anything more to me. You do understand that, right?"

"Yeah, I get that," he said a bit gruffly, as if he were disappointed. "Doesn't mean that I like it."

"Are you trying to tell me that if there were a chance for us to be something more, you'd want that?"

He was quiet for a moment. "Yes, I think I would. I don't know why, but something tells me that we would be good together, that we would be right together. There is this incredible pull that I get from you, Kristin. I don't much understand it, but I feel it."

I frowned. "I appreciate you saying that, Hugh, and maybe I do feel the same way. I can't quite explain it either, but it can't be more than it is between us. I can't ask you to be my consort; it wouldn't be fair to you."

"Why not?"

I laughed. "Look, why don't we discuss this later? Would you be available tonight?"

"Actually, I have to go out of town for a couple of days, but when I get back, let's discuss this, shall we?"

"Okay, then when you get back, we will talk about it."

"That sounds like a plan." He paused. "You know that since you've been out in public, people—and I mean human people—are going to want to know more about you. Are you ready for that?"

I inhaled slowly and then released it. "It's time. I think humans need to know more about us. They know we exist, but I think it's time that they see just what we are about and hear from me so that they know that it's not our people they need to worry about."

"Does this mean that you are willing to work with me more? That you'll share some stuff with me? Or do I need to get it from the papers?"

I chuckled. "I'll give you some things, but let's take it one step at a time, okay?"

"Okay."

"You have a good trip; I'll talk to you when you return."

"Stay safe out there, Kristin."

"I will."

We got off the phone after that, and I went up to my apartment. Did I want to take Hugh on as more than he was? Did I want to bond to him in that way, to make him officially my human consort? Many people of my kind did that these days. Especially after the international counsel ruled that turning humans was not acceptable—especially females.

Yes, there were quite a few of them around now, but we had ruled it illegal to change any more. It was too dangerous to have a bunch of human-turned vampires around. Not only did the process water down our bloodlines, but it created problems. Especially when the turned were women. Both males and females were sterile after being turned, which was a good thing. I couldn't imagine what would happen to our breed if they were able to have half-breed babies.

My mind shifted to my old friend Olivia. We had been the best of friends before I learned of this world, and when she learned of what and who I was, she had climbed right on board the crazy train. Olivia had been kidnapped and turned by my sister before Lena and I knew each other. Angelina had needed our help, and turning Olivia was the only way she could think to get it. During that time, we had learned a great many things about the abilities of female turned. The fact that they could control elements might have been a good thing, but there were many downfalls to them.

Initially, it was thought that they would lose their humanity once turned and become raging monsters. We had learned that if they mated shortly after turning with the ones that they were bound to, that they would retain more of their humanity. Olivia had, for a while, at least.

Several years after she turned, we noticed that she had more of a taste for blood, more of a need to kill. Like me, she had been a police officer sworn to protect. She got to the point she didn't bat an eye at draining a human of his blood or making him a puppet for her. Gabriel, her mate, and once a very close friend to me—practically a brother—had said that she would most likely change again, but that he could control her. I had serious doubts about that.

I'd finally had to tell her that she needed to leave. That she could no longer stay at my side because I couldn't keep covering up her destruction. It had torn our friendship to shreds, and the relationship that I had with Gabriel had also become strained. To the point that we no longer spoke. I didn't even have any idea where they currently were, or if they were sided with us. For all I knew, they could be dead.

We knew that human-turned were still made, and we had punished several of them—both maker and turned. The only ones that we didn't always punish were the human-turned males that were willing to work with us. They seemed to retain their humanity better than females, and Donovan and Mick were the perfect examples of it.

Mick had been my human police partner many years ago when I had first learned of this new world. He had learned of what I was by accident when he had observed me taking down several vampires on what would have seemed like a routine traffic stop. These vampires had known where Alex was being held, and once I had received the information, I had killed them.

It had been tense for a while with Mick, and even though I tried to protect him, he had come further into our world. So far in, that after his wife and child were killed in a car crash, he had asked to join us. He had pushed just long enough that I finally relented, and we found a nice woman by the name of Joanna to bond with him, and then once turned, they mated. They were also double-bonded to friends of Joanna for safety.

The two of them were good together, and as far as I knew, happy.

Now Donovan and Mick traveled with their mates and worked for me locating other human-turned and reporting back to me.

I climbed into bed, staring at the windows as the shutters began to descend to block out the rising sun. My mind was heavy as I thought of Olivia and Gabe and the friendship that we once had. I wondered for a minute where they were; maybe it was time to find them and reach out. Check on them, see what they were doing. More importantly, find out which side they were on. I had a sad feeling that it wasn't mine.

I closed my eyes, my mind drifting back to simpler times of laughter and love. Of children being born or couples being happy. I remembered many moments with Trent, and with Alex, and then my mind finally settled on Julian. I could almost smell his scent—leather and cinnamon—feel his touch. No matter what had been happening in our lives, when Julian and I were together, things were better. Our relationship had always been complicated from the moment we first got together, and while at the end of his life, we weren't a couple, we never stopped loving one another.

The memories were bittersweet as they rolled through my mind. For the first time in a very long time, a tear eased down my cheek. So many loved, so many lost.

~

"Well, it looks like your idea might have worked," Hazel commented as I met with the elders the next evening.

"I have to agree," Henry added. "I have heard nothing but good things about you being out last night."

"Do you think it was enough?" Scarlett asked. "Or are you planning on doing that again?"

"I plan on doing it regularly. I think me being out there in the open several times a week would be good for us."

Beckett shook his head. "It still seems like a dangerous plan."

"It is," Clayton commented. "But it might be wise. News has spread like wildfire that she was out at the club last night. Many of our breed are happy to see that, although I have heard from a few elders that they feel it was irresponsible."

"Irresponsible?" I echoed back. "I hope you told them that it is probably one of the most responsible things I have done in a while. Thirty years ago—even twenty years ago—Alexander didn't hide. Yes, he was careful about where he went, but he did what he wanted, when he wanted. He didn't have a bunch of sentinels following him everywhere he went either."

"Those were different times, Mistress," Henry said. "Very different times."

"I know they were, Henry. I think we need to keep it up for a little while longer, at least. Portage needs to know that I'm more accessible. We need someone to come forward and try to get to me."

"And if something should happen to you, Mistress? Who will take over then?"

Garrett would be the wiser choice, but he wasn't even transitioned yet. He was only twenty. Rex could do it, being my son, and Alex's grandson, he had the rights, but I wasn't sure that Rex had the temperament to do the job.

I exhaled slowly. "Let's not worry about that yet."

"If you are going to be out in the open, we need to worry about that."

"Then let me think about it. Garrett is too young, and I'm not sure Rex is suited to the position."

Clayton rubbed his jaw. "I might have to agree on Rex. While he is a strong male, he can get a little aggressive with some things."

"Another reason you should mate, Mistress. If you have the right male at your side, then they could always take over for you in the interim until Garrett comes of age and figures things out," Scarlett said.

"Or there is my sister," I said slowly.

Hazel laughed. "Your sister would turn our breed into a bunch of lustful party animals."

"I'm not so sure about that," I replied to her. "Angelina knows how important our breed is. Twenty years ago, I would have agreed with you, but now she has become a crucial part of our society, and she's just as strong as me."

"Well, not as strong as you," Beckett stated. "But she might be an option. I still think a mate would be a better choice."

I frowned. "Stop with the mate bullshit, Beckett. I already told you I would think about it, but it's not going to happen overnight, so let it go already."

He shook his head, but let the matter drop. A few minutes later, we discussed the human media, and I told them I was trying to come up with a plan for that, but that I would talk to them before I said anything to them directly. After they all left, Clayton stayed behind and spoke softly.

"Do you have any ideas on who you could take for a mate?"

"Not you too, Clay!" I lamented as I leaned back in my chair and twisted it from side to side.

"I'm not trying to pressure you, Kristin." He paused. "But if you would consider it, I could fill that position."

I was slightly shocked by his suggestion. "Clayton, I didn't think you were interested in overseeing the race. It took me a long time to convince you that I needed your help here at my side to begin with. What has made you change your mind?"

He shrugged a shoulder. "I guess being here and helping you has changed my mind. I believe in the changes you have made, in the way you fight for our breed."

"And your mind has been changed enough that you would want to mate to me?"

He grinned. "I'm not sure there is a man, vampire or human, who wouldn't want to mate with you, Kristin. You are a beautiful, passionate, thoughtful, and strong woman. It's been many years since I have been mated; perhaps it is time to consider doing so again."

HUGH

I had been gone for three days, and I was finally on my way home. My trip had turned up some useful information, but not as much as I had hoped. I had learned of a town in North Carolina, along the coast, where there was a large population of vampires. While most of them wouldn't speak with me, there were a few that would—briefly.

The conversations that I had confirmed information that I already knew. The two factions were heading to war, although many were on the fence as to which side to take. Many believed that their way of life should continue as is, but there were a few others that looked down on me as if I were only a meal to them.

At least Kristin had finally said she would talk to me. Maybe now I could get the answers that I needed.

I sighed as I went into my apartment and told the television to turn on the news. The screen appeared in the living room and then shifted to the bedroom as I entered there. The big local news story was of the mistress who had once again graced the public eye by having a meal at one of the local taverns. There were more photographs, a few videos of her speaking with people in the estab-lishment, and overall, seemed positive.

The reporter brought up questions as to why she was now coming out into the public eye and wondering what it meant after years of secrecy. The media was finding out tidbits of information and had learned that she had once been a police officer. While I had known that, I hadn't thought to look into it. We now had a team of people investigating everything they could find about that time in her life. It had given us a place to start, and we were building a timeline on her.

The news clamored for any story on her and shared everything they learned. They had even found people still alive that she had worked with and spoke with them. They were a step ahead of us, but that was going to change tonight.

I showered, changed clothes, and then was back out on the street, calling for a transport to take me to her hotel. It was close to midnight when I arrived, and while most hotels would be quieting down at this time of night, the activity level here was abundant. The bar was packed, and more vampires were hanging out in the lobby than the last time I had been here. Was this all part of her plan? Was she doing this to bring business into her hotel?

I saw Ryker and her son near the elevator when I entered. Ryker nodded to me as I approached them, but Rex practically sneered at me. "What are you doing here?"

"I came to see the mistress," I told him. I should have told him I was going to see his mother, but I still had a hard time wrapping my head around the fact that he was older than me.

"Does she know you're here? Did she summon you?"

The temptation to get into his face was so fucking strong, but I held back. "She told me to come to see her when I got back in town." That wasn't exactly a lie; we did say that we would talk when I returned.

Someone called Rex's name, and he glared at me as he stepped away. Ryker laughed. "Don't take it personally; he doesn't like humans, period; it's not just you."

"I'll try to remember that. Can you let her know that I'm here?"

"She already knows. Jett saw you come in. I'll take you upstairs."

"Thanks, Ryker."

We made our way up the elevator, and he let me into her apartment. "She'll be right up. If you need anything, let me know. I'll be out here."

I told him thank you and was surprised that I'd been allowed into her place alone. I stood near the living room and glanced around before I headed toward a collection of photographs on a side table. I lifted an older one of her with three men in the photo near a blue car. I recognized Alexander from photographs we had on file, but the other two men were unknown to me. I stared at her; her hair was blonder back then and much shorter. She also had on a police uniform, and I smiled and squinted at the picture. I could just barely read the name on the patch, Fawn Hollow Township.

She was younger in this picture too, although you wouldn't know it. I only knew it by the clothing that they wore and the fact that her hair was once again blonder and shorter. In this one, she stood with a tall male who had short blond hair. He was wearing a police uniform, and she was holding an infant. Would that be baby Rex? If it were, wouldn't that make the man in the photo Alex's son? What was his name? I couldn't remember. I thought I had read it somewhere, but it didn't come to me.

There were about a dozen pictures, and I studied them all. Alex, his son, and two other men showed up in her pictures quite often. I studied the one photo as she leaned against the blue car, again dressed in uniform. The man beside her leaned back, his arms crossed, his face devoid of emotion. Beside them was a large dog. Neither of them looked particularly happy in the photo, and I wondered why she displayed it. What was the story behind this one? Who was the other man?

The door opened, and I turned to see Kristin stepping in. She was dressed in black slacks and a dark-purple blouse, again almost see-through, and I felt my body come alive. I stepped away from the photos. "I hope you don't mind; I was looking at your pictures."

"Not at all." She strolled toward me, a smile on her lips. "I'm glad you came."

"Are you?" I asked as she paused in front of me.

"Yes, why wouldn't I be?"

"I don't know. I guess I am just trying to figure out why I'm here."

She looked puzzled and then laughed. "I assumed it was because you wanted to see me. You did come here uninvited tonight. It's not like I summoned you."

"I did want to see you. It's funny, while I was away, I didn't think much about you—no offense—but the moment I got back to town, it was like this sudden need to be close to you came over me. It's almost too hard to refuse, which is strange to me. I've never felt like that before, and I don't know what it means, Kristin. I know that when I'm around you, it just feels right, but I'm not sure how you feel."

She averted her gaze and stepped around me. "That is a hard thing to answer, Hugh, and I'm not sure I'm prepared to answer it right now."

"You said that when we saw one another again, we would discuss this whole consort thing."

She poured herself a drink, then peaked a brow toward me as she held the bottle, and I nodded before she poured another one. She brought my glass to me, then went to have a seat in one of her single chairs. I took the one opposite her so that we could see each other directly and not be tempted to touch one another.

"Hugh, do you want that? To be a consort? You might not understand what that really means."

"Explain it to me then."

She frowned as she stared at her glass. "If I bond to you, which can be very dangerous for you, especially with my blood, then in a way, I will own you."

"Own me?" I laughed briefly.

"Yes, once a bond forms, it never goes away unless it is replaced by another bond, or one of them dies. I could call for you at any time, and you'd likely be unable to resist it."

"Why would you call for me?"

"For company sometimes, but mostly for sex or feeding."

I chuckled. "Well, it's not like I'd turn down the sex. You know I wouldn't." I paused. "I wanted you to feed from me before, but you didn't."

"No, I didn't."

"Why?"

"I told you why. I was enjoying the fact that it was just you and me, just a man and a woman. I didn't want my nature to come between us. I didn't want to use you that way."

"What if I want you to use me that way, Kristin?" As I asked that, I wondered why this was so important to me. I'd never thought of myself as being subservient, but wasn't that what I was asking from her? To be a servant to her in the way of sex and blood?

She tilted her head to the side, studying me carefully. "Is that what you really want, Hugh? If you enter our world, you become a part of it. Till death do *you* part."

A nervous laugh bubbled up in my chest. "So, it's like being married to the mob."

She grinned. "In a way."

I thought about what she had said. There was a part of me that didn't want to do it, but there was another side—a larger side—of myself that was practically begging for it. I'd never been the type to want to be married, so what made me want this so badly? Was it because I wouldn't actually be married and could still go about my life, but still be a part of hers? Would I be able to resist her if she summoned me? Would I want to if I was bound to her? Another question stopped me cold, and my gaze sprang back to her.

"What did you mean about your blood being dangerous?"

"My blood is powerful, Hugh. Even many of my kind can't handle it."

"What do you mean, they can't handle it?"

"It kills them."

My mouth opened and then closed again. I glanced around the room. "You're saying it could kill me?"

"Yes, it could."

"How will we know? How much would I need to take?"

"We wouldn't know if it would hurt you until you took it, and it would only be a couple of drops."

"If it is strong enough to kill your own kind, don't you think it would definitely kill me?"

"It's a possibility. It has never been tested."

"Wait, are you saying that you don't share blood with anyone? I thought vampires shared blood all the time."

"Normally, they do, but I'm different. My sister and I are different, and our bloodline is very strong, toxic to most. So no, I don't normally share blood with others. I take, but I don't give."

"Why is your blood different than others?"

"I can't explain right now."

"You can't, or won't?"

She stared at me for a few seconds before replying softly, "A little of both."

I laughed nervously. "Alright. So you are saying that if I wanted to be your consort, I would have to live through taking a few drops of your toxic blood?"

"Yes."

"Would it change me?"

"Not really. As I said, it would bind you to me. I could communicate with you easily; I would know where you were and could find you whenever I wanted."

I stared at her, and the rational side of my mind was saying get the fuck out of here, but that more influential part was ready to raise my hand and say sign me up.

The logical part pushed through. "Can I think about it?"

"Yes," she said immediately. "I think that would be wise."

"Does this mean that we can't have sex anymore?"

She smiled. "Oh, we can have sex. In fact, I'd like that very much." She sipped from her glass, then set it down before standing and coming to me. She took my glass from my hands and pulled me to my feet.

For a moment, we looked at one another, our fingers laced lightly together, and I watched her eyes shift to a lighter blue. "Your eyes are so incredible."

"Thank you," she replied huskily as she wrapped an arm around my neck to bring my mouth to hers.

The instant that I kissed her, it was like a dam had broken open, and I couldn't seem to get enough of her. I speared my hands through her hair, holding her lips tightly and plundering her mouth until she whimpered and pressed her body closer to mine.

I began to walk her backward toward her bedroom, peeling her clothing from her body as we went, and she managed to get my shirt off of me between rushed kisses.

Her slacks dropped to her ankles, and she stepped out, her feet still tucked into her heels, and I spun her around and bent her over as I ground my hips against her ass. My hands ran up her thighs, between her legs, and peeled back the silk panties that she wore. The feel of her soft, wet flesh made my knees almost weak, and I struggled with the belt on my pants for a second before I could free myself. In one quick movement, I sheathed myself deep within her, loving the fact that she was still in her heels, but nothing else.

For a few moments, I enjoyed the feel of her body wrapped around mine as I moved within, and then I withdrew. She spun around so quickly that I didn't see it coming, and I was on my back a second later in the middle of the bed. She yanked my pants off, removing my boxers and then crawling up my legs.

The look in her eye was predatory, and I shivered slightly as my dick throbbed. She seated herself over me, ground her body against mine, and then took my wrists, pinning them above my head.

Our eyes locked as she stared down at me. "Are you still offering your blood to me, Hugh?"

At that moment, I would have done anything to feel her fangs deep in my neck. "Yes. Fuck—yes."

My gaze was instantly locked on her mouth as she peeled back her lips, and the fangs descended. A shiver of excitement coursed through my body as she leaned forward. The sharp teeth scraped my skin, and she licked under my ear. "Last chance."

"Take me—fuck—please," I begged as I pushed my hips forward, deeper into her.

I barely felt them enter my neck before a wave of ecstasy crashed over me, and I almost climaxed. As quickly as it began, it ended, and Kristin was gone from me. She stood eight feet away, her light-blue eyes wide, her mouth partially open, a drop of blood at the corner of her mouth.

Before I could even think to speak, Angelina appeared beside her, grabbing her arm. "What?"

Kristin tore her shocked gaze from me and looked at her sister for a few seconds. Maybe I should have been concerned that I was lying there naked in her bed with a raging hard-on while two sisters had a silent conversation, but I didn't have time. A second later, Angelina was at my neck, and the intense feeling rushed through my body again, my hips thrusting forward to find something—anything—but only finding air.

Angelina stood slower than her sister. Slow enough that I could watch her move, and she stared at me in wonder as she wiped the crimson liquid from her bottom lip, her fangs visible behind her top lip.

She spoke with a voice so soft that I wasn't sure that I heard her right.

"How did we not know he was a reborn?"

ANGELINA

"Did you know that he was coming here tonight?" I asked my sister as we took the elevator up.

She shook her head. "No, I haven't spoken to him in a few days. Last I knew he was going out of town."

"Looks like he's back now." She laughed. "I'll make sure you aren't disturbed for a little while."

She looked perplexed as we stepped off the elevator.

"Hey, is there a problem? You want me to get rid of him, or even better, show him a little of my old-fashioned charm?"

She laughed. "No, I was just thinking about my last conversation with him. He was asking why I didn't take his blood, and we started discussing the whole consort thing. I have a feeling it's going to come back up tonight."

"Why not take him as a consort? You could still keep him even if you mated."

"Yeah, I know, but part of me is wondering if it's a good idea or not. What if just a drop or two of my blood kills him? We've always thought it would kill a human, but we've never tested it before. I like the guy. I don't want to kill him."

"But what a way to go," I joked, and she rolled her eyes. "Hey, talk to him. Tell him the dangers, and let him make up his own mind. If he walks away, he walks away, but at least get another rocking night out of him."

"I will," she told me and disappeared into her apartment.

It wasn't an hour later when I heard her panicked voice in my head and rushed to her bedroom. I had visions of Hugh being dead in her bed but found quite the opposite. He was rather ecstatically alive and extremely excited, although thoroughly confused.

"What is going on?"

"Angelina, taste his blood." My sister looked like she was going to pass out, her skin pale, her eyes wide and so light blue they looked like mine.

"What?"

"Just do it!" she shouted into my head, and I flashed to the side of the bed and latched on to his neck. His body arched off the sheets slightly as his hips jerked forward.

The blood that filled my mouth was slightly different, as if watered down, but it was so consistent to ours with its deep savory tang that I immediately recognized it. I stood slowly, in awe at the man in front of me.

"How did we not know he was a reborn?" I hadn't meant to speak the words aloud, but I was too shocked to do otherwise.

"It wasn't my imagination?" she asked me privately.

I shook my head as I turned to her. *"No, it is not your imagination. Holy shit, Kristin!"*

"Can one of you please tell me what the hell is going on?" Hugh sat up, his formidable erection deflating slightly as he realized that his good time had effectively been cut short.

"I think you need to get dressed and come out to the other room so we can have a discussion." I grabbed his pants off the floor and tossed them to him. I turned to my sister who was still staring wide-eyed at Hugh, the color now shifting back to her natural blue. "You too, get dressed. I'm going to get Cam."

"No!" My sister finally snapped out of her daze.

"Yes, someone else needs to help us decide what to do here," I told her, and her shoulders dropped slightly.

"I'm serious, ladies; what the fuck is going on?" Hugh asked as he shifted to the side of the bed. "Is there something wrong with my blood?"

I laughed as I left the room, calling over my shoulder, "Or something so totally right."

When I came back a few minutes later, Kristin was staring out the window into the night in her living room, and Hugh was pacing near the bar.

"What's so important?" Cameron asked as the door closed behind him.

"We need you to taste his blood," I replied, and Hugh's shoulder rose as his back straightened in alarm.

"Oh, fuck, no! No one else is taking a drink from this draft until you all tell me what the hell is going on."

"You do realize that he could take it before you could even inhale your next breath, right?" I asked as I cocked my head and grinned.

Hugh frowned at me, but it was Cameron that replied. "Don't worry. I'm not going to take your blood without your permission." He turned to me. "Explain, Lena."

Kristin turned from the window and approached Hugh. "Hugh, I need you to trust me for a moment and let Cameron taste your blood. Just from your wrist, and only a little bit. I promise once he does, I'll explain everything. I just need to make sure before I attempt to make sense of this."

"Fine, because *you* are asking nicely, but you have to promise that you're going to tell me what the hell is going on after he does."

"Yes, I will tell you everything." She squeezed his arm, shivered, and then quickly stepped away from him.

Cameron gave me another hard glance but went to Hugh's side. "May I have your wrist?"

"Jesus, Cam, stop being a douchebag gentleman and just bite him for Christ's sake," I growled at him.

"Lena, cut it out," my sister snapped.

"Yeah, go ahead." Hugh held his hand out toward Cameron, and Cam shared a glance with Kristin before he shifted and latched on to Hugh's wrist. Hugh's body went stiff for a moment and then relaxed as Cameron withdrew and licked his wrist.

In Cam's eyes was wonderment. "Well?" I asked him.

"His blood is almost identical to yours," he responded as he let his gaze drift over Hugh. "Not as strong and definitely not toxic like yours is now, but similar."

"Ours wasn't toxic when we were younger. It's only been the last twenty years or so," Kristin responded.

Hugh put his hand up, his gaze staring at his wrist briefly where the puncture holes had already closed. "Alright, enough of this. Tell me what the fuck is going on. Why do you think my blood is like yours? How can that be possible since I'm human?"

"You might want to have a seat and a drink," Cameron said to him with a smile, and then he grew thoughtful. "Hugh, I'm Cameron, by the way, an old friend of the family." He turned away from him and took a seat, still looking thoughtful, and Kristin went to the bar and poured us all a round before handing them out.

"What was your last name again?" Cam asked Hugh.

"McMurphy," Hugh said as he accepted the drink from Kristin, who practically pole-vaulted to the other side of the room the moment he took it.

"How old are you?"

"Thirty-nine."

"When is your birthday?"

"What the fuck is this?" Hugh growled. "Just explain what the hell you all are talking about."

"I promise I will; I'm trying to put the pieces together so that we have the complete picture, and I can explain it properly."

Hugh sighed. "My birthday is in three weeks."

"What is your father's name? Is he still alive?"

He shook his head. "No, he died when he was forty, and his name was Bryan. I never knew him."

146

"Natural causes?"

"I think the autopsy said a massive aneurism."

"What about your grandfather?"

"Dead at forty, too, his name was also Hugh."

Cameron began to smile. "Your great-grandfather?"

"I think his name was Galen Donahue. I don't know how old he was when he died, but he was killed in a fishing accident; at least that's what I heard from my grandparents. My grandfather was adopted."

Cameron pointed at Hugh and grinned. "There is the connection."

"What connection?" Kristin asked, looking as confused as I felt.

"Hugh, your great-grandfather was a friend of mine. You're right; the story of how he died was tied back to a fishing accident. He bled out while out to sea, and because he was considered a sailor, they gave him a burial at sea the same day he died. His body was never recovered, and your great-grandmother learned that she was pregnant shortly after he passed."

"Well, shit," I murmured as Kristin leaned back against the wall, looking completely stunned.

"I don't get it," Hugh said as he glanced between us.

"Hugh, your great-grandfather was a vampire. I knew Galen. When he died, he must have bled out quickly, so quickly that he couldn't heal fast enough. The people he was with were human, and they didn't know what he was. They put his body to rest in the sea, but they never staked him."

"Why would they stake him if he was already dead?"

"Because it keeps the soul from being reborn. When a vampire is staked, their soul is destroyed and returned to earth in ash. Because he wasn't staked, his soul was reborn into his own son. Your great-grandmother found out she was with child just hours before she learned of his death."

He looked utterly befuddled. "Wh—what are you saying? I'm a vampire?" His eyes zipped around the room, landing on each of us before going back to Cam. "If I am, why wasn't my father?"

"It's much more complicated than that. Your great-grandmother died in childbirth, and humans took your grandfather to raise. There was talk of going after him, but it was decided that we would wait until he was older. Sadly, he slipped out from under us, and we lost track of the family.

"When your grandfather was married, he carried the gene of a reborn vampire but never knew it. If a vampire male does not go through the transition by the age of forty, they die."

"And then what happens?" he asked.

"Well, we have to assume that the soul moves on to the next one in line. In which case was your father. Your father didn't know his father, did he?"

"No, my grandmother learned of her pregnancy after my grandfather died."

"And you?" Cameron asked quietly. "That's how you didn't know your father; you were conceived right around the time of his death. You carry the reborn gene, the blood of a vampire, and unless you transition over to a full-blooded vampire soon, you will be dead in three weeks, Hugh."

Hugh fell back in his seat and began to laugh. "You're kidding, right? You're trying to tell me that I'm some third-generation reincarnate of myself?"

"Kristin and Angelina are," Cam said, and Hugh glanced between us.

Kristin spoke softly. "Many years ago, my name was Calista; her name was Anastasia. She was my daughter, and we were killed within a minute of each other but not staked. We came back as twins."

Hugh's jaw hung open, and his mind was in so much turmoil that I couldn't even try to comprehend it. *I think his brain is going to explode,* I whispered into Kristin's head and saw her lips twitch.

"I know this is a lot to take in, Hugh," my sister said. "The fact that you are a reborn might be why you feel so drawn to me."

"Do you think so?" he asked, still looking like someone had just pulled the rug out from under him.

"That also explains why you were smoky the last time you were with him," I stated to my sister.

"Smoky?" he asked. "I don't smoke."

"Ah, your scent is very smoky, but not like fire smoke, more like barbeque-flavored," Kristin responded.

Cameron turned to Kris. "You haven't fed from him before?"

"No, I almost did the last time."

"That's why he threw out his bonding scent then."

"Jesus, you guys are blowing my fucking mind right now. Bonding scents and reborn blood. Reincarnation is *not* a real thing."

"It is in our world, but there are very few that are known about," Cam told him. "We find one occasionally but not often. That is why Kristin is so important to our race. She and her sister are incredibly strong because of their reborn genetics."

"You would be incredibly strong, Hugh," Kristin said softly. "If you decided to transition."

"How long do I have?"

"Until your fortieth birthday, plus or minus a day or two, we think. Males of our species who do not turn never live to see a week past forty; some have gone a few days early."

He stared at us, one by one. "You guys are serious? Like you aren't trying to prank me or something, right?"

"No pranking, Hugh," Kristin said and then turned to me. "Why don't you guys give us a little while to talk alone?"

"Sounds like a good idea. It's going to take him time to digest it all." Cameron stood and held out his hand. "And if you need someone else to talk to, let me know. I'd be happy to help you."

Hugh stood and shook his hand but didn't say anything, and Cameron and I quietly left. Without saying a word, we went into my apartment and sat down. Cameron started laughing. "Well, shit, I think I know who Kristin should mate with now."

"You aren't suggesting she mate with Hugh? If he transitions, he'll be a toddler."

"Do you remember when you and Kristin came together, how your powers flourished and strengthened? You two were so strong

149

together, especially if Julian was around to assist. Can you imagine what a mated reborn couple could do?"

I leaned back in my seat. To be honest, I'd never even considered it. "I'm not sure I could picture that."

Cameron laughed again. "I'm not sure I can either, but damn, I'd love to see what happens."

ZANDER

"*L*ooks like your mistress is enjoying herself." Laura spun her computer screen toward me with the flick of her wrist, a picture of the mistress in the center. Her dark-blue eyes had been staring right at the camera, her lips in a seductive position.

"She's not *my* mistress," I stated briskly as I looked away.

Laura rolled her eyes. "*The* mistress then. I was saying *your* mistress because you and your father are so hell-bent on destroying her."

I glanced at the clock. "Don't you have to get going?"

She closed her computer by putting her hands together as if closing a book and jumped to her feet. "You sure you don't want to come?"

"No, but thanks. My father and I have a call scheduled for later. You have fun, though, and tell everyone I said hello."

She blew me a kiss and dashed out the front door. After I heard her transport leave, I pushed a few buttons on my watch and brought up my computer screen. "Search mistress in Philadelphia."

Since she first showed up in the news, I had devoured everything that I could about her. I had dissected every inch of her body and the people with her—but mostly her. I had reread the articles until I practically knew them by heart. There were a few new ones, and I slowly savored the words as I learned that she had once been a cop. The media had a list of all her arrests and snippets of interviews with co-workers.

I was addicted to knowing more. A vicious obsession deep inside my gut that made me crave everything I could get about her. I told myself it was to help my father, but even I had to wonder if that was true.

Of all the pictures I had seen of the mistress, there was one that I returned to continually. It had been taken outside of the club after her night of dancing. Hair clung to the sides of her face, and her arms were thrown in the air as if excited. There was such a look of freedom on her features. Was that what she was feeling then?

Was I projecting my wish upon her? Was she kept prisoner for protection? Wasn't that what my father said he was doing to me? I felt as if my entire life, I'd been held prisoner, my body and mind— completely controlled by my father.

I stared at a picture of her eating, and I searched each of the faces with her. I paused on one man who looked slightly familiar. Had our paths crossed previously? Was he working for my father, or had I met him in another capacity?

I scrolled back to one of the images of her kissing a man outside the hotel where she lived. It looked staged, not real. Maybe to someone who didn't know any better, it might seem real, but for some reason, I knew better. It was like something inside of me knew the moment I looked at it, and I had come back to it several times. Why would I think that of that photo?

There were a few more pictures of her with the man, his face always serious, and in one shot that was up-close, I paused. He looked overly concerned, as if he were waiting for something bad to happen. I'd seen that look before, and I sat back in my seat as it suddenly dawned on me. "Well, I'll be damned."

I did recognize the man. He was with Alexander the night my father killed him. This man had been beaten to within an inch of his life. Then he had been dropped on the side of the road not far from where Alexander's mate had lived.

Was he protecting her as he had Alexander? That made sense. We had figured out that he could hide his presence, and sometimes Alex's. Now the two of them together made perfect sense. How many times had she been outside of her guarded walls with him while he covered her presence? I was willing to bet hundreds—if not thousands since Alex died.

I wondered briefly if my father was aware of that information. I was tempted to call him but thought better of it. Perhaps if he were more open with me about what he wanted me to do, I might have felt like sharing more with him.

I flipped through the images one more time before I closed the screen and went to sit on the deck. I could have used a night out of this place. I was sick and tired of this stupid beach house, but this is where my father wanted me—for now—hidden among a large group of our breed, slowly chipping away at them to come to our side for the upcoming war. Not that I was actually doing anything; I wasn't doing shit. I had people working for me that were doing all the work.

I frowned. What the hell was I doing, and why was I doing it? I leaned my head back and closed my eyes, trying to calm the frustration that churned inside my mind.

A picture began to form slowly, and deep in my gut, the frustration turned to anger. The feeling so intense that I didn't understand it as I tried to look around inside the mental image. There were people scattered around the area—no room, it was a large room, or maybe an entryway. Yes, an entryway with a large chandelier hanging above their heads. Like usual, no one's face was clear, but there were quite a few people present. A hand reached for me, and I batted it away. Words were spoken loudly out of anger that made odd vibrations in my skull. No matter what I did, I could not understand them.

Then ever so softly as the image began to fade, a woman's voice drifted through my mind; the words were so full of anguish. "Don't go." My eyes popped open in surprise. That was the first time I had ever been able to hear the words, and they had been clear as a bell.

Was I going someplace? Had I gone someplace? Was this past or future? Had that been Laura asking me to stay? I didn't think so, but why couldn't I figure this out? What was holding me back from seeing the faces, from hearing the rest of the words?

I tried to force the vision back, but I couldn't grasp it again. The two words that I had heard echoed through my mind, and I suddenly felt like I was going mad. I honestly thought that if I didn't figure this out soon, I would lose my mind completely. I got to my feet, pacing back and forth as I wiped my face with my hands and rubbed them over my head in frustration.

I forced myself to breathe slowly, to calm myself as I stared out into the night and listened to the waves crash along the shore. My eyes drifted to the stars above me, and I felt something on the edge of my consciousness. I tried to grab for it, tried to reel it in, but it vanished like all the rest of my visions.

One day I would figure it out. One day, I would know for sure who the woman was, would know if this was past or future. Until then, I'd keep waiting, waiting for my father to tell me that he was ready for me. Ready to complete whatever destiny he thought I was here for.

I sighed as I continued to stare at the sky and slowly began to count the stars.

KRISTIN

*C*ameron and Angelina left, and Hugh and I stared at one another for a long time. I felt the questions cranking around in his head, but I was too busy trying to answer my own.

How had I not picked up on his bloodline earlier? As I sat here, his scent filled the room, and I could easily recognize it now. Was that only because I had sampled it and could put a taste to the scent?

That moment when his blood had coated my tongue, my senses had jumped higher than they had in a very long time. Liquid heat had rushed down my throat, and the taste had almost electrified me. My first thought was that something was wrong, and that's why I distanced myself. My second thought: This can't be happening—no, it wasn't possible.

But it was, and Hugh was one of us. Who would have thought that the reborn gene would pass through generations? Had anyone known that? If that was the truth, how many humans walked the earth that should be living among us? Was that why Hugh and I were drawn together?

I was attracted to him, but I believed his attraction was stronger for me. I felt a longing from him, but he said he was driven to be near me—to have me. Was that because his vampire blood was screaming to come to life? Had it been dormant for so long that it was urging him on? Had I possibly lost my fucking mind?

"I'm not sure what to think right now." He finally spoke, his voice husky.

I tried to smile, but it was more of a grimace. I took a seat beside him and took his hand. "I can understand that; to be honest, I'm a little confused too. What you have just learned is incredibly intense and will change your life forever. Knowing that you are one of us, or could be, is heavy knowledge, but even heavier than that is the knowledge that your current life has an expiration date, Hugh."

"You know, I was just thinking the other day that I felt like there was a ticking time bomb in my chest. It's one of the reasons that I have gone in for physicals every three months for the last two years. I don't want to die, Kristin."

"You don't have to now, Hugh."

"But I'm not sure I want to be one of you either."

I chuckled. "Yes, I'm sure. Our way of life is different, very different. You know, I was brought up as a human, too. I had no idea that I had vampire blood in me, much less reborn vampire blood running through my veins. It wasn't until I was in my mid-thirties, and Julian and Alexander found me."

"Who is Julian?"

I let go of his hand and went to retrieve a photo off the shelf. When I came back, I handed it to him. "This was me back then, and of course, you probably know Alexander; that is his son, Trent, and the other man is Julian."

"I noticed he was in quite a few of the pictures, and I wondered who he was. I thought maybe he was Alexander's son."

"No, he was Alex's best friend. In reality, Julian should have been the master, but he passed that torch to Alexander."

"Why?"

I shrugged. "He just didn't want the trouble. He preferred to be out on the road, working with the breed. He hated being cooped up, and he didn't have the diplomacy that Alex had when it came to dealing with groups of people."

"Why do you sound so sad when you speak of him? Did you love him?"

I stared down at the image of Julian. "I think every person has a great love story; Julian was mine. Although it was never easy for us, and while people would think that we should have been together, we just weren't right for each other. Something was always dividing us. It was like the timing was never quite right."

"So you were never mated to him?"

"I was, a very long time ago, as Calista. Julian was Angelina's father back when she was that little girl that we called Anastasia."

"That was your first life?"

"Yes. When I came back, I was almost identical to who I had once been, although I was stronger, both physically and mentally. When I was a cop and I was investigating a murder that turned out to be vampire-related, Julian and Gabriel, another sentinel for the VMF, came to town to sweep it under the rug so humans wouldn't learn of their existence. Only, I got in the way, and Julian realized that I was his long-lost mate."

The memories of that time crashed over me, and I stood hastily. I returned the picture to the shelf and let my gaze drift over the other photos to give myself a moment. When I returned, I had myself back in control.

"The point of what I was trying to say was, I know how weird this must feel to you. I remember clearly the night that Alexander told me what I was. It was very overwhelming, but I bet if you look inside of yourself, a lot of things will make sense. It did to me. You are probably stronger than most people that you know, and you don't need to work out as much as they do to retain that strength. You don't get sick, and you don't need as much sleep. You probably eat more red meat than any other kind, and when you do, those are the meals that you are most satisfied with."

"Yes, to all of that. You know, a year ago, when DHS and ICE came together to form a task force to investigate vampires, I was the first to raise my hand. I was completely intrigued by them and felt like I had to learn everything that I could. There is so much that is not known, like being reborn. No one knows about that."

"That is a very closely guarded secret, Hugh. You can't tell anyone about that. Could you imagine what the humans might do if they found that out? Right now—if they kill one of our kind, they don't always stake them. We have to believe that those souls are coming back and that one day they will help to build our society to be strong and great again."

"Or take over the Earth."

"No, we have no intention of that. Portage wants that, and that is why I need to remain strong so that I can keep him from doing that."

He sighed. "What am I supposed to do about my job, Kristin?"

"Well, I think right now, you're going to have to decide what to do about your life, Hugh."

His laugh was rough and shifted into a groan halfway through as he lifted his glass and threw back the rest of what was in there. He stared at the glass. "Is that why I can't get drunk? I've tried many times, but I just can't seem to get there."

"Yes, that is why. The blood in you that is ours burns off the alcohol almost instantly."

He shook his head and stared around the apartment as his shoulders rose high and fell. "I think I need to head home. I have a lot to consider."

"That might be a good idea, Hugh."

He stood, and I took his hands. "I'm here if you have any questions, but I need to ask you a favor."

"What's that?"

"I need you to keep what you have learned tonight quiet. You can't put this information into any reports. You understand that, right?"

He looked contemplative for a few moments. "Yeah, I guess I do understand that. I won't do anything right now."

"Thank you."

"I do have a question for you, though."

"What? Anything."

"If we have similar blood, would yours still be toxic to me?"

"I don't think so."

"Can I try it?"

I shifted back from him. "I don't think tonight would be a good idea for that. With your blood in me so soon, it would instantly bond you to me. I think you need to decide if this life is what you want. If you do decide to transition, we'll discuss it later."

"How would I transition, if that's what I decided?"

"One of our males would turn you. They would take your blood, bind you to them, and you would do the same. Usually, after a bond is complete, your transition would happen quickly. Typically, it's the father that does it, but in this case, we could find you someone else."

"You couldn't do it?"

"Women generally don't. I have been told that it is rather painful that way."

He nodded, and his hand touched my face reverently. "I can't believe that I am like you. Maybe that is why I have this undeniable need to be close to you. I thought it was just because I desired you."

I took his hand and kissed his palm. "I desire you too, Hugh, but I do believe it is our blood that is calling to one another—calling you home."

"Then probably better for me to think on this without you around."

"Yes, I agree."

I showed him to the door and instructed Ryker to take him down. Hugh and I locked gazes as the elevator door closed, and once it did, I frowned. Well, crap! What the hell was I going to do with this?

I went into Angelina's apartment; Cameron and she were sitting in the living room.

"Where is he?" my sister asked.

"He went home to think." I plopped into a chair. "I don't think that I need to tell you two that we need to keep this quiet until he decides what to do."

"Like that is even a choice," Lena said on a laugh.

"He believes it is," I told her. "And that decision is his to make."

"What kind of decision is there?" she asked. "He either lives forever, or he dies."

"I agree with Kris," Cameron said. "While it might seem like an easy answer, he doesn't know anything about us. I'm sure that after he considers it for a little while, he'll make the right decision."

"Yeah, to turn and mate with Kristin." My sister's words brought me up short.

"Say what?"

"Cameron and I were just discussing how incredible it would be if you were mated to another reborn. Can you imagine the power you would have? Didn't we just talk about this?"

"Whoa, whoa, whoa, hold your horses, you two. It was less than two hours ago that I was wondering if I wanted to even bond to the man to make him a consort. Now you want me to mate with him?"

"Think about it, Kris." Cameron leaned forward. "You and your sister are a force to be reckoned with when you combine your strength. Can you not imagine how strong you would be as not only mated, but mated to another reborn? One with abilities."

"We don't know that he will have any," I stated.

Angelina frowned. "Yeah, actually, we don't know that. My ability to break compulsion is nowhere as impressive as hers, and male human-turned don't have abilities. What makes us think that Hugh will be any different?"

"But what if he is?" Cameron asked. "Even if he doesn't, I think having two reborn mated together might be a good thing."

"Maybe," I murmured.

Cameron turned to my sister. "Maybe Angelina should mate with him; then she can see what it does. If it makes her stronger or brings out another ability, then maybe you can break the mating and take him for yourself."

"Hey now!" my sister said, putting her hand up. "No fucking way! I was mated once." She glared at Cameron. "And that was enough. I have no interest in mating with anyone else, even if it is on a trial basis. Who is to say that anything would come to him, and then I'd be stuck with a mate. No, thank you."

"I thought you liked him, Lena." I grinned at her. I got what she was saying. I'd never ask her to do such a thing, never.

"I said I wanted to screw him, not get saddled with him," she hissed.

Cameron and I laughed, and the door opened. Joshua popped his head in the door. "Mistress, you are needed downstairs. We have a development."

"I'll be right there, Joshua," I told him, and he closed the door behind him again. "I don't need to mention it again, do I?"

"No, we'll keep our mouths shut."

I got to my feet. "Let's just hope that Hugh does the same."

"Why didn't you compel him not to talk?"

"I don't know. Maybe I should have, or maybe I need to see what he does on his own." I headed toward the door. "I'll talk to you all later."

In the hallway, Joshua joined me, and we entered the elevator. "What's going on?"

"There was a scene down at Dangers in the Darkness."

"What kind of scene?"

He glanced at me. "A few of Portage's men showed up there."

"Why?"

"Looking for you," he stated gruffly.

A smile came to my lips slowly. "Oh, goodie! Let the fun begin. Maybe we should go out tonight."

Joshua turned to me. "Or maybe we shouldn't. Let's not push it. Yes, they came here, and they were looking for you, but that doesn't mean that we should tie a ribbon around your neck and hand you over."

"You know that's not what I meant. I'd be interested in what they want."

"To kill you, Kris. That's what they want," he barked out.

"Not immediately. I have a feeling that if Portage's men could get their hands on me, they would take me to him." The elevator door opened on our main office floor, and I stepped out. I was instantly stopped by a firm hand on my arm.

161

"And if you think for one fucking second that I am going to let that happen, you have lost your damn mind, woman. There is no way I am going to allow those men to take you to him; no fucking way, Kristin. Have you forgotten that I saw what they did to Alex? I watched every single moment of his torture, and I heard his heart stop. I breathed in his damn ash! I refuse to allow that to happen to you."

Joshua had always been passionate about my safety, but this bordered on mania. I rolled my shoulders back and glared at him. "Do not forget who you are speaking to, Joshua. I am well aware of what you saw when Alexander died. I have seen it in your head more times than I care to. It's time that you got over that and put it behind you. His death was not your fault. In the meantime, do not ever call me something as common as a woman again. Do you understand me? I'm your mistress, and you would be well to remember that."

He instantly looked contrite and shifted back two steps, letting his hand drop to his side as his chin touched his chest. "I'm sorry, Mistress. It will not happen again."

"See that it doesn't," I growled over my shoulder as I headed toward the conference room.

Lorna and Lainey both glanced at me quickly but averted their eyes. It wasn't often that I jumped down someone's throat, but I was coiled tightly right now. Over the last ten years, the people who worked for me had become more than employees; they had become friends. Maybe it was time to put some distance between us and remind them all who I was and what I was capable of doing.

I stepped into the conference room. Two of the virtual video monitors were cued up for me as the elders sat around the table along with Rex, Garrett, and a few others.

I scanned the room and then sat back in my chair. The next course of business was going to be dealing with Portage. "Show me."

HUGH

$\mathcal{I}$ let myself into my apartment and sank to the couch. My mind was in a tailspin, and I was fighting to keep it from crashing. How could all of this be possible? The strange thing was that it made sense in a really sick kind of way.

A dream that I'd had many times over the years filled my mind. I was on an old fishing boat, which had never made sense because I'd never gone fishing in my life. The waves had been rough and were splashing over the side. Something broke, a large pole of some kind that had heavy ropes attached to it. One of the cables sailed through the air toward me, a large hook on the end of it. The knot on the line had knocked me back as a wave had me off-balance, and a massive hook had dug through my side as if I were soft butter. I had screamed, and the hook yanked back as the pole that the rope was attached to jerked the other way. The hook had ripped me practically in half. My body fell back against the side of the boat as another wave tossed us roughly, and I went right over into rough water.

The water had been brutally cold, churning in every direction, and I couldn't find which way was up. My energy lagged from loss of blood, and I felt myself falling deeper into the darkness. Every single time that I had that dream, I woke up clawing at my throat as if I were sucking the salty water down instead of air.

I rubbed my hands down my face. Was it possible that the dream was how my great-grandfather had died? If what they said was correct, then that could be a memory from my soul and not a dream at all. My great-grandfather hadn't been put to rest at sea; the sea had taken his life.

This was ridiculous. Was I believing this crap?

I went into my bathroom, stripped down, and got into the shower. I sighed as my phone began to ring, and I grunted, "Speaker." As soon as I heard the click, I said, "Hello?"

"Hugh?"

"Yeah, Tom. Why are you calling me so late?"

"Because I just got word that some rogue vampires showed up in Philadelphia. We are pretty sure they are Portage's people, too. They were causing a scene down at that club that the mistress had been seen in."

"When was this?"

"About an hour ago. Video showed up on the news channels, and it's everywhere on the net. I guess they were sending a message to her."

"What was the message?" I asked as I lathered soap over my face.

"They attacked a few of the creatures—um, vampires—in the club, said they were looking for a certain dance partner. They killed four of them viciously on camera! But that's not the worst part. They killed nineteen humans on the streets, bled them out right there for everyone to see. Left their bodies in the gutters like trash."

I pulled out from under the water where I'd been rinsing. "That was on the news?"

"No, thank god, the news didn't show the human deaths, but they can be found online."

I winced. The news had been banned from showing those particular types of scenes. "How did the other ones get on the news then?"

"We don't know. The news station stated that it just showed up on its feed, overwriting a show that was on. They had nothing to do with it. Someone took over their airwaves and posted it without them knowing."

"Is it still out there?"

"Yes, we are trying to pull it, but it's going to be hard to get all the copies. It went viral in seconds. I just sent it over to you."

"Alright, let me finish my shower, and I'll look at it."

"Have you spoken to Mrs. Armstrong again and gotten anywhere? Is she willing to start helping us?" He sounded exasperated and pissed off at the same time.

I almost laughed. "I'm still working on her. I'll give her a call later after I watch the video, see if she has anything to say about it."

"Let me know after you do. I'm afraid that this is going to escalate quickly. If they would just work with us, we might be able to deal with this together and keep harmless people from being caught in the crossfire. In the meantime, tell her to stay the hell inside and stop causing scenes. It's like she was inviting them to come and cause trouble. We don't need this shit here!"

"Yeah, I'll tell her." Not that I thought it would do any good. I was pretty sure she wasn't going to listen to me anytime soon. He hung up after muttering about our world going to hell in a handbasket, and I finished my shower.

Back in my room, I called out for the video that he had sent over and watched it on my large television screen. The deaths of the four vampires were exceptionally violent, and I noted on each one of them how they not only had their throats slashed or heads entirely torn from their bodies, but their hearts had been staked. It was like it was snowing around the club with all the ash that filtered through the air, the strobe lights glistening on the flakes as they drifted through the air like confetti.

I sat there watching it over and over again, studying the people in the video. I recognized two of them as being henchmen of Portage, but the other five that were on the video weren't people that I knew. Most likely underlings that carried out the dirty work.

I put my earpiece into my ear. "Call the mistress." It rang twice and went to voicemail.

"Hey, I'm not sure if you are aware, but someone was trying to send you a message tonight—at least I think they were. Nineteen humans were killed before your friends showed up at the club. I was just calling to make sure you were aware of it. I'm assuming that you are, but just in case. Right now, my task force is up in arms. I'm sure it's going to be hell tomorrow. Can you give me a call back? After knowing what I know, I'm having a hard time trying to figure out what I'm supposed to do with this come tomorrow."

I hung up the phone and waited as I went through a few emails, several of them about the incident tonight. My phone rang, and I answered without thought.

"Yeah?"

"Hey, lover boy." A seductive voice came over the line, and I frowned.

"Angelina?"

"Ah, I thought maybe I could confuse you for a moment."

"No, your voice is rather distinctive. Where is your sister?"

"She's busy, as you can expect. She told me to call you and tell you thank you. We were already aware of them showing up at the club. We were not aware of the human carnage that they left in their wake."

"What is she going to do about it?"

"Who wants to know? The cop or the bad vampire boy?"

I laughed slightly. "Maybe both. Is she going to do something about this?"

"Of course, she is. Man, Hugh, you have a lot to learn about my sister."

"I'm sure. What is Kristin planning on doing?" She didn't reply right away, so I continued. "Look, the people I work with know that I'm in contact with her. They wanted me to try and form a relation-ship with her so that she would come to trust us."

"Is that the only reason you've been hanging around?"

"No, I happen to like Kristin, but I do have a job to do."

"For how much longer, I wonder," Angelina said softly. "I mean, you're going to be dead soon if you stay with your job."

"Thanks for the reminder. Right now, my concern is for the people that are being tossed out like garbage into the middle of the street. I need to know what she is going to do to stop that. If I don't learn something, this task force that I head up is going to come banging on her door in a not so nice way."

"Is that a threat, Hugh?"

"It's not a threat, Angelina. It is what will happen."

"And you're in charge of this task force, huh?"

"One of the people in charge."

She grew quiet again. "I'm sorry that she can't speak with you right now, but she's getting ready to go out dancing. Strange isn't it that she would want to do that when all of this is happening?"

"She's going out to meet them?"

"I didn't say that. I said she was going out dancing."

"Dangers in the Darkness? That's where she's going?"

"Yep, she sure loves that place."

"Why are you telling me this?"

Her voice grew soft as if she didn't want anyone else to hear her. "Because if you want to see firsthand what this war is about, and what she is like, then you might want to be there to watch." Her voice grew louder. "Well, you have a good night. I'll let her know you said hello. Hope to see you soon."

She didn't even give me a chance to respond before the line went dead. I thought about it for a whole two seconds and then jumped up and got dressed. Before I left, I made sure to put my gun on and grabbed an extra magazine to slip into my coat pocket. Because of my job and the task force that I worked on, I now had that special ammunition that could put a vampire down. It wouldn't kill them, but it would hurt like hell.

I was out the door ten minutes later and grabbed a transport. I had it drop me off a block away from the dance club, and I moved into the shadows to wait. Hopefully, they weren't here yet.

It was twenty minutes later when a larger transport pulled down the street and stopped in front of the club door. I recognized the first two out the door and then saw Angelina step out and put her nose into the air. She smiled and looked right at me. Damn, I was hoping that I could have watched from a distance without anyone knowing I was here.

Kristin was right behind her with Joshua, and she took two steps toward the club before she spun around, and her eyes lightened so much that they almost glowed in the darkness. Words exploded into my mind. *"What the hell are you doing here?"*

Well, no use hiding now. I stepped out of the shadows, and Joshua and someone else stepped in front of her. She pushed them aside and met me halfway.

"I asked you why you are here."

"I told him to come," Angelina said as she joined us.

Kristin spun on her sister. "Why would you do that? Are you trying to get him killed?"

"I thought he should know," she said quietly and looked behind her at the group on alert.

"Jesus, Angelina, this is not his business."

"Yes, it is," I replied. "I'm trying to help you stop a war. If there is something that I, or the people I work with, can do to help, then we need to do it."

"Your humans cannot do anything to stop this war, and if you try to get in the way, you will all be killed." Her eyes seemed to glow, and I couldn't tear my eyes away from them.

"Then tell me how I can protect them. How can I protect the humans, Kris?"

"Why should I care about them?" she snapped, and I shuffled forward slightly, only partially afraid that she would tear my head from my shoulders.

"Kristin, you were a cop once. To me, that means that you cared about people, that you wanted to help them. Are you trying to tell me that after all these years, you no longer have any of that blue blood left in your veins? Has it all been burned away with violence, sex, and control?"

Her eyes began to shift away from the eerie silver to a darker gray, and she averted her gaze for a moment. "Of course I care, but I care about my people, too!"

"Then let me help you." I stepped forward and took her by the shoulders. "Let me stay here to see what happens. See if there is something that I can do to help protect my people. I need to understand this."

She stared at me, and I wondered what she saw. After another two seconds of quiet, she stepped toward me and lowered her voice. "I'll let you stay, but you have to do something for me."

"What?"

"*You have to take my blood first,*" she whispered into my mind.

"What? You want me to do that here, now?" I answered her out loud because I didn't know how to do it any other way.

"Kris, is that a good idea?" Angelina asked quietly.

"Of course not, but I need him protected. This is the only way I can do that."

"How is that going to protect me?"

She pulled the sleeve of her blouse up and bit her wrist. "Drink, and you'll find out."

I stared at her wrist, a part of me immediately wanting to drop to my knees and lap at the crimson on her wrist, the other trying not to freak out.

"Do it, Hugh," Angelina said softly. "You'll be okay."

Kristin's eyes glowed almost silver for a moment, and I heard the next word slip over her lips. "Now." I didn't have any other thoughts as I lifted her wrist to my mouth and licked at the blood.

It burned the inside of my mouth, but the flavor was nothing like I'd ever tasted before. It wasn't the metallic taste of normal blood; it was sweet, almost creamy. I sucked once hard, and then Kristin pulled her wrist away from my mouth and licked the holes. My body began to tingle, but it wasn't in a painful way; it was as if it were coming alive.

"Watch him," Kristin snapped at her sister and turned to head into the club.

"How do you feel?" she whispered toward me.

"Not bad," I answered. "I think."

Angelina hooked her arm in mine and turned me toward the door, where eight pairs of eyes were staring at me in a mixture of confusion and awe. Ah, shit.

ANGELINA

ristin handed me her phone when she came out of the conference room. "Call Hugh and tell him thank you for letting me know about the human casualties."

"Why aren't you calling him?"

"Because I need to change. I'm going out."

"What?" I barked as I rushed after her to the elevator.

"I'm going out to the club. I need to see what they want, and I can't do that sitting on my ass in here."

"Is that wise?"

She shrugged. "I don't really care. Look," she turned to me, "I started going out so that I would get a response from Portage. I got one. It's my turn to respond. This was my plan; it's what I wanted."

"But what are you going to do?"

"See what his messenger has to say. I know he won't show up; he's too damn chicken to do it himself. So I want to see what message they have for me."

"The message is going to be simple. He wants you dead."

"Jesus, what's with you guys? Portage does not want me dead; he wants to control me, and if he can't do that, *then* he will want me dead. I'm not going to let him have either of those wishes."

The elevator door opened. "Get changed; you're coming, too."

"Oh, goodie!" I squealed with false delight. As I went into my apartment, I brought up Hugh's number and called him. I know she said to tell him thank you, but this might be a good way for him to see what she could do and what was in store for him when he transitioned. I did not doubt that he would.

As we all gathered in the lobby to leave, I guarded my thoughts. I knew that Kris would be pissed that I had told him about it, but I knew what I was doing. At least, I thought I knew what I was doing. I had jumped on Cameron's bandwagon and believed that if he transitioned and mated with her, it would be good for all of us—especially her.

When we arrived, I searched the air as soon as I got out of the transport and found him lurking in the shadows of an alley. Did he honestly think that he could hide there and we wouldn't know? He had so much to learn.

I knew she would be angry, but damn if I didn't feel her fury flash through me like wildfire as I admitted that I had told him to come.

She argued with Hugh and me for a moment, but I knew that he had won her over eventually. He would never know what his comment of blue blood had done. Once upon a time, she had said that her blood was blue because of her need to help others. She had been devoted to her job and loved helping the humans in times of need.

I studied Hugh; was that why he had gotten into law enforcement, too? Did his blood run blue?

"Kristin, let him stay, give him your blood. You can protect him then, and if for some reason they get him, you'll be able to find him through the bond."

"What if it kills him?"

"Then blame it on Portage and move on," I replied quickly and felt a little uneasy at my own words.

She inhaled slowly and released it. "I'll let you stay, but you have to do something for me."

Oh, please do not let her blood cripple him, or worse yet, kill him. What a scene that would cause out here if it did.

I felt his apprehension, his body warring with itself as her blood bubbled to the surface. He wanted to take it, but he was afraid. I felt her compulsion reach out to him in her one word, and he took her wrist and sucked from the bite mark she had left on herself.

My body tensed as I waited to see what would happen. Would Hugh fall to his knees and start holding his throat as the blood burned through his esophagus? I wasn't the only one anxious; she was too.

Hugh swallowed a few times, and then he rolled his shoulders back as if he were making himself stand taller. Hallelujah! It hadn't killed him. Holy crap—it didn't kill him!

"*I told you!*" I sang into her head.

"*You're lucky,*" she seethed back.

"*Oh, I believe he is the lucky one,*" I replied happily.

"Watch him," she said to me as she spun and returned to our group. Oh, shit, I had forgotten about them.

"How do you feel?" I asked him as she left us.

"Not bad, I think."

Well, he sure looked good—too good. As I took his arm, my eyes scanned over the group.

"*Why isn't he dead?*" Josh growled into my head.

"*Oh, that's a story for around the campfire later, my dear Josh.*" I grinned saucily at him. "*Keep your focus on her and forget about Hugh. I will look after him.*"

Josh shook his head and spun to catch up to Kristin, who had just disappeared into the club. Dominic was at the door, and he stared hard at Hugh.

"He's the mistress' consort," I stated to him as I smiled brightly. He nodded and let us pass as he basically eye-fucked Hugh in a not-so-good way.

Inside, the club was jumping as if nothing had happened here earlier. A few of the patrons seemed nervous to see her arrive, but you could feel the pride of others filling the air as she walked through the crowd as if it were just another night of fun. I laced my fingers with Hugh as we threaded through the bodies packed on the dance floor and headed toward the stairs.

I felt his curiosity as he looked around, but he remained quiet as we took the stairs, and the DJ lowered the music to make his announcement. "The mistress is back in the house!"

I noticed that I hadn't been announced this time, but I had a feeling that had more to do with the earlier threat than him being neglectful. The crowd of partygoers roared with excitement, and I glanced back at Hugh. He seemed shocked by the way the people began to chant her name and whistle for her.

"*She is very loved,*" I whispered to him.

"I see that," he replied vocally.

"*Speak back to me with your mind,*" I answered him, and a line marred his forehead.

"*How?*"

"*Just like that. Direct your thoughts to the person you want them to go to, and if their mind is open to you, they will go through. Works best with people you have shared blood with.*"

"*I haven't had your blood.*"

"*Yes, but I have had yours, and what yummy blood it was.*" I grinned at him, and he laughed slightly.

We climbed the stairs behind the rest of our group, Conner and Jett glancing back to check on us. At the top, Kristin stood at the balcony, and everyone made a semi-circle around her. Hugh and I stood directly behind her, and I kept my fingers intertwined with his. I had brought him here, and I wasn't going to be responsible for him being hurt or doing something stupid.

The music continued, and the people danced as if nothing had happened or was about to. Our party remained still and watchful, none of us moving to the musical notes that we had previously enjoyed. Tonight was not for fun.

We had been there for almost thirty minutes, and I was getting bored. I was just about to suggest we get a drink when Kristin tensed, and Josh immediately stepped toward her. She lifted one hand from the railing only a few inches and flicked her fingers toward him. He stopped in his tracks. His hands fisted at his sides, and Hugh glanced between him, Kris, and me, a brow up in question.

"*She doesn't want to be hidden. She needs to be felt.*"

"Angelina." Kristin's voice was a strong command in my head, and I shuffled forward a few inches, placing my palm between her shoulder blades. I still had ahold of Hugh's hand, and when I made the connection with Kristin, I felt a wave of power fill me and flow into her. Her shoulders tensed, and her head snapped to the side, her silver eyes wide and so damn bright that I blinked in surprise. She took in the hold I had on Hugh and turned back, her lips lifting in the start of a smile.

I had been right. Even as an un-transitioned, Hugh's power was staggering. This connection between the three of us was even more powerful than when we used to connect with Julian. My god, had we found the perfect weapon in Hugh?

Kristin lifted her hands; they began to glow slightly like her eyes. Something none of us had ever seen before, and someone behind me gasped. "All of those not of my blood, freeze." Kristin's voice slithered over the sound of the music.

All around us, bodies stopped in the exact position that they had been upon command. It was rather comical to see legs bent, bodies twisted, and arms raised wildly in the air.

"What the fuck?" Hugh whispered.

"Pretty awesome, isn't it?" I replied, and Lorna snickered behind me.

The only sounds in the club were now of the music blaring, the heavy *thump, thump, thump* of the bass seemingly out of place with all the motionless bodies. The lights continued to pulse, flashing around us in odd patterns, and very softly downstairs, the pitter-patter of feet filtered up to my ears.

A clap echoed through the club, and then another one and another one. A deep, joyful laugh filled the air and seemed almost louder than the music. Three men stepped into view, and then five more behind them. They wove through the statues below, knocking into a couple and shifting them to make pathways.

"Nice trick, Mistress," he called up to her as he stopped clapping, and I felt my heart slam against my chest. "Too bad it didn't work on us."

Kristin's reply was calm and steady. "I didn't expect it to. I assumed you would have brought a shield with you."

A shield? How had she known that they would have had a shield? Which one of them was capable of blocking like that? The last I knew, only female human-turned could control air like that, so was there someone else here that we couldn't see? Or could she feel something that I couldn't?

"Well, I'm so glad that we were able to meet, although you did interrupt a fine meal."

"I'm so sorry. I did hear that you and your friends have quite an appetite." Kristin spoke in a sweet voice as if they were talking about fine dining.

"No worries, Mistress. I'm not sure why I haven't been to Philadelphia before; there is so much to see, so much to taste," he said with an audacious grin.

Kristin cocked her head to the side. "Adam, what is it that you want? I know you didn't ask for this meeting because you wanted to discuss Philadelphia cuisine."

She knew his name? How the fuck did she know his name? Josh and I peered at one another as if he was thinking the same thing.

"I wished to talk, Mistress, but you are right, not about the local cuisine. Although now that we are here, and we have this great music, I am kind of hoping I might get a dance with you. I hear you like to get your groove on." He glanced around him. "But it might be more fun if we are closer together, don't you think?"

Kristin's face was turned slightly sideways, and I saw her begin to smile. "But of course, if that is what you'd like, I'd love to dance. I've been standing here waiting for the right partner to arrive."

"Well, wait no more." He grinned up at her.

She took a step forward, and Josh tensed. I felt several of the others prepare to move, but she nixed that with one word as her fingers flared beside her. "Remain."

She stepped away, and my hand fell unchecked from her back.

"*Why can't I move?*" Hugh asked me mentally; his voice almost panicked.

"Because she compelled us all to stay here. She really can ruin all the fun sometimes."

"Is she seriously going to dance with him?"

"Yep."

Josh growled low as Kristin reached the top of the stairs. "Why don't you come up here; we can dance on the top floor."

He glanced through the glass floor. "Looks a little crowded."

"Move!" she commanded, and the people on the floating floor began to come alive but not to dance. They walked like zombies off the floor and over to the side.

"Plenty of room now." She smiled down at him. "You can bring your men if you wish, but I will only dance with you. I'm kind of a one-man woman, you know?"

A wide grin filled his face as he let his eyes practically strip her naked. I felt Hugh growing anxious beside me.

"Calm yourself, little boy."

"What if he tries to kill her?"

"She can take care of herself, trust me—trust her."

He sighed; I felt it more than heard it. While we weren't able to walk toward her, we could move. Our group shifted uneasily as Adam climbed the steps. He was tall, maybe six foot three, with dark-brown hair and dark-green eyes filled with malice.

He reached the top and glanced at our group, then back to his own. He had come up alone, cocky little fucker. His men below looked nervous, their gazes jumping from us to him, and then to Kristin.

She held her hand out to the dance floor. "Please."

"Oh, no, I'm a gentleman. Ladies first, Mistress."

The smile she gave him was so out of place for the moment. It was almost sweet, adoring, and I wondered what the hell was going on. I tried to reach out to her, but her mind was blocked. Had she blocked it, or was he doing something to her?

Hugh squeezed my hand, glancing at me as if he knew I was unsure of something. I tightened my grasp on his hand, preparing to break her compulsion if need be and get moving. That was my gift. I could break any compulsion that she created, especially if I had helped to create it, and I could break any other compulsion put on me by other people.

Kristin stepped ahead of Adam onto the dance floor. The two of them were now cocooned inside the circular glass enclosure with only one opening, the bridge that led back to the VIP section. They circled one another as the music *thump, thump, thumped* around us. My heart was now beating as hard as the bass was.

He put his hand out to her as if he were a gentleman, and she took it. A second later, he had spun her around and had her back to his front. His arm was wrapped tightly around her body, and I started to open my mouth to break the compulsion.

Only Kristin glanced toward me and smiled as her eyes flashed brightly once, and her hips began to move to the beat.

KRISTIN

*H*ugh's words echoed through my mind. When was the last time that I thought about my blood being blue? It had been years. He was right; sometime during the previous thirty years or so, I had let go of that ingrained need to protect anyone who wasn't part of our breed. It was time to stop that. Maybe it was time to find my blue blood again.

My breed wasn't the only ones that needed protection, especially with this war raging down on us. Humans would get killed, and maybe I could do something to stop that—maybe—or perhaps Hugh could help me stop that.

I didn't want to admit how nervous I was for him to take my blood. I didn't want anything to happen to him, and I sure as hell didn't want to kill him here on a side street in Philly. As my blood entered his mouth, his tongue swirled over my wrist, and I felt him start to come alive. My blood raced through his body, almost yipping in delight.

There was power deep inside of him, and I knew then that he would be a powerful vampire if he chose to turn. But now was not the time to think about that, nor was there time to answer the million questions running through everyone's mind.

I was here for a purpose, and I needed to keep my focus on that. As we entered the club, I felt a flutter of nervousness enter my system, and I shoved it aside. I could not be fearful of what was to come. I had to remain focused, to be in control of what was to happen.

We waited. We watched. Finally, I felt them. More importantly, I felt Adam. Oh, I knew him. I knew him very well. Once upon a time, he had worked for Julian out of the western VMF office. He was also the one that I believed killed Julian, and I had a very special deep-seated hatred for the man. I didn't show it though.

I felt the other presence, one I recognized as being similar to Olivia. There was a female human-turned here, and she was holding a shield up to protect the men from my compulsion.

As Adam moved through the mass of frozen people below, my control was at its peak. I was determined to survive this. I had no doubt that a message would be left and that they would not try to harm me—not tonight. It was the people with me that I most worried about. Hence the reason I moved away from them.

Adam was arrogant as he climbed the stairs to the top floor. His attitude was dark and egotistical, his mind twisting on the things he would like to do to me. He wanted to hurt me, but he also desired me as a woman. His thoughts were loud as he pictured tying me down and taking his pleasure. Brutally forcing himself on me.

I would use that knowledge to my advantage. That's why I let him wrap his strong arm around me. It's why I pressed my ass to his groin and rubbed it against his hard erection. While one arm was like a vise around my waist, the other hand roamed my body, touching every-thing that he could. My stomach wanted to revolt, and I had a vision of taking him to the ground and yanking his heart from his chest.

My group was almost frantic in their worry, but as I stared at my sister, I felt her calm. She knew what I was doing, and she knew I was okay. She calmed, and as she did, it helped the others to do so also. Well, all of them except Josh and Hugh. Both of them looked as if they were about to lose their minds.

Adam ran his fangs up the side of my throat. Oh, please, take a little nibble. I dare you, I wanted to say, but I held my tongue and kept my mind locked down tighter than I ever had. These men had compulsion in their minds, I could feel it, and I knew that only someone powerful could leave that mark. Was I strong enough to break that compulsion and add my own? Maybe I couldn't, but could I compel over it?

I wasn't sure what these men had been compelled to do. Could they breach minds? Cameron could read anyone's thoughts, anytime. So, it was possible that one of them could, too.

Maybe I should have insisted that Cameron come with us tonight. Perhaps he could have read the men, tried to figure out what they were up to. Maybe see what they knew about Portage. Next time, I would request his presence—if there was a next time.

"So, what is it that you want, Adam?"

"Other than to fuck you until you can't see straight?" he growled into my ear. I put my hand over his as it cupped my breast and squeezed it, playing into his fantasy.

"You'd like that, wouldn't you? To take me over and over again, hard and long."

"Fuck, yeah," he hissed as he pushed his hips forward. "What about you and I go at it, right here, right now. They can all watch the mistress in her glory being pleasured."

I laughed softly. "As incredibly sexy as that sounds, I think I have to pass—tonight at least. What message do you bring me from your master?"

It wouldn't hurt to keep playing on his fantasy. He did believe that Portage was his master and that he would become the master of our breed.

"What? No pleasure? You just want to be all business?"

"Tonight, it must be. The hour is late; the sun will be rising soon."

"Aw, there is that." He groped my breast again, pinching my nipple before sliding his hand between my legs and cupping my sex. Even with as much as I hated the man, my body responded to the raw sexual need it felt. His touch might disgust me, but the image of having him within my body was sharp.

"So, tell me, Adam, what message do you have for me?"

"The master wants you to come to him," he said gruffly as he spun me around in his arms and quickly lifted me. I locked my legs around his waist, coming face-to-face with him. Liquid hatred ran through my veins, and I fought to control it and keep my eyes from changing to silver.

"Now, why would he want me to do that?" I asked playfully as Adam pushed my face to the side and put his mouth to my neck. Bite me, you son of a bitch; just bite me once.

My head was thrown back as if I were enjoying what he was doing to me, my eyes cracked open, and I saw the fury on Josh's face. My gaze shifted to Hugh; his hand was fisted at his side, his body shaking. Was it possible for him to break the compulsion? If he did, they would strike him down in an instant.

I wanted to tell him to calm, but I didn't want to chance opening my mind for the slightest of a second. I glanced at my sister and then back to Hugh. I saw her nod just the slightest bit. Thank god, she understood me without saying a word.

"He wants you at his side so that you two can come together," he said into my ear. "Although before you are his, you will be mine."

I laughed, the sound high-pitched as if I were delighted with the thought. Give me a fucking break. "If he wants me at his side, then he needs to come to me. I will not be beckoned like a commoner. If he wants me, he needs to show me the man he is."

He laughed huskily. "You know he will not do that. I think he fears you, Mistress. Don't tell him that I told you that. He thinks you will come to him on your own."

"I don't think that is going to happen anytime soon," I said with a smile.

He pressed our bodies against the glass wall behind us. "What about us? What about we blow this joint?"

I touched his face, staring into the eyes that I had dreamed of pulling from their sockets. "You will have to wait."

"For what?"

I smiled shyly, glancing over his shoulder. "Until I don't have my men with me."

He turned and looked at our group and laughed. "Is that human yours or your sister's?"

"Mine."

"I never pictured you to slum it."

"Hey, a girl has her needs," I purred.

"I could fulfill those needs better than any human." He shoved his hips forward as if to prove a point.

"I have no doubt that you could, but that is not going to happen— at least not tonight." I stared at him, my voice going low as I leaned my mouth toward his. I licked at his lip, nipping once gently, and he growled. I bit again, just hard enough to acquire a drop of his blood; the taste made my stomach roll with revulsion. "Now put me down and leave. Your message has been received. On your way out of town, you will not kill any more humans."

He stared at me and slowly let my legs fall to the glass floor. In the reflection of his eyes, I saw the glow of mine.

"Tell your master that if he wants me, then he must come to get me himself." I leaned forward, my lips almost touching his again. "Do you understand me, Adam?"

He blinked as if he were trying to fight my compulsion, but he couldn't. I was too close for him to resist it, and I was far too strong for him to win the fight.

As I pulled back, I dropped the compulsion before he and his men picked up on it. The process had taken only a few seconds, and they would be none the wiser. Even he would have no concept of what I had done, only that I had kissed him.

"I will relay your message," he said and leered at me as he stepped back. "Until we meet again, Mistress."

"Until we meet again, Adam."

He walked backward a few steps and then turned and left the dance floor. He paused a few feet away from Hugh and laughed again, shaking his head. "A human consort. The master will love that."

He stared at me as he took the stairs, his eyes devouring my body as he went. On the bottom floor, he shoved two frozen vampires out of his way. They toppled over to the floor. One of his men drew a stake and slammed it into another dancer before they all laughed. Adam grinned one more time at me and then went to the door, his men following him. I stepped off the dance floor. "Return," I said to the people who had once been there, and they filled the floor again. "Move," I said to my people, and they all shifted their feet.

Once everyone was back in place, I lifted my hands to my sides. "Resume," I called, and suddenly the place came back to life. I stared down at the two people on the floor as they looked around wildly, wondering how they had gotten there. The ash of the third one filtered down, and I prayed he had not been mated to someone here. After a moment of confusion, everything returned to normal with the crowd.

"What the hell were you thinking?" Josh said to me the minute I turned toward him.

I glared at him. "Watch yourself," I stated under my breath.

A muscle in his jaw flexed repeatedly as he ground his teeth, and I began to take the stairs down. Everyone followed me, and once we were outside, we all piled into my transport, even Hugh.

"I know a lot just happened back there," Lorna said, "but can someone please explain to me why he's still alive?" She pointed at Hugh.

I glanced around at the occupants, knowing that they were all wondering the same thing. My sister had a smirk on her face, and I rolled my eyes as I sighed.

"There is nothing to explain." I shrugged a shoulder.

"Bullshit," Joshua said from beside me as he took my hand and laced my fingers with his. He might be mad at me, but he would still protect me. "I've been feeding you for years, and one mouthful of your blood nearly killed me. How can he handle it? He's only a fucking human."

"Is he?" Angelina said quickly.

The faces in the transport all snapped toward Hugh, and Ryker leaned forward and sniffed at him, suddenly laughing. "No way!"

"What?" Paxton quickly asked as she sniffed the air.

Ryker looked at me, then Angelina, and back to Hugh. "He's like you."

"What? That's not possible." Josh glared around me and stared hard at Hugh.

I sighed. "Look, this cannot leave the transport right now. Hugh *is* like Angelina and me. He's a reborn, or he will be if he transitions."

Jett snickered from the other side of the transport. "Lucky son of a bitch."

"How is that possible?" Josh asked gruffly and then looked at me as if he expected me to know that specific answer. His eyes shifted to slants as his tone deepened. "How long have you known?"

"Only a few hours, calm your ruffled tail feathers, Josh."

"When is he going to transition?" Lorna asked, eyeing Hugh in a different way than she previously had been.

"I don't know that I am," Hugh stated and shocked everyone in the vehicle beside Angelina and me.

"Why would you not?" Jett said on a laugh. "Did you not see what the mistress was able to do back there? A reborn has incredible power."

I glanced at Hugh as Angelina whispered into my mind, "*You felt it, didn't you? When I touched you, and he was holding my hand, it was so much more powerful than before.*"

"*I did.*"

Hugh spoke again. "That's a huge decision to make, and I need some time to make it."

"I don't know. If it were me, I'd be jumping on it without hesitation," Ryker said. "I noticed the power you lent to the mistress."

"What power?" he asked, and I glared at Ryker for a moment.

"Must you always be so perceptive *and* vocal, Ryker?" I said to him. "Yes, I noticed it."

"What power?" Hugh asked again.

Angelina turned to him. "Did you happen to observe that when I touched Kristin, she seemed to come alive with energy, and her eyes glowed even brighter?"

"Yeah, and her hands were glowing slightly, too," Paxton said in awe.

"Yeah, well, *that* has never happened before. That was because of you, Hugh. When I touch her myself, I lend her my strength. It's like adding another battery to hers, and her power grows. I was holding your hand when I touched her. You, Hugh, have incredible power inside of you. I cannot imagine what you will be like once you join us."

"I don't know that I will," he stated again.

My sister and I shared a look. Oh, he would. He was going to transition over even if I had to do it myself. After tasting his strength earlier, I was determined to have him on our side. Cameron was right, mating with Hugh would be smart. Now to make him realize that.

JOSH

The woman was going to be the death of me. Yes, I was aware that I was only her employee, someone to feed and protect her as needed, but I couldn't help that my feelings were so much more.

I cared about her from the very depth of my soul. My need to protect her was almost obsessive—I knew that. What I had to remember was that I wasn't free to voice such things in public. It had been a long time since she had spoken down to me as she had in the hallway outside the conference room. Maybe if we had been alone, she might not have been as strict with her words, but they had the desired effect that she was striving for. She put me back in my place.

That didn't mean I had to like it. I also didn't like the fact that Hugh had shown up at the club. He had no right to be here. I didn't like the man, and it wasn't just that he was sleeping with Kristin. Something about the man bothered me.

When he took her blood, a tiny part of me was prepared to hide my glee that he was going to drop to his knees and keel over. Only that didn't happen. He seemed to not only tolerate it but enjoy it. What the fuck? How was he able to do that? Was her blood not toxic to humans as we had thought? That was the only possible explanation

I could come up with at the time. I would speak with her later when we were alone, and I could be open with her.

I felt her tension when we first entered the club, and then I felt her control take over. That was one of the things that I respected so damn much about her. She could remain calm and in control, no matter what shit was going down.

I wasn't surprised that she froze the place; however, seeing the slight glow on her hands had my lips parting in awe. The connection between Kristin, Angelina, and Hugh had added something to her ability. A small part of my mind dwelled on that as the rest of me stayed focused. As Adam came up the stairs and she stepped away from us, demanding us to remain where we were, I thought I'd lose my mind.

She was never supposed to lock us down. Ryker, Conner, and Jett were just as pissed, and Paxton wasn't thrilled with it either. She had even locked down her sister and her human, although if need be, her sister could break out of her hold.

I knew that Kristin harbored a deep-seated hatred for Adam. I had been there when she and Alex had learned of Julian's death. There was a rumor that Adam might have been involved in the death of Trent, but no one was ever able to confirm that. How she remained so in control while that filthy animal put his hands all over her body was a mystery to me. I would have wanted to take his head off if it had been me.

But that was the difference between us. My first thought was to protect her and then myself. To take out anyone who had ever hurt either of us. I tried so hard to break the control she had over me, but at the same time, I knew that she was doing it to protect us. Had we not remained where we were, we all would have been at her side, and people would have been hurt, possibly killed. Most of those killed would have been the partygoers here at the club, and she would not allow that. It was her job to protect them, as she protected us.

The moment Adam and his cohorts were gone, I was in her face, livid with having been held back. When we got back to the hotel tonight, I was going to have words with her.

Inside the transport, the question was brought up about how Hugh survived her blood and the shock of hearing he was a reborn weighed heavily on me. I now understood the attraction between them. Kristin's blood had found a common link. It wasn't that he was a male she found herself interested in, but a vampire who had not been unleashed yet. That was how her blood had not hurt him.

Lucky fucking bastard, I thought to myself as I glared out the window. I should be happy for her. I should be glad that she had found a proper man that she could possibly mate with, a man that would strengthen her, please her. Yet, I wasn't.

Back at the hotel, Kristin said goodbye to Hugh. No kiss, no hug, just a quick goodbye and that she would talk to him later and that he should remain quiet about what he saw tonight. Would he? I wasn't so sure.

I followed her into the hotel and to the elevator. I expected her to hit the floor for the conference room, but she asked to be taken up to her apartment first.

"I thought you would want to speak to the elders," Angelina said.

"They can wait a few more minutes. I need a shower first. I have to get this nasty scent off me," she growled.

I laughed under my breath, and we remained quiet until we got to the top floor. I followed her into her apartment, and she glanced back at me once, brow raised. "Go ahead, tell me how disappointed you are in me. How pissed off you are that I held you back."

She began to remove her clothing on her way to her room, and I paused just outside her door. "I am pissed. What if something had happened?"

"It didn't," she told me as she dropped her blouse to the floor and kicked it into the corner near her hamper.

"Yeah, but what if something had, Kristin? You locked all of us down, and his men were all moving around easily. They could have come up the stairs and staked us all."

"Had they made one move, I would have released you all," she stated.

"How would you have known if they did? You were too busy getting it on with Adam. I thought you hated that man."

Her face turned toward me slowly as she dropped her bra to the bed. "Do you think that I was not aware of what all nine of them were doing downstairs?"

"Nine? There were only seven."

"Oh, no, there were nine. Adam had seven people with him, and then there was one under the stairs that you couldn't see. That was the person who held the shield to protect them, a human-turned. You couldn't see her, but I could feel her, Josh. I knew what they were doing and how each of them was feeling. They would not have made a move without Adam telling them to, and he had been instructed to give me a message, not kill my sentinels."

"He could have had his own agenda."

"He could have, and he did. He wanted to tie me down and rape me brutally. That is his thing, but he wouldn't because he had been compelled to do one thing. Give me a message and then leave and bring it back."

"He was compelled?"

"Of course, he was," she replied and stepped out of her pants. I forced myself not to check her out as she stood there in only burgundy panties. I had seen her naked a thousand times, and most times, it didn't affect me. Tonight, I had the urge to show her how I felt again. Maybe place my bonding scent upon her. The little bit of blood that she had left in my body screamed out at me to close the distance and take her.

"Don't even think about," she said over her shoulder before she went into the bathroom.

"Think about what?" I asked her as I followed behind her.

"What you were just thinking of doing. We will not be together anymore, at least not right now."

"But you'll bond to him?"

She raised a brow at me after she called out for the water to turn on to the correct temperature. "I assume you mean Hugh?"

"Yes. Why didn't you tell me he was a reborn?"

"I told you, we had just learned about it earlier tonight. I hadn't had much of a chance to think about it myself, and I wasn't sure what to do about it."

"Now what are you going to do?" I leaned back against the vanity, crossing my arms over my chest.

"Make sure he transitions."

"Are you going to force him to?"

She shrugged. "If I have to, maybe."

"Are you going to mate with him?" She looked at me as she stepped out from under the water.

"I don't know, Josh, I might. I'd like to think that he might be up for that. There is a connection between us, and being that he is a reborn, and you saw his strength tonight, I think it might be good."

I pursed my lips.

"You don't agree?"

"I agree that he might help your power, but there is something about him that I don't like or trust."

"You don't even know him, Joshua, and you have been barking about him since the moment he arrived."

"Don't you think it's strange that he showed up now? That he came to us asking about our powers now right when things were changing?"

"No."

"How can you not? The man works for the government, a government that wants to control us. Portage is knocking on our door, trying to take your power, and here comes this guy that no one knew about. He shows up; you two hit the sack, and then look at that, he's a reborn, and you're looking at mating with him."

"You say that like he has this devious plan. He's a reborn, Josh, and his blood goes back years. It was his great-grandfather that died a vampire and was reborn into his grandfather, his father, and then him. None of the other men even knew what they were. We are lucky to have found him."

"Are we?"

She finished rinsing her hair, and I waited patiently as she turned off the water and wrapped a towel around her hair and her body.

"Yes, we are. I think Hugh coming to us now is a good thing. Perfect timing."

"So you are seriously considering mating with this guy?"

"Not that it is any of your business, but maybe. We have to wait and see what Hugh decides. He might want to transition, but maybe he wouldn't want to mate with me."

I laughed. "Yeah, I don't see that happening."

"Why not? Because you secretly wish that you could? Because several of the other men here wish that they could?"

"Maybe."

"Sorry to disappoint you all, but it's going to be either Hugh or an elder. You are too important to me. Besides the fact that our blood is too different, I need you focused on my safety as the mistress. Not as my mate."

"Fine," I muttered and stared at the floor.

She came to stand in front of me, taking my face in her hands. "You know I love you, Joshua. I will always love you for what you are to me, for what you do for me, and for the way you feel about me. I can't give you more; you have to accept this." I nodded, and she continued. "And you also need to start watching your tongue. No more outbursts in public or I am going to have to punish you. Understand?"

"Yes," I replied. Little did she know that she was already punishing me in ways she could not imagine by even considering mating with Hugh.

ZANDER

"I just got word that Adam met with the mistress. Things are going exactly as planned."

"Yeah, and how much blood was shed?"

He laughed. "Well, not much inside the club during the meeting, but I don't care how much. Those people were of no consequence to me."

Of course, it wasn't. "How did the meeting go? I saw the video you sent earlier about his request for a meeting. Did he have to kill those people?"

"Zander, don't be soft. Those killed at the club were followers of hers. You would do well to remember that. The meeting itself went rather well. Although I do believe that Adam would have liked to have gotten time alone with her. He has something of a lustful crush on her. Maybe after I am done with her and have control of her power, I can allow him to sate his vicious whims."

I frowned. What did I care of that nonsense? "What about your request?"

"She refused to come to me, of course. I didn't expect her to accept my invitation. She had the gall to tell Adam that if I wanted her, I would have to come to her."

"What if you did? What if you went to her? Wouldn't that surprise her?"

"Aw, no doubt it would, but I will not play by her terms. She might think she is the mistress and ruler, but she is not. She will come to me. It will take some time, but I have no doubt she will come to me."

"What makes you so sure?"

"Zander, do you still need to question everything?"

"No, I'm not questioning it. I'm trying to figure out what you are up to and how I can assist."

"Your time is coming." He sighed. "You never have been a patient man."

And my patience was wearing thin with this whole thing. Why couldn't he just go to her, bring her back, then take control of her power? If he was so powerful, and she was nothing, then what was he waiting for?

"Yeah, well, you're right. I'm not patient, and I'm bored out of my fucking mind. I need more to do."

"Soon."

"How soon?" I snapped as my temper vibrated through me.

His voice lowered. "As soon as I say it is time."

"Whatever," I muttered.

"I will speak with you again soon, Zander. I told you that you would be important, and you are. You are what will bring her to me."

"Me? Why the hell would she come to you because of me?"

"Because I have something that she will want."

"Yeah, what's that?"

"I have you, dear son. I have you."

He hung up before I could even utter a sound. I stared at the phone in my hand. What the hell was he talking about?

I threw the phone against the wall, watching it shatter into a million pieces. My frustration was at an all-time new level. Laura appeared in the doorway from our room.

"What's wrong? Why did you just smash your phone?"

"Because I'm tired of waiting for that man to tell me what the hell is going on. He thinks I'm just going to keep sitting here while he tells me to wait. I can't keep doing that. He wants to take over her power, control the breed. Well, he needs to let me help him."

Laura came to my side. "Zander, relax. Your father knows you want to help, sweetheart. When the time is right, you will." She leaned forward and kissed me, then pulled back and winked.

"Are you leaving now?" I asked her as I took in the dress she wore.

"Yes, you sure you don't want to come? I think you could use a night out."

"I'm sure I could, but I wouldn't be good company tonight. Besides, I need to clean this up and get myself a new phone. Although if I don't replace it, I won't have to take his calls anymore."

"Stop being silly. You need to take his calls. Otherwise, you won't know when it's time to help him."

"Somehow, I think I would get the message," I muttered, but she didn't reply. She waved a quick goodbye and was gone.

I exhaled loudly and went to retrieve the pieces of my phone. I should have just put my earpiece in and not picked up the actual device. When he had called, my phone was closer than the earpiece, so I had grabbed that. After I collected almost all of them, I set them on the counter in the kitchen and froze.

My gaze locked on the phone, but the counter was different. Instead of the brown and black granite that we had, I could see a wooden counter and another phone, a very old model, shattered into pieces. Beside it was a mallet of some kind. I almost felt like I could reach out and touch the pieces, but I couldn't. Suddenly, hands scooped up the remnants of the vision before me and discarded them into a trash can, the movements a mixture of anger and regretfulness. This was the first time that I could remember something that gave me a date in history.

Those types of phones hadn't been around in a very long time. The devices we used now were smaller, more technical, but maybe it wasn't a phone. Maybe it was something else.

The image was gone when I blinked, and I couldn't pull it back up. All I could do was rehash it like I had rehashed two dozen more over the last couple of weeks. They were coming faster, more frequently, and starting to clear up visually. How long would it be before I could see all the details? See the faces that appeared before me? Hear the sounds of the voices that went with the moving lips?

Maybe I should have gone out with Laura tonight. I could use a distraction. Where did she say she was going? Out to dinner near the boardwalk? What if I met her there? Would she mind? I doubted that; she would probably be happy that I came. On my way, I could purchase another phone.

I went to change clothes and then called a transport for myself. On the way to the boardwalk, I had the driver stop at a store, and I collected a new phone in minutes. Now that I had a new phone, I could call Laura and tell her I was going to be there, or I could surprise her.

I opted for the surprise. I had the driver drop me off in the center of the area and felt around. She was here, and it wouldn't take me long to find her. I could tell that she was happy, laughing, having a good time with her friends. Hopefully, they would be able to pull me out of the funk I was in.

I stepped into a bar along the boardwalk to find it was filled with our kind. I nodded at a few of them and made a beeline for her table. Laura stood, surprised to see me, and her gaze darted to someone at the table before she came around to me, pasting a smile on her lips.

"Zander! What a surprise."

I kissed her cheek, then glanced over her shoulder at the man she had exchanged a look with. He was tall, young for our kind, with brown hair. Beside him was a pretty woman with big expressive dark-brown eyes. The pair of them watched me carefully. Were they doing so because they had heard of me? Or for another reason?

When had I become so concerned with how people looked at me? When did I start wondering what people knew of me? What might get back to my father?

I waved to everyone else at the table as Laura asked for another chair to be brought over. Everyone shifted around as I took a seat, and Laura started to go around the table and introduce the people I did not know, which was most of them.

When she got to the man and woman, I felt her tense as she glanced my way. I had already picked up on the fact that the woman was a human-turned. Did she think I would do something to her? I couldn't care less if she lived; as long as she did what was asked of her, I wouldn't care.

"Zander, this is Gabriel and his mate, Olivia." I nodded to them, not recognizing their names. They said hello, and then she continued around the table as if she hadn't been nervous about introducing them.

As we drank and ate, periodically I would glance at the couple. Olivia had thrown her head back to laugh at something, and I froze, my eyes dropping to the table as a vision of a woman standing in the middle of a mini-tornado came to mind. A laugh filled the air around me; there were others there, but I couldn't see them. I could feel them. The laughter was the same, and my head popped up. I opened my mouth to speak, but Laura's hand landed on mine, and the question vanished instantly.

I glanced at Laura; she was smiling and laughing at something. She darted a look at me, then smiled brightly before leaning forward to kiss me and let go of my hand. The vision that had filled my head had vanished along with my words, and as hard as I tried, I couldn't recall what it was.

I leaned back in my seat, trying desperately to recall them, and wondering what I might have wanted to ask Olivia—but it just wouldn't come back to me, and I stared at Laura. How had she made me forget?

LENA

*J*t had been a hell of a week. Kristin had been in rare mistress form, barking orders at everyone she came in contact with and keeping herself behind closed doors. I knew that she had been in meetings with other masters around the world, and I figured it had to do with Portage and his message, but she wouldn't even talk to me.

Our group had remained quiet about Hugh, and I had to wonder if Kristin had somehow compelled everyone without my knowledge. I didn't think that she did, but stranger things had happened.

One of those strange things was the absence of Hugh. Kristin had neither seen him nor spoken with him all week. Was she not wondering what he was thinking? What was he planning on doing? God knew that it was driving me nuts not knowing.

That's why on Friday night while I was bored, I decided to give him a call. He answered on the second ring, "Hello?"

"Well, hello there, sexy."

"Angelina, how are you?"

"I'm just ducky, but more importantly, how are you? Did we scare you off last weekend?"

His husky chuckle slithered through the link. "No, you didn't. I've been busy at work. Your friends coming to town caused quite a stir. I've been putting out fires all week."

"Yeah, I guess it would have."

"I am glad you called. There is something that I have been wondering all week."

"Just one? If I were you, I'd have a list of a thousand."

He chuckled again, and I smiled into the phone. I did enjoy the sound of his laugh. "Oh, I do have a lot, but one that I need to know the honest answer to."

"Then, please ask."

"Did Kristin do that compulsion thing on me to get me to drink her blood?"

"Yes."

"Why?"

"Because she needed to know you would be safe. First off, humans can't go into the club, but consorts can. She also knew that if things went down the wrong way, and for some reason, they decided to take you, she would have been able to find you since you two had formed a bond."

"Did we? I mean, did we literally form a bond?"

"Yes. Kris had your blood earlier in the night; taking hers completed that bond. Had it been days between, it might not have worked as well, but she would have still been able to find you. She can always feel those who have ingested her blood."

"So she did that to protect me, not try to convince me to turn?"

"Why? Has it convinced you?"

"No, I didn't say that."

"What *has* her blood done to you?"

"Made me wonder, that's for sure. After I took it, I felt more alive than I had in years, but that only lasted a couple of days. Now I'm feeling weaker; I guess more like my normal self."

"Or you could be in the first stages of failing, Hugh. It would be smart to make your decision soon."

"You say that like I'm just signing up for a club, not changing my entire existence, Angelina."

"We are a very elite club, Hugh. The cream of the crop, especially Kristin and I, and you saw just how special she is."

"Are you special like her?"

"Do you mean, can I compel the world around me to stop moving? Sadly, no. I can compel someone that I am close to, or have shared blood with, but I can't control an entire room full of people."

"What can you do then?"

I sighed wearily. "Nothing as special as my sister. I can break a compulsion if one is put on me."

"You guys don't have the same gift? I would have thought that you would since you are twins."

"Actually, if you think about it, Kristin and I are opposites, or we used to be. To be honest, Hugh, we are guessing at all of it. There are so few of us that we don't know why some have stronger powers, and others don't."

"That means that we don't know if I will have any."

"What we do know is that you will be able to lend your strength to Kristin. That is what will be important."

"Why?"

"My god, you ask a lot of questions." I sighed.

"Hey, you called me. Is she there, by the way? Did she ask you to call me?"

"No, she's not, and no, she didn't. She doesn't know that I am speaking with you."

"Alright, so tell me how I would make her stronger."

"By mating with her."

"Like marrying her, right?"

"If you want to put it that way, yes, kind of."

"What if I don't want to mate with her?"

"Why would you not? You happen to enjoy having sex with her; it's not that different. You have sex; you exchange blood; you go about your days, and you help her when she needs it."

"Yeah, but what would my days be like? I mean, I would have to leave my job, so what would I do?"

"That I don't know, besides learn our ways and help her when she needs it."

"Could I keep my job?"

"Could you only work at night?"

"Um, no." I could practically see the frown on his handsome face. "I guess I couldn't then."

"Perhaps after you got into our world a bit, you could be the liaison between your human friends and us, or co-workers, or whatever they are to you."

"You think that's possible?"

"Anything is possible, Hugh. Would Kristin go for the idea? I think she would once she trusted you. It might take some time, but I think she would come around."

"Are you saying that she doesn't trust me? If that's the case, why would she want to mate with me?"

"I didn't say that, but I will tell you that she does not trust easily. You need to earn that trust."

"How is she?"

I shrugged, although he couldn't see it. "Being a bit of a brat right now."

"A brat?" He laughed. "I can't imagine that."

"Oh, trust me, my sister can be a brat, a bitch, a bore, and all those other *B* words that you might come up with. She's under a lot of strain right now with the breed and other masters."

"Has she heard from Portage again?"

"No."

"What is she doing tonight?"

"I think she is in a meeting right now. Why? Do you want to come over and have some fun with her?"

"I thought maybe we could talk."

"Boring—" I sang into the phone. "Why don't you come over and get her all hot and bothered. She could use a good sexual release. Might put her in a better mood."

"Do you people always talk about sex so blatantly?"

"Are you asking in general of our population or me in particular?

Because to me, it's like taking a shower, something that you need to do regularly, just more enjoyable."

He laughed. "I have to tell you, Angelina, I do enjoy talking to you."

"Well, I'm glad to hear that, Hugh. I enjoy conversing with you, too." Although if I had the chance to have you in my bed, I might not ever let you out again.

"Maybe I'll come over."

"Please do. I'll let Ryker know to expect you. If she's busy, you can visit with me. I'm bored out of my mind. Maybe I can help you get ready for her."

"You're a beautiful woman, Angelina, but I'm not sure I could handle both of you."

"It would be fun to try," I said to him before I hung up. Not that I wanted to share him with my sister. No, I most certainly didn't. I'd prefer to have him all to myself. Maybe if I were lucky enough to mate to him, some stronger dormant power would manifest itself in me.

Not that I was normally envious of my sister. I hated her job, hated what she had to do, but sometimes it did suck to be in the background.

I heard her apartment door close and went to speak with her. She was sitting on her couch, her head in her hands.

"What has you so doom and gloom?"

"Nothing." She wiped her hair back from her face. "Everything."

I snickered as I sat down. "Talk to me."

She flopped back on the couch. "There have been issues all over the globe, small skirmishes, nothing major, but just enough to be a nuisance. All of the masters are looking at me and demanding to know what I'm going to do about it since I decided to wave a red flag in Portage's face."

"Tell those old pricks to take care of their own territories."

"Yes, I have, but they all blame me for starting the uprisings with my stunt with Portage. Which they are right about. Had I not baited him, this might not be happening."

"No, we'd all be sitting around waiting for the other shoe to drop.

Fuck them, Kristin. You're the only one who has done anything proactive. They should be backing you up, not giving you problems."

"Maybe." She sighed heavily.

"Well, maybe I have something that will cheer you up. Hugh is on his way over to see you."

"How do you know?"

"Because I just spoke to him. I figured one of us needed to, and since you have been so busy with breed business, I took it upon myself to get you a booty call. You should be thanking me, not giving me that stern look."

"I'm not in the mood for a booty call," she muttered.

"How are we sisters?" I asked her, and she snorted a laugh.

"Did he say anything else?"

"Do you mean about turning? Not really, but he did ask some questions, and I told him about the possibility of mating with you."

"Why would you do that?"

"Because he has the right to know. If he is going to turn, I know that you will want him to mate with you."

She made a gurgling noise in her throat. "To be honest, I don't want to mate with anyone."

"But think of the power that he holds. The power that will combine with yours."

"I know, but that doesn't make this any easier. I also hate saying to him, okay, we'll turn you, but then you are mine to do with as I please."

"What man wouldn't want that?" I asked teasingly.

"Hugh," she said.

"Maybe you are right. Hugh does seem to have a strong mind, but I think that if he knew all the stakes, and you explained to him how you feel, he might decide to do it. It's not like you two have to mate for life. Just mate with him until this war is over and then find someone else that you want to be with."

"You know that's not how I do things. I want to care about the man that I am with."

I laughed. "I'm pretty sure that you didn't feel that way about dear old dad when you first mated with him, and if the stories are true, you were drugged when you mated with Trent. So I call bullshit on that. As for Alex, I know you always cared about him, and I know why you mated with him, at least the second time." I stood. "Look, just get the guy to transition, mate with him, use him while you need him, then boot him to the curb."

Then I can have him for myself. I finished in my head and found myself perplexed at my thoughts. I didn't want to be mated either. What I did want was to see if mating to a reborn would bring about any other abilities. Was that wrong to want to use the man that way? Wasn't that what I was asking my sister to do?

"Look, go shower, get something pretty on, and when he gets here, have wild animal sex, and then talk to him about the transition and mating. See what he says."

"Fine, I'll do that, but the wild animal sex might need to wait until after we talk. I know what Hugh tastes like now, Angelina. I'm not sure I can hold myself back from taking more."

"Maybe he won't want you to."

"Before I take more from him, he needs to make a decision."

"Then tell him that," I told her as she walked away, and I left to find Ryker and let him know Hugh should be brought to her room when he arrived.

I stood in the elevator, my arms crossed, and tapped my toe restlessly. I hoped that Hugh would turn, Kristin would mate, and then she would get this fucking war over so she could move him along and I could enjoy him for a little while.

Was that too much to ask for?

KRISTIN

I was personally getting tired of everyone telling me what I should be doing. The other masters wanted to know how I was going to get Portage under control, saying that my blasé attitude about him did not look good. Jacques Berger had defended me, saying that I had taken a positive step. A few others believed that too, but all of them still wanted to know what was next.

Well, I was going to wait to see what happened next. The other masters didn't like that idea, but what were the choices? If I pushed, more humans would get killed. I'd already gotten several calls from Tom Singer from ICE saying that he needed to speak with me. That was a call that I was avoiding.

My board elders were up in arms about what had happened and harping on the fact that I should take a mate. Four more elders had been paraded past me, and I wanted to strangle them all. I wasn't sure why they all wanted me to mate with a stuffy elder. Yes, they were powerful with their age, but they lived in the past. They weren't able to see the future and what our society could be. Two of them had even expressed the fact that they thought I was wrong in not wanting to control the humans, and those two made me somewhat nervous.

What if they were working for Portage? What if this was some elaborate scheme to get control from the inside?

That is what made me the most nervous. Right now, I didn't know who I could trust.

My people were antsy. I could barely walk from my apartment to my office without someone asking how I was and when we would go out again. Maybe I needed to go back to the club and let them have some fun. Or perhaps they all needed to grow the fuck up and do their jobs.

Josh was the worst. He was moody and quiet. I could easily read his mind, but I forced myself not to because it was the same old crap. I wasn't sure what I could tell him to get it through his thick head that we would never be more than we were right now. I needed to start working on finding him a mate of his own; it was time.

The latest two to get on my case were my sons. Rex was pushing for me to take a more direct course of action and go after some of Portage's men. Capture some of the upper-level ones and torture them until they gave him up. I refused to do that or flat-out kill any of them if I didn't have to—well, except for Adam. I would gladly kill Adam just for the fun of it.

Garrett, on the other hand, remained neutral, like he typically did. He was still so young, only twenty now, and it would be at least another twelve to fourteen years before he transitioned.

My two boys were as different as night and day. Both of them so much like their fathers. Rex jumped to conclusions and wanted to rush into things; Garrett was calm, reserved, and mentally calculated every step that he should take. There was no doubt that Garrett would make a better leader than his brother.

The problem was, this had come up in conversation with them the other night, and Rex had lost his shit. Again, like his father, he became moody and disgruntled. He immediately claimed that if something happened to me, Garrett would not be in any position to preside over the breed. He did not like the fact that I said Clayton would oversee the breed until Garrett became of age.

Part of me felt as if I were playing favorites, but I wasn't. I loved both of my sons for different reasons. I knew without a doubt that Garrett would be able to oversee our society much better than his brother.

When Angelina joined me in my apartment, she told me that she'd spoken with Hugh. That was another thing that had weighed heavily on my mind. I wanted to know what he was doing, what he was thinking, and perhaps it was a good thing that he was coming over. We did need to talk. Over the last week, I had respected his privacy and stayed out of his head. Although I mentally checked in with him from time to time just to make sure he was alright.

I did want Hugh to transition and be with me, but I needed him to come to me on his own.

I took her advice and showered, dressed in something pretty but comfortable, and was pouring myself a drink when Ryker stepped into my apartment to announce that Hugh was here.

When he entered, the two of us stared at one another, neither of us all too sure of what to do next. I could feel uncertainty swirling through his mind, but at the same time, he was glad to see me.

"Would you like a drink?" I finally asked.

"Sure."

I poured him what I was having and brought it around to him. "Have a seat. How are you doing, Hugh?"

"I'm okay, I guess. How are you, Kristin?"

The laugh that left my throat sounded a little strangled. "I'm not sure how to answer that. It's been a rough week."

"I'll tell you about my hell week if you tell me about yours." He grinned over his glass as he lifted it to his mouth.

"Is this a personal interest or professional?"

"Right now, tonight, this is personal. I have been thinking about all of this. I need to understand a little more about what to expect or what you are expecting of me."

"I don't expect anything of you, Hugh. Our world—is your world. You belong in it." I paused. "But I can understand your hesitation. I remember learning about our world when Alex told me what I was and who I was. It seemed surreal, but it made sense deep inside of me. I never doubted what I wanted once I embraced that feeling."

"How soon after you learned did you transition?"

"I don't recall the exact time, but it wasn't long, a couple of days. It did take me much longer to go through the final transition."

"Why?"

"Women transition differently than men. We all go through the transition normally in our thirties. Once a female bonds to a male, our transition starts, but it is not completed until we become pregnant."

"Wait, you all have to get pregnant to transition?"

I nodded. "Yes, I was mated to Alex for a while after I first learned of what I was, but I wasn't ready to give up my life as a cop. Alex wanted me to quit and join him officially as his mate and help him oversee the breed."

"But isn't Rex your first child? I thought he was Trent's son."

"He is. Alex was kidnapped; Trent and a few others came to protect me, and Trent broke the bond that I had with Alex to spare me the feelings of Alex's torture. As a mated couple, you can feel anything the other feels if they are not protecting themselves mentally. Unfortunately, when Trent broke the bond, we accidentally mated."

Hugh laughed. "How do you accidentally mate?"

"They drugged me because they knew I would fight it. No one thought about the fact that when Trent took my blood to break the bond, it would also drug him, and one thing led to another."

"How exactly do you mate?"

"Share blood while you are having sex. It's the exchange of all bodily fluids at once that brings the connection to a head. Right now, you are bound to me, and that is because we shared blood, but we aren't mated."

He studied me. "Do you want to mate with me, Kristin?"

"To be honest, I do not want to mate with anyone, Hugh, but if the choice were you or another elder, I would choose you. I enjoy your company, and it is quite obvious that our desire is strong for one another."

"Does the fact that I am a reborn play into your decision?"

"Very much so. I believe that you hold a very intense power that will only make me stronger. I believe in the days ahead, I will need all the strength that I can obtain. Would it be using you? Maybe, but I'd prefer to think of it as the two of us banding together to protect all those people who need our help—human and vampire alike."

"I appreciate the fact that you are so forthright with your thoughts, Kristin. No beating around the bush."

"I never have been one for coy games. If you do decide to transition, I will not force you to mate with me. I would accept your decision if you chose not to, but I would require you to remain bonded with me and to remain at my side while we fight this war, at least for a while."

"Does Portage seriously want to control all humans?"

"Yes. He sees humans as vessels to feed off of, to play with, and nothing else. They are toys for enjoyment. There are a lot of people that feel that same way. Some are afraid to admit it, but many would side with him if the tide turned and he started rising to the top." I paused as I glanced around my apartment. "I have to thank you for reminding me of something."

"What is that?"

"You reminded me that once upon a time, I believed my blood ran only blue. Over the years, since I left law enforcement, I have forgotten what it was like to live as a human. I forgot the oath that I took all those years ago to protect them, to protect all those that required such. I do not want to see humans hurt, and if we go to war, many of them will die."

Hugh observed me for a few seconds as if he were mulling over my words, and then he smiled. "I'm glad to hear that, Kristin. I really am." He shifted so that he was turned slightly toward me, his light-blue eyes studying me carefully as he hesitated. "I have a proposition for you."

My right brow popped high. "Alright."

"If I were to transition, and I decided to mate with you, would you allow me to leave your side once the war was over if things were not going well between us? I mean, I get why you want me to mate with you, for the power, but what if we find that we don't have anything else between us besides great sex?"

I chuckled. "Hugh, once things have calmed down, I would release you. I would release you before that as long as you took an oath to stay at my side and to help me. It's not like it is with humans. No messy divorces, you can just do it."

"Alright, that is good to know. Would you also allow me to become a liaison between your society—um, our society—and the human world? I think since I have lived in that world for so long, I might be able to help the two work together."

I cocked my head to the side, wondering if there was an ulterior motive for his request. He did have insight into their world, just as I had. That would be something else that we had in common. Both of us raised in the human world. "I would consider it. It might be good, but you would have to prove yourself to me first."

"How?"

"By showing me that I could trust you. If you transition, your world will change; you will join our world, and our world is full of secrets and abilities. As much as you might think you can straddle between the two, you can't. I know this firsthand. It might seem like you can, and for a short time, you will be able to, but then time passes, and things change. Remember when you first started in law enforcement, and you were gung ho. Eventually, you became a bit jaded in your views, right?" He laughed and nodded. "Yeah, well, imagine how jaded you can become when you realize what you are compared to what they are. What is important in our world and what they whine about."

I inhaled slowly. "I know that you came to me when this all started and wanted to know our abilities and who our people are. I can't have you sharing all that information with the government; it would be dangerous for everyone involved."

"Why?"

"Hugh, can you honestly tell me that your task force, or government, doesn't want to use some of our society members as weapons?"

"No, I cannot tell you that. They do."

"And what can you tell me about some of my members being kidnapped? Where are they being held?"

"Held? What are you talking about?"

I studied him and didn't see or feel any deception. "We have had quite a few of our breed recently disappear. It might be Portage, but I think your government is collecting some of our people for their own purposes."

"I don't know anything about that, Kristin. I honestly do not. If they are, I have absolutely nothing to do with that."

"Yeah, well, we can't allow them to have any more knowledge than they already do. If they knew what I was capable of, what would they do to try and force me to use it for their own reasons? That is not my purpose. My purpose is to use it for our breed, to protect our society and the humans that interact with us."

"I understand that, Kristin." He stared at his drink for a minute. "I get it. I would respect your wishes. I would work with you to determine what they should be told and what they shouldn't be."

"Well, I might have you work with my son Garrett. He will be the next one in line to take over, should the day come that I cannot."

"Garrett? What about Rex?"

I laughed. "Rex is not always rational and can be rather impulsive at times. He is a lot like his father."

Hugh chuckled. "What would they say to me mating with you?"

Ha! Rex was going to have a fit. I honestly wasn't sure what Garrett would think. I shrugged. "I don't know, and I don't care. They have no voice in the matter."

"Does anyone else know about me?"

I shook my head. "No, my sentinels have kept their mouths shut. We were waiting for you to decide." I reached out to him mentally, feeling inside his body. "And not that I want to add pressure to you, but your decision must come soon. Your time is coming near its end; I can feel it within you."

"You can?"

"Yes."

He blinked a few times as he glanced around. "I don't want to die, Kristin."

"I believe you."

"Would it be odd to admit that I'm scared?"

"Not at all. I believe that fear is a very powerful motivator. As long as you don't allow it to consume you."

"I'm not sure I've ever been afraid before, not like this."

I reached for his hand. "There is nothing to fear, Hugh. We are not going to hurt you; we will help you, and you could use your experience to help both societies."

I saw the wheels literally turning in his mind, saw the decision fill his eyes. "Okay, then I'll do it. I'll transition, and—"

I put my hand up. "One decision at a time. Let's get you through the transition, and then you and I can talk about the future."

"What if I already know the answer?"

"Do you? I mean, do you really know the answer?"

"I'll transition, and I'll mate with you. If we are going to spare the human society from pain, I want you to be as strong as you can be. I am taking you for your word and your previous oath that you are going to do everything you can to protect humans. If having a deeper connection with me will help, then you can have everything that you want and need from me."

I stared at him, measuring his words with his actions and the temperament of his body. The words he spoke, he meant, but something within warred slightly with it. Not enough to cause hesitation, but enough that I could sense it. Was that only fear of the unknown?

"Thank you, Hugh." I squeezed his hand.

He set his glass down and cupped the side of my face. "No, thank you, Kristin. Thank you for allowing me the privilege and honor of being by your side."

"The honor is all mine," I told him before his lips brushed over mine.

ANGELINA

I was down in the bar, drinking my woes away when Kristin reached into my head. *"Can you please gather everyone?"*

"Everyone?"

"Yes, everyone. I have an announcement that I need to make."

"Is he—"

"Yes."

Before I could reply, she cut the link and locked down her mind. I twirled my glass for a moment; this was a good thing. An excellent thing. If it were so great, why did it bother me then?

"Jett," I called his name, and he lifted his head from where he'd been whispering with Novah. I waved him over as I finished what was in my glass.

"Yeah?" he asked as he stopped in front of me.

"Can you get all the high sentinels together? Kristin wants to have a meeting. I'm going to go find the elders, Rex and Garrett."

"A meeting?" he asked, his brow rising slightly.

"Yes. She has an announcement."

He grinned. "On it."

I watched him walk away and then sighed as I got up to corral the elders and her sons. This was going to be interesting.

215

Thirty minutes later, everyone, and I mean just about everyone who had any business in the main office, was hanging out in one of the smaller ballrooms on the ground floor.

Lorna, Paxton, and Ryker were murmuring in the corner, while Josh stood moodily off to the side. He was going to have to get over himself. Maybe now that Kristin wasn't using him all the time for blood, I could use him for myself. It would be nice to have just one male to feed on, although where was the fun in that?

The doors opened, and Kristin walked in, holding Hugh's hand. Murmurs drifted around the room, mostly from the elders. Rex grunted next to me. "What the hell is he doing here?"

"Oh, dear boy, just wait and listen," I chided him playfully. "Your mommy is about to change history."

"What the hell is that supposed to mean?" he snapped back. He really was like his father, well, the bad parts of his father. Trent had been rather calm when people weren't pissing him off. I rolled my eyes at Rex as I walked away, and then I took a seat off to the side to watch the show. I wished I had popcorn; it would have been nice to have a treat while shit hit the fan.

"Thanks for coming, and I'm sorry for interrupting your night," Kristin said to the room.

"Mom, why is he with you?" Rex asked as he jockeyed to the front of the group.

"Because this is about him," she stated. I felt someone step beside me, and I glanced back to see Cameron. He put his hand on my shoulder and squeezed in the way of a hello.

"What the hell does any of our business have to do with a human?" Beckett growled loudly.

Kristin gave him a hard look and began to speak to everyone. "Hugh might seem to be human, but he's not. He's a reborn."

There were a few gasps in the crowd, and Rex looked instantly constipated. "No, he's not."

"Yes, he is, Rex, and if you'd keep your mouth shut for a few minutes, I'll explain." She glared at him for a moment longer, and he shifted uneasily on his feet. Hugh looked uncomfortable standing beside her, and I sure hoped that changed once he had transitioned. We couldn't have a timid vampire standing beside my sister.

"Last week, I fed from Hugh and realized instantly that his blood was very similar to mine. With the help of Angelina and Cameron, we were able to figure out that Hugh is a third-generation reborn. His great-grandfather, Galen Donahue, was one of our breed. Hugh's grandfather was adopted, and both his grandfather and his father never knew what they were because they were raised by humans, as Hugh was."

"Are you serious, Kristin?" Clayton asked as he stared Hugh up and down. "I knew Galen."

"I did too," Scarlett added.

"I think all of the elders knew him," Henry commented.

"And you probably know how he died. Hugh told me earlier tonight that he has had the recurring dream of being mortally injured on a boat and being thrown overboard by a wave. He died at sea, and his heart was not staked."

"You're saying that his soul was reborn three times?" Hazel queried, her voice suggesting that she didn't believe it.

"Yes, I am. You're welcome to have a taste to see for yourself."

"Is his blood toxic?" Scarlett asked quickly.

Kristin shook her head. "No, not right now. Neither mine nor my sister's was toxic for years."

Scarlett stepped forward. "I knew Galen rather well, and in a personal manner. I would like proof."

Kristin turned to Hugh. "Do you mind?"

He shook his head and held his wrist out to her. Scarlett hesitated only a moment before she put his wrist to her mouth and took a sip of his blood. Her eyes widened, and a smile crept over her lips.

"I remember that blood," she said softly as she took Hugh in. "And you do look like him, sort of."

Hugh returned her smile, and she turned and melded back into the group.

"So, what does this mean?" Beckett asked.

"It means that Hugh is prepared to go through his transition. He only has a couple of weeks before his human life will end, so he will do it soon."

"And after he turns?" Garrett inquired.

"Then Hugh and I will mate," Kristin stated.

Murmurs exploded like a pipe bomb in the room, and Kristin looked at me as Henry put his hands up to quiet everyone.

"Is that smart? I mean for you to mate a newly turned vampire that doesn't know our ways?"

"Angelina, can you come over here, please?"

I stood, knowing that the show was about to start. I joined them upfront, and I took hold of Hugh's hand before placing my hand on Kristin's shoulder.

There were gasps around the room, and people shuffled about. I heard Paxton speak near the back. "That is so damn cool."

Kristin's hand once again glowed as did her eyes, and even Rex looked somewhat awed. Kristin dropped her hand and winked at me. I let go of Hugh and went back to stand beside Cameron.

"As you can see, Hugh's strength is deep, and he's not even turned yet. I cannot imagine what his power will be like once he does." She let her eyes scan the room. "I know that a lot of you wanted to know how we would win the war; I believe that this might be the answer."

"When will he transition?" Lorna questioned.

"Soon. He has some things to deal with in his human life before he joins us. I want to put two sentinels on him during the nighttime hours. Of course, none of us can watch him during the day, but neither can our enemies. Until he changes, Conner and Ryker you have been assigned to his protection."

Conner and Ryker exchanged a glance and a nod, not to mention a smirk on Ryker's part.

"I'd like you two to make sure that he gets home tonight and stay there until you need to return for the day."

"Yes, Mistress," Conner replied.

"The rest of you I will speak with later," Kristin stated and turned, taking Hugh's hand and walking out of the room. Conner and Ryker hurried out the door behind her.

The minute they were all gone, the room erupted in excited chatter. Some were talking about how incredible it was that another reborn existed. Others were discussing what it could mean for us, and a few were questioning the future mating. Josh and Rex were in on that one, and I frowned at them both as I joined their little circle.

"I suggest you two both get on board with this. You know you will not change her mind, and going against her right now will only piss her off. This is going to be good for our breed, and it's going to be good for her. That is all that matters."

I turned and walked out with my head held high. She was all that mattered, but I sure as hell wished she weren't.

Kristin was in the front lobby, saying goodbye to Hugh. She stepped forward and kissed him tenderly, and I fought not to frown. He glanced my way and winked before he walked out the front door with Conner and Ryker.

I approached my sister. "Did you compel him to do it?"

"No, he made that decision all on his own." The two of us began to walk back to the elevator. "We had a long and detailed discussion, and he admitted that he didn't want to die. He wants to be a liaison between our two societies."

"I might have been the one to give him that suggestion," I said.

"And it's a good one, once I know I can trust him. He needs to understand that not all of our abilities should be common knowledge, especially mine. I think he understands that, but I need to give it some time to see how things go."

"What do you think he'll be able to do?" We stepped into the elevator. "I mean, do you think he'll have any special abilities?"

"I don't know, and right now, I don't really care. He lends me enough power that it makes me quite formidable."

"That it does," I replied. "When is Hugh going to do it?"

"Next weekend. He wants to wrap some things up at work. He told me he was going to put himself on a leave of absence while this all happens. Once it's done, he'll see how things are and decide what to do with his job."

"I guess that's a good idea." The elevator arrived at our floor, and we stepped out to find Rex glaring at Kristin outside her door.

"Well, I think I will let you handle *that*," I said, and she put her hand on my arm.

"I think you should stay with us." She spoke aloud and then continued into my mind. "*So I don't throttle my firstborn.*"

"What has gotten into you?" Rex snapped at her.

"Me? What the hell has gotten into you?" she retorted.

"I'm trying to protect our way of life, and you're going to let some guy from the government right into our world. Are you crazy?"

Kristin brushed past him and into her apartment. "I am far from crazy, Rex. Yes, he might work for the government right now, but he will be working for me, for *us* very soon."

"I don't trust the guy, Mom."

"You don't know the guy, Rex."

"You are being so damn irresponsible. Dad used to call you flighty; I can see why now."

She was in his face a split second later, and I wondered if I should step in between them. "You were only thirteen when your father died, Rex. What memories you have of that time do not mean anything."

"Bullshit! Dad always said that Alex should have been training you to take over. He knew that you would fuck everything up."

Kristin picked her son up by the throat and put him against the wall so fast that I barely saw it. Oh, shit, she just might throttle him. I grabbed ahold of her arm, but she was no match for me when she was this angry. "Your father had issues, Rex. He was not stable, and I will not have you bringing him into our conversation. You know nothing about what happened back then."

"I know you're the reason he's dead!" he shouted.

Kristin's eyes flared silver and then dulled as she released the grip on his throat and lowered him to the floor. "Rex, I was not the reason he died." She sighed heavily and stepped away from him, hanging her head for a moment. "Rex, your father wasn't right."

"You're the one that is not right."

Kristin turned slowly toward him. "Rex, I never told you this, but your father killed himself. He wasn't murdered."

His face paled and then became a mask of anger. "You lie!"

"No, I don't, Rex."

I was afraid to move, afraid to even breathe for a moment. When the room remained quiet but full of crackling tension, I finally stepped forward. "Rex, what she says is true. I saw him. I saw him fall upon his own stake as the sun rose."

Rex stared at me in disbelief. "She's making you say that."

I shook my head. "No, Rex, she isn't. Your father wasn't well. We don't know exactly what was wrong with him, but he took his own life. He did it in the sunlight so that in case he missed the stake to his heart, he would burn. I watched him and tried to get to him in time, but I wasn't able to. I was ten feet from him when he pierced his heart and turned to ash before my eyes. No one made him do it; he did it himself."

Rex looked shredded as I spoke, but then he turned vengeful eyes on Kristin. "You compelled him to do that, didn't you? You made him kill himself."

"What? No, I most certainly did not! I wasn't even around. I was traveling, had been traveling for over a week. I had nothing to do with his death, Rex. I was gutted when I felt the bond snap and his life force leave him—utterly gutted. I loved your father very much."

"You're a fucking liar. I will never believe that he took his own life, never!" Without another word, he raced from the room, and Kristin dropped her chin to her chest.

"Well, that was fun," I said with sarcasm.

"Jesus, Lena. I never wanted him to know about that, but I don't think I had a choice but to tell him."

"I think you're right. Rex needed to know. Look, I'll talk to him later and calm him down. I'll let him see the memory, then maybe he will believe me."

She gave me a small smile. "Thanks. Look, I think I am going to crawl in bed. It's been a long day, and I have a feeling the week is going to be another week of hell."

"Yeah, I think you might be right. Go get some rest."

She disappeared into her room, and I let myself out. I was tempted to find Rex now, but I think he needed some time to digest the information before I gave him the visual to go with it.

With a heavy sigh, I let myself into my apartment, wondering what the next weekend was going to bring.

HUGH

*A*dmitting that I didn't want to die was hard, but once I had admitted it to myself, I felt a little bit better. If Kristin was willing to bring me into her world and let me be a part of it, that was good. It was almost like my life was clicking firmly in place, and a part of myself began to relax.

I knew that things would be tough, and there was a lot that I would need to learn, but knowing that I was going to be learning from her was excellent. It only made sense to accept her proposal of a mating. If things didn't work out with us, then I would be free to go to someone else. Would I want to? Or would Kristin and I be happy together?

I knew I liked her a lot. Would I come to care more for her? Possibly love her? Did that even matter in their world—my new world to come? Did they fall in love? I knew they were passionate, but where did love fall into everything?

I thought a lot about it over the next week. Kristin had told me that there would be some opposition to me mating with her, and I saw that firsthand during the impromptu meeting she had called last week. Some didn't believe that I should be part of their breed, much less mated to their mistress.

On Friday night, I stood in my apartment and stared around me. All of my stuff would be moved to the hotel. Kristin had told me that I could have my own apartment if I wished for it, or I could share hers. I was tempted to take her up on her offer of having my own place, but if I was in for a penny, I was in for a pound. I had never been one not to give something my all, and the best way to learn would be to immerse myself in it and her.

Ryker and Conner were waiting for me in the living room when I stepped out with my last suitcase. I was bringing just enough to get me started. They would collect the rest of it and bring it later.

I had told my boss that I needed some time off to deal with a few health issues. I had a couple of weeks to figure out the best way to come back and explain what had changed. I did not doubt that they would be as shocked as I was. In the meantime, I would become the best reborn vampire that I could be.

"You ready?" Ryker asked.

"I guess," I told him.

Over the last week, I had come to know Ryker and Conner pretty well, and I liked them both. Ryker a bit more than Conner, who tended to be quiet, but they both enjoyed watching sports, so we had that in common.

Conner and Ryker collected the other few bags that I had, and I took one last look around my place. Goodbye to the old life, and hello to the new one. I was tense on the way back to the hotel, and Jett met us in the parking garage, taking my bag from me.

"You know I can carry that," I said.

He grinned over his shoulder. "Well, Mr. Master-to-be, it would be an honor to do it for you."

I laughed. "Yeah, I don't know about that title."

"Get used to it," Ryker joked.

"Does this mean that I will be considered a master after I mate with Kristin?"

"Yep," Ryker said. "She became the mistress when she mated with Alexander. I guess it will be the same when you do it."

I nodded and felt butterflies flit around my gut. We rode the elevator to the top floor, and Jett turned to me. "You'll get access tomorrow when we put your DNA into the system after it changes. Then you will have access to just about anywhere in the building."

"Sounds good," I told him.

The elevator door opened, and they stepped out. My feet felt stuck to the floor, and Ryker glanced back. "What? You getting cold feet now?"

I laughed slightly and forced my feet forward. "Maybe just a little bit. Does it hurt?"

"What, to transition?" Ryker asked back.

"Yeah."

He shook his head. "Nah, there is nothing to it." Jett and Conner chuckled, which told me that Ryker had just lied his ass off to me.

"I will kick your ass later if you just lied to me."

"We'll see if you can do that." He grinned as he held the door to Kristin's apartment open.

Inside, the room was full, and many of the people didn't look too happy. Well, damn. Was this a welcoming committee or an execution?

Kristin came to my side, a genuine smile on her face as she spoke. "Hello, Hugh."

"Hey, Kristin." She cupped my cheek and winked. While we had talked over the phone several times, we had not seen one another since last week.

"We decided to have Clayton oversee your transition," she said as a man stepped forward and held out his hand.

"Welcome to the family. I'm Clayton Lakin, one of the elders on the board."

I shook his hand. "Nice to meet you."

Kristin looked slightly nervous as she glanced around, then back to me. "Are you ready to get started?"

"I guess. Is everyone going to watch?"

Kristin laughed. "No, they were all just leaving, well, most of them. Ryker and Conner will remain along with Clayton."

"Will you be here?"

She shook her head. "No, this part you do on your own. I'll see you later after you rest."

"Okay," I replied solemnly.

The group started to file out of the room, mixed emotions on their faces. Angelina was the only one that approached me, and she placed a kiss on my cheek before she met my gaze and winked.

After everyone else left, Kristin stared up at me with apprehensive eyes. "Are you sure?"

I inhaled and released it slowly as I took her face between my palms. "Yes. I am."

"Thank you, Hugh. Your life is about to become so much more. You will never know how much this means to me."

"You're welcome," I said softly.

She leaned forward and kissed me once, staring into my eyes with her pretty light-blue ones before turning and leaving without another word.

"Well, let's get this started," Clayton said. "Why don't you take off your shirt and go lie down on the bed."

I stared at him. "Um, you don't expect me to have sex with you, do you?"

Clayton laughed and slapped me on the shoulder. "No, son. Far from it."

"Okay," I replied slowly and then went into Kristin's room, removed my shirt, and kicked off my shoes. I sat on the edge of the bed as the three men came in, and for the first time since I'd made the decision, I was petrified.

"Relax, Hugh. It won't hurt as bad as you think."

"I'm not worried about the pain; I'm just wondering if I am making the right decision."

Clayton took a seat beside me. "You are about to enter a world that you have only ever dreamed about. Yes, your days will be different, and your nights will be full. You'll see things, hear things, taste things, and feel things like you have never experienced. Your emotions will be high one moment and low the next. You will encounter love in a way you never thought possible, and when you hate, it will threaten to consume you."

"Is that all?" I laughed uncomfortably.

"Oh, no, there is much more, but until you have lived it, you can't comprehend it. The decision that you are making is one that has been in the works for three generations. You do hold great power, Hugh; I can sense it in you, and you are going to be a force to be reckoned with, especially beside Kristin."

"Do you really think so?"

"Yes, but I will tell you this now, Hugh. If you ever hurt her, I will drive a stake through your heart so fast that you will never see it coming, and if for some reason I do not, there will be a line behind me of people who will."

"I won't, sir. I promise I won't."

"Then, shall we begin?"

I inhaled slowly and then released it. "Okay, what do I do?"

"Lie back. I will feed on you. I will take a lot, and it won't feel as good as when Kristin does it. After I do, you will take my blood, and then you will take some from Conner and Ryker. Not a lot, but it will bind you to them to protect you. Your transition will begin once you take my blood, and it will take a few hours to complete."

"So, in a few hours, I'll be like you all?"

"Yes, you will. Then you will feed from Conner and Ryker to complete those bonds, and also to learn how to feed properly. After that, you will need to feed well, and we can bring you any female you want, or—" He paused. "You can mate with Kristin immediately."

I wasn't sure I was ready for that, but I was prepared to take the first step. "Let's get this show on the road; we'll figure those things out later."

Clayton snickered as he glanced over his shoulder, and Conner and Ryker were suddenly there, holding my arms. Before I could process it, Clayton was at my throat, and his fangs dug deep into the side of my neck. He wasn't kidding about it hurting; I thought he was trying to shred my neck, but I forced myself to keep still and quiet.

He drank until I began to feel dizzy, and the pressure holding me lessened. My body was shifted, and I heard words that didn't make sense, and then there was something at my mouth. I opened my lips, the taste of fresh air after the rain filling my nose as something wet and warm ran into my mouth. I swallowed immediately and realized it was blood. My mind and body warred with itself, but instinct kicked in, and I latched on the wrist and sucked hard.

After a few mouthfuls, the wrist disappeared, and I felt fangs dig into both wrists almost simultaneously. That didn't hurt anywhere like what was going on in my mind and torso, though. My body was on fire. It felt like everything inside of me was burning, and I was about to go up in flames. I clenched my jaw and held back the cries of pain that threatened to spill forth.

After a while, the pain began to subside, and I drifted off to sleep. When I started to wake, I heard voices, and I opened my eyes, expecting them to be in the room with me, but they weren't.

I lifted my hands and looked at them, seeing every line on them as if I were looking at them under a magnifying glass. I heard a laugh in the next room. It was so loud, as if I were sitting right next to the person. I glanced around the room; everything was crystal clear. The hum of a motor reached me, and then doors opened; did I hear the elevator? Holy shit!

I heard the footsteps approaching the door and sat up just as she reached the threshold. "How are you?"

I knew she was speaking softly, but it sounded like she was shouting.

"I can hear everything, feel everything."

She smiled and stepped inside. "You'll learn to control it so that you aren't overwhelmed. It will take some time, but you'll figure it out."

Her eyes drifted down my chest, and she smiled before she called to Conner and Ryker. They came into the room, both grinning widely.

"Welcome to the family!" Ryker roared, and I winced. "Sorry, I forgot about that."

"Yeah, it's okay." My voice sounded slightly different, but not by much. What else was changed in me?

"You need to pop those pretty new teeth out and feed from us," Conner said as he stopped in front of me.

I glanced back at Kristin, my eyes slipping over her body. Her scent was sweet, creamy like sugar and butter, and suddenly I had a hard-on like I'd never had before.

"Whoa there, big guy," Ryker joked. "You take from us first, and then you can have her."

"How do I get them to come down?" I practically growled.

"Tell them to feed," Kristin whispered as she stepped farther into the room. "Tell them it's time to feed." She began to unbutton her blouse slowly, and I whispered the words into my head.

I felt my jaw tingling, felt the teeth begin to lengthen as she parted her blouse. Ryker put his wrist out, and I stared at it, then her. I didn't want his wrist; I wanted to be at her throat. I wanted to be deep within her.

"Take it, Hugh," Kristin whispered.

I snapped on to his wrist faster than I could have imagined and heard him laugh. I sucked twice and then shoved his wrist away to grab Conner's. When I finished, I literally felt their blood drift through my body. It was like I could tell the difference in every drop as it raced through my veins.

"Go," I growled as I stood. One of them laughed, but I didn't care which one. In two steps, I had her in my arms, and my mouth was heading toward her neck.

I was about to latch on when she threw me off of her like I was nothing. "Lie down."

I hissed but did as she requested. She removed her clothing, and it took every ounce of strength not to go back to her. I might be strong now, but she was still stronger than me.

She crawled on the bed, undoing the jeans I wore and yanking them off my body. My hands clenched at my sides to keep from grabbing her. Once she had me undressed, she stared down at me, and I inhaled a deep breath through my nose and almost lost my mind. Her arousal was so fucking strong, and the entire room smelled like butter and sugar combined. A hunger I'd never felt before unleashed in me, and I could no longer resist.

I grabbed her arm and pulled her to the mattress, rolling over to cover her body with mine.

She smiled and touched my face. "Kiss me, Hugh."

I leaned forward, touching my lips to hers, and I felt it to the tips of my toes. Every ounce of my body tingled, and the kiss deepened. Her hands drifted lightly over my body, causing my nerve endings to fire like crazy. It was overwhelming but so damn good. So fucking good.

I pushed her legs apart, and she grinned at me as I shifted my hips between them. The undeniable urge to be inside of her was too much for me, but she was ready. She was so damn ready.

For a few moments, I moved inside of her, feeling it through every part of my body as we touched and kissed. As I moved faster, I zeroed in on her neck, and she turned her face slightly to the side. "Take my vein, Hugh."

She didn't need to tell me twice. I latched on, sucking hard and filling my mouth with the most incredible flavor I'd ever tasted. My body quivered as I pulled from her vein again, and I felt her lips on my neck. She licked over the vein throbbing there, and I shoved my hips harder toward her. She slid her fangs into my throat and pulled at the same time that I took my third swallow.

My body convulsed, every muscle in it going taut as we completed some crazy circuit, and the two of us suddenly hit that orgasmic pinnacle together. My mind was blown; images flashed through it that made no sense; sounds exploded to the point that I almost wanted to hide from them. Never had I felt anything like this before. Never had I experienced one-tenth of the feelings that I had just had with her.

Kristin withdrew her fangs and licked my neck as I did the same to her. I leaned on my elbows and stared down at her.

"What do you think?" she asked with a smirk.

"I think I could do that all day long," I said with a laugh. "Is it always that good?"

"Yes, sex is always incredible."

"Damn, that right there makes it all worth it."

She chuckled.

"So, is that it? Am I like you now? Are we mated?"

"Yes, that's it, and we are." She suddenly looked serious and then rolled her eyes.

"What's wrong?"

She sighed and pushed me so that I would roll off of her. "As much as I would love to stay here and do that a few dozen times, they need me for something."

"But you'll be back?"

"Yes, you rest. I'll have food brought up to you, and then you can feed more later. Or I can have another woman brought in for you to feed from."

I felt my forehead line. "You'd let me feed from another woman? Wouldn't I want to have sex with them too?"

"Yes, you would, but remember, sex is different with us than with humans. It's not unusual for us to have multiple partners, even while mated."

"Well, if it's okay with you, I think I'll stick to just one woman right now," I told her. That was something that I was going to have to get used to.

I was full of energy, and something was simmering under my skin. I suddenly felt the need to be alone and didn't understand why. Kristin disappeared into the bathroom. A few moments later, she came out, let her eyes drift down my body, and then smiled. "I'll be back as soon as I can."

"See you then," I told her. I listened to the door close, and I found myself getting up and retrieving my pants. From the pocket, I removed my cellphone and dialed a number that I didn't quite know. The phone rang twice before a man answered.

"It's done."

"Done?" the man said.

"Yeah, I'm in."

"When you say in, how far do you mean? Did they turn you?"

"They not only turned me, but I'm mated to the mistress."

An evil laugh burst through the line. "Mated to the mistress? Are you serious?"

"Yes." I frowned, wondering who I was talking to and why I was telling them this.

"Good job, Hugh. Excellent job. I knew you were the right one for this task. Now, when you hang up the phone, delete this number from your call history and forget that you spoke with me. You will wait for the next set of orders. Do you understand that?"

"Yes, Master, I do." The phone line went dead on a laugh, and I did what I was told. A moment later, I blinked and stared at my phone.

Was I going to make a call? I stared at it longer, wondering why it was in my hands and when had I picked it up. Was something wrong with me? Had something gone wrong in the transition? How could I not remember retrieving my phone?

I set it down on the bedside table, the echo of an evil laugh vibrating through my mind as I lay back and closed my eyes, trying to remember when I had ever heard that sound before.

THE END

Hugh is part of Kristin's world now, and things are about to get wild. How long will it take for her to realize that she had been played? What will Josh do once he realizes that he had been right about Hugh all along? How soon before Portage comes calling on Hugh again? Will Angelina be able to protect her sister and her own heart? And what will happen when Zander can't stand waiting any longer and decides to take things into his own hands?

Prepare yourself for another step in The Blue Blood Returns Saga with Hugh's story: Blue Blood Compelled. Find out what his last year was like before he came to meet Kristin and what happens after that surprising phone call.

HUGH: BLUE BLOOD COMPELLED

1 YEAR EARLIER

J took a seat at my desk, glancing over my small work area to see if anything new was there. Not that I expected anything, it was rare to have any type of paper left on our desks. Most of our stuff landed on our phones or virtual tablets. Even my voice-mails from the office line went to my cellphone. However, we did have quite a few storerooms full of metal cabinets that contained folders in them and a shit ton of boxes with printed copies of reports, photographs, and other evidence that had accumulated over the years.

Evidence was now collected and scanned into images and stored on one of our secure servers. Once that was done, it was triple-checked to make sure that all the identifying marks were collected properly before the physical evidence was destroyed. If the evidence was needed for prosecution, it could be rendered again with machines to make it look identical to the original, then once again destroyed. There was no wasted space for weapons and drugs. All interviews were also done through video and sometimes audio methods.

I couldn't imagine how law enforcement in the past had kept everything straight when it was all on paper. Even things typed into the computers were printed out and stuffed into binders or folders. It boggled my mind how much had changed in the last twenty-five years.

The concept of digging through those folders full of information to find a specific detail was utterly foreign to me. These days, we could search for a keyword, and the computer would bring up anything that would be valid to our case. As we investigated a case, we added the audio and video along with any crime scene details, persons involved, and photographs. Then the computer system would tell us what we needed to do next. It also helped connect dots that we might not have seen otherwise. Plus, we were always in touch with our cases and our bosses—well, sometimes a little too much on that last part.

I heard someone approaching and looked up to see Bruce Cochran, my sometimes partner, heading toward his desk. "Morning, Murph. You're here early."

"Yeah, not sleeping so well these days."

He smirked. "Jocelyn keeping you up?"

"Nah, we split up a few months ago. I think it's because I'm getting old. I don't seem to need as much sleep as I used to."

"Murph, you're not even forty yet; you're not old." He grinned at me. "Wait till you're my age, and then we can talk. Besides, not sleeping has nothing to do with age. I'm forty-five, and I sleep like a baby."

"I hear you."

"Hey," he said as he took a seat at his desk. "Did you see the news this morning? Two more massacres overnight."

"Wait, two? I heard about the one in New York City, but where was the other one? Or were they connected?"

"No, there was another one in Atlanta. The news was talking about how they are comparing these to the active shooter rampages they used to have in the early two-thousands."

"Well, shit, that's not good."

"I know." He shook his head. "They need to figure out a way to keep those fucking creepy creatures in check. We should round them all up and slaughter every last one of them."

I frowned. "Why do you say that?"

"Because they are blood-sucking freaks, that's why!" He laughed as he took a seat.

"Yes, but they have been around a lot longer than we have. Maybe we are the freaks. You don't see any of them overweight and with a ton of medical problems."

He stared at me and then flopped back in his seat. "Holy shit, you're a vamp-fan."

I put my hand up. "Hold on a second; I'm not saying I'm a fan. I'm saying that they have been around for a very long time, and we are just coming to learn about them. How have they stayed hidden for so long? Think about that. Until recently, they kept to themselves. Yeah, we'd see and hear about some weird shit that happened that we couldn't quite explain, but they weren't in-your-face about their business."

"True, but now they are."

"Don't you ever wonder what has changed?" I had thought about that quite a bit recently. Truth be told, it had been on my mind more often than I cared to admit. As far as I knew, vampires had been around since the dawn of time. The fact that their existence was now public knowledge was slightly awe-inspiring.

Yes, they were deadly creatures, as we had all come to learn very quickly, but they intrigued me. What had their lives been like all these years? How had they stayed under our radar? Why stay under the radar? What was happening in their world for them to come forward and make themselves known now?

Bruce broke me out of my reverie. "Who cares what changed. What I want to know is how we are going to get rid of them."

"Seriously? Aren't you the least bit interested in learning more about them?"

"Fuck, no!"

"See, I am. I find the fact that these people have been living amongst us for all these years rather fascinating. How could we not have known? Maybe some people did, but the majority of people didn't. It makes me wonder what else is out there."

He stared at me funny. "What? You mean like werewolves and elves and demons and shit?"

"Who knows." I shrugged. "If vampires exist, maybe they do too."

He sneered. "Let's hope the hell not. One nasty creature is enough to deal with, and I can't believe you referred to them as people. They are far from civilized human beings."

I was about to comment on that when all the virtual screens in the office flashed and then beeped, alerting us to an incoming message. "All agents are requested to attend the meeting at nine a.m. sharp. Please acknowledge your receipt of this message." Our boss' voice came from the speakers, and Bruce and I looked at one another.

"Wow, been a long time since we were all called into a meeting," Bruce said. "I wonder what's up."

"It probably has to do with what happened last night," I replied. "Maybe they want us to prepare for that to happen here in Philly."

"Maybe." He pushed a button on his virtual screen to acknowledge the message, and I did the same before I glanced at my watch to see it was still before eight. I had enough time to go over my to-do list and see what needed my attention before the meeting.

Five minutes before nine, another announcement rang through the room, reminding everyone about the meeting, and several of the agents began to converge on the stairs to head down a floor to our conference room. Bruce and I joined the group, and I listened to the mutterings of those around me as they all tried to guess what the topic of the meeting would be.

We had known about the vampire race for less than two years, and when we had first learned about them, everyone was up in arms. The news media went wild with footage of their killing sprees, and the general human population had been running scared. Many were locking themselves into their homes with fear of going out in public. It sounded similar to how the people had reacted back when the COVID-19 virus went viral, and the pandemic shocked the world. I was just an infant then, but I'd learned about it in school. The public had been issued a massive quarantine order, and for months people stayed inside while fear ran rampant throughout the world.

It was like that after the vampire presence became known. Some humans had come forward to say they had been aware of the vampires' existence for a while, and they defended them as a peaceful society that had been existing amongst us for hundreds, if not thousands, of years. While the stories had been never-ending, few facts had been shared with us and even less that were confirmed.

The conference room filled with over a hundred agents, and Bruce and I glanced at one another questioningly. I had expected our floor to be here but didn't expect the entire building of agents to be present.

Our boss, Steve Windwood, stood at the front of the room with Zack Easlick, the head of Immigration. What the hell were these two doing together? While we did work with ICE occasionally on homeland terror cells, we didn't generally meet up with one another at this level.

"Alright, can I have everybody's attention," Steve spoke into the microphone in front of him. "I know you all have a lot to do, so let's get this over with quickly."

The room grew quiet as everyone gave him their attention.

"You all know Zack Easlick from ICE. We have been working together on a new project, and it's time to make that project common knowledge and build a solid task force. Over the last couple of months, we have seen the rise in violence with this new species—you know, the vampires. The violence is expanding and not just in our major cities, but our small towns too. It doesn't stop there either; it is the same around the globe. We have all witnessed the carnage either personally or via video footage, but it is time that we get a handle on this situation. That's why we are starting a new task force that will focus solely on vampires and those humans that work with them. This task force will not only be about dealing with the violence but what we can learn to help us understand these people—or whatever they are—and figure out what we can do to stop this and keep them in line."

Zack approached the microphone, and Steve shifted to the side. "I know you all are wondering what the hell ICE is doing here, and I sure wish we weren't, but we have learned that many of these beings are moving between countries. We also know that they have a governing body that exists in multiple countries around the world —think a United Nations kind of thing. We want to work with DHS to find out what they are up to, how they control their own, and try to stop them from any world domination plans that they might have."

I frowned as I thought about his world domination wording. I didn't know that was their purpose, and I peered to the side to see Bruce shaking his head and leaning toward another guy on his left as he whispered something to him.

"We are looking for volunteers who want to work on this task force. Between our two agencies, we should have enough people interested in learning more and seeing what we can do to stop the violence. We have seen the damage that this race can do, and we need to figure out how to stop it or control it before it is too late."

Steve stepped forward again. "If there is anyone who wants to be part of this task force, raise your hand. If you are even slightly interested, raise your hand so we can talk more."

My hand went up, and Bruce started laughing as he slapped my shoulder. "Figures you would, Murph."

There were about twenty-five of us that raised our hands. "Okay, those of you who have no interest, you are excused. The rest of you stay put, and we'll give you some further details."

Bruce clapped me on the shoulder again. "You have fun with that, buddy. It looks like I'll be dealing with our case alone today."

As they left, there was muttering and laughter; those of us who stayed shifted toward the front of the room. I knew most of the people in the group, but not all. Some of them were from the forensics division, others from the technology department.

"Thank you to all of you for staying," Steve said as he stepped away from the microphone now that the group was smaller. "What we are looking for is a group of people who can work side by side with some of the ICE agents to pull this task force together. It won't just be centered here in Philadelphia either; we will be nationwide, and we will work with other countries to share information."

"What is it that you hope to gain with this task force?" a woman from our IT department asked.

"Well, we want to know what these people are, who these people are, and what they can do. We are going to need people who aren't afraid to come face-to-face with them and are curious enough to push to get answers."

"Even the tech people?" she queried.

He nodded. "Yes, we are going to need databases built that can track, technical equipment to oversee investigations, and we're going to need people who can help us or oversee engineering of weapons that can used against them."

She nodded as did a few others. "Do you plan on having us interview these people, vampires, whatever they are?"

"Yes, we do. Just like how you would cultivate any confidential informant, we are going to need to build relationships with them to see what we can learn. We know that they have long lives; we know that for some reason, they have decided to make their world visible to us; we just don't know why. We need to know if they are planning on trying to take over the world."

I laughed. "Sir, somehow, I doubt that. If they have been around all these years—centuries—whatever, why would they decide that now was the time to take over the world?"

"I agree with you, McMurphy. I don't think that they are either. I believe something else is going on, but there are others at the top of the food chain that are concerned. We have heard rumors that they are fighting amongst themselves, and that might be what has them coming forward. Maybe whatever they are dealing with, we can help put a stop to it so that no more humans die in the crossfire."

"Do you think that's possible?" I asked. "I mean, I have a feeling that if they are warring against themselves, they don't care who gets killed."

He sighed. "Or they could be using us as examples. Who knows. That's the point of this whole task force. We *want* to know."

I glanced at the guy beside me, Warren Bates; we had worked a couple of cases together in the past. He seemed as interested as I did in what they were saying. We listened for a few more minutes, and then Steve told us to put in an official request to join the task force. We'd no longer carry our current caseload and would instead focus one hundred percent on the vampire race. I was totally in.

After Steve excused everyone, he called out and waved me toward the front. "Hugh, I'm glad you stepped forward today. I was hoping you would."

"Why is that, sir?"

"Because I'd like you to start as being the head chair of the task force for our side. You'd be working with Tom Singer from ICE to oversee everything. Would that be something you'd be interested in?"

"Wow, of course, sir, but why me?"

"Since the day that their existence has become public knowledge, you seemed to have had an interest in them. You haven't appeared all gung ho to wipe them out but instead, showed an interest in learning about them. To be honest, I think there is a lot for us to learn and a whole lot more of them than we think there are. I want someone who is smart, on top of things, and isn't biased one way or the other."

"Well, I can do that, sir."

"Good, put your official transfer request in, and I'll make sure it happens. On Monday, you will report to your new office on the tenth floor. We'll get started then."

After we shook hands, I went back up to my desk and opened my virtual computer to bring up our inter-office site. I filled out the form, and right before I clicked the submit button, I paused.

Did I really want to get involved with this world? Was it a sick fascination that I had, or was it something more? I wasn't sure why, but for some reason, it felt like it was more, and I clicked the send button and sat back in my chair, feeling like I was about to open Pandora's box.

Ready for more?
Find out in Hugh: Blue Blood Compelled coming in September.

Hugh: Blue Blood Compelled (The Blue Blood Returns Series, Book 2)

*T*ake a short trip back in time to find out how Hugh got involved with his task force and then learned about the secret society before he was summoned to meet with Joseph Portage and began a new mission.

Kristin knows that there is more going on than meets the eye with Hugh. Now she must deal with the issues of the breed and the secrets of her new and powerful mate. A warning from an old friend will put Kristin in a tailspin. Past and present will converge in the flash of the strobes and the thump of the bass.

With the rest of the VMF gang working to find Portage and protecting Kristin, there are ups and downs for all of them, but Josh is hell-bent on figuring out what Hugh's secret is.

Portage has his way in now, but that is only step one of his plan to control Kristin and take over the breed. While Zander continues to get frustrated with the dreams and his father, he finally decides to take off on his own and figure things out. It's not until he arrives in Philadelphia that he will start to find answers—but they will change everything.

ABOUT THE AUTHOR

Stacy Eaton is a USA Today Best Selling author and began her writing career in October of 2010. Stacy took an early retirement from law enforcement after over fifteen years of service in 2016, with her last three years in investigations and crime scene investigation to write full time.

Stacy resides in southeastern Pennsylvania with her husband, who works in law enforcement, and her teen daughter. She also has a son who is currently serving in the United States Navy and has two grandchildren.

Be sure to visit www.stacyeaton.com for updates and more information on her books.

Sign up for all the latest information on Stacy's Newsletter!

ALSO BY STACY EATON

Paranormal Romance:

My Blood Runs Blue Series

My Blood Runs Blue, Book 1 **

The Pulse of Blue Blood, Book 2 (Short Story) **

Blue Blood for Life, Book 3 **

Mixing the Blue Blood, Book 4 ***

Blue Bloods Final Destiny, Book 5 ***

The Return of Blue Blood Series:

Kristin: Blue Blood Returns, Book 1 (June 9)

Hugh: Blue Blood Compelled, Book 2 (Sept 22)

Zander: Blue Blood Reborn, Book 3 (coming soon)

Lena: Blue Blood Desired, Book 4 (coming soon)

Garda ~ Welcome to the Realm

Domestic Violence – Crime - Suspense:

Whether I'll Live or Die**

Barbara's Plea

You're Not Alone**

Romantic Suspense:

Liveon ~ No Evil ***

Second Shield ***

Distorted Loyalty**

Six Days of Memories ***

Second Shield II: The Return ***

Contemporary Romance:

Tempt Me Too**

Finding the Strength

Finding Love in Special Places:

Stacy's Short Story Series

Finding Love on Christmas Vacation

Finding Love on the Summer Surf

Finding Love with Dear Santa (Oct 2020)

Heart of the Family Series

Mistletoe & Cocoa Kisses, Book 1 **

Roses & Champagne Kisses, Book 2 **

Orchids & Hurricane Kisses, Book 3 **

Carnations & Hot Toddy Kisses, Book 4 **

Heal Me Series

Cured, Book 1 **

Revived, Book 2

Mended, Book 3

Rescued, Book 4

The Celebration Series

Tangled in Tinsel, Book 1 **

Tears to Cheers, Book 2 **

Heathens to Hearts, Book 3 ***

Rainbows Bring Riches, Book 4 ***

Sweet as Sugar, Book 5 ***

Making Mom Mad, Book 6 ***

Sparklers or Spankings, Book 7 ***

Raffles to Rattles, Book 8 ***

Flirting with Fireworks, Book 9 ***

Working under Wheels, Book 10 ***

Masquerading at Midnight, Book 11 ***

Blessings & Beans, Book 12 ***

Velvet & Vows, Book 13 ***

The Celebration Series Box Sets:

Part One: Books 1-5

Part Two: Books 6-9

Part Three: Books 10-13

The Sometimes Series:

Sometimes You Win, Book 1**

Sometimes You Lose, Book 2**

Sometimes You Play The Game, Book 3**

The Sometimes Series: Win, Lose & Play Set **

Pleasure Your Fantasies Series

Mistletoe Fantasies, Book 1 **

Whispered Fantasies, Book 2

Secret Fantasies, Book 3

The Twisted Love Series

with Amy Manemann Co-Author

Love Lorn, Book 1 (Manemann)**

Love Torn, Book 2 (Eaton)**

Love Inked, Book 3

Love Drowned, Book 4

Love Carved, Book 5

Love Trapped, Book 6

Love Crossed, Book 7

Love Twisted, Book 8

Love Lies, Book 9

Rise Again Warrior Series

Mission: Believe, Book 1 **

Mission: Accept, Book 2 **

Mission: Repair, Book 3

Loving a Young Series

Wesley, Book 1

Henley, Book 2

The Unexpected Series

Unexpected Packages

Unexpected Arrivals

** These books are also available on Audio

*** These books are coming to Audio soon

List Updated 5-26-20